ML

Kapralov, Yuri
Castle Dubrava

DO NOT REMOVE
CARDS FROM POCKET

CASTLE DUBRAVA

CASTLE DUBRAVA

YURI KAPRALOV

E. P. DUTTON, INC.   NEW YORK

For Faith, Katya, Andrei, Collin, Sonya, Jasmine, and Rosa

Published in the United States by
E. P. Dutton, Inc., 2 Park Avenue, New York, N.Y. 10016

Library of Congress Cataloging in Publication Data
Kapralov, Yuri.
Castle Dubrava.
"A Joan Kahn book."
I. Title.
PS3561A573C3   1982   813'.54   82-5100
                                                              AACR2

ISBN: 0-525-24143-4

Published simultaneously in Canada by
Clarke, Irwin & Company Limited, Toronto and Vancouver

10 9 8 7 6 5 4 3 2 1

First Edition

BOOK ONE

one

$\mathbf{N}$o, do not wake up," a deep, friendly voice whispered. "Not yet. Sleep a while longer and enjoy your freedom."

I will do just that, she decided and held her breath. In her dream she was flying into a cloud of blue mist; suddenly it disappeared. She looked at a landscape; an iridescent garden where her nerves were attuned to the music and the multicolored lights. She had a feeling of joy, of total happiness and fulfillment. She was nearing a paradise of senses, populated by cuddly, lovable animals and beautiful plants. The ground on which she was either floating or walking felt like the softest velvet.

She knew there was a final destination somewhere beyond the ancient bridge, across the pond, somewhere beyond the flowers and statues. The unusual mansion with its Doric columns—that's where the mystery was. The mystery of which she was almost a part, the mystery that transcended centuries.

A few blinding flashes of light.

Another voice broke in. Firm, businesslike, and insistent. It urged her to wake up, to face the day, and to do so now. It reminded her that today, of all days, she had to be in her office at ten. She had a most important meeting with Budda at ten-thirty. She had to wake up because her entire eight-year career of demanding and exasperating work was on the line.

She fought the second voice until the feeling of joy and freedom began to fade. Her body was becoming heavy and the ground was changing from velvet into hard, jagged stones.

Reluctantly, Sally opened her eyes.

This bright morning everything seemed to be slightly different. Life had somehow altered during the night; it was easier to breathe. The oppressive feeling of uncertainty that Sally had been trying to shake off for nearly six months had lifted as if by magic. She no longer feared her confrontation with Budda, no longer even feared for her career. Her reputation was firmly established. In any case, there were other top agencies in New York that would be happy to grab her.

The large crystals hanging over her bed sent hundreds of rainbows across the carpet. Her striped gray cat purred contentedly near her pillow. No more melancholy, no more rains and nightmares! She opened her curtain completely and looked at the bluest sky she had seen in weeks. The sound of bells was coming from the church at the end of her block, near Lexington Avenue.

Sunday. Today was Sunday. Sally wished very much that it could have been Sunday, but it was Friday, and she had to cope with reality.

She arrived at her corner office on the twenty-ninth floor of the Pan Am building at precisely ten o'clock. There was a small bouquet of roses on top of her round, glass-topped desk, courtesy of her secretary. There were stacks of tapes and folders full of radio and TV scripts, contracts and proposals. She sat in her black leather armchair, looking thoughtfully at the roses. She then called her secretary.

Frank, her secretary, was a bright, immaculately groomed young man who had been with Sally for nearly two years and who had never made a mistake in whatever he was asked to do. He also knew everything that went on in the agency—not a small achievement considering that the agency currently numbered over a thousand employees: which copywriter slept with which group head; who in media was being axed; why the computer had been acting so strangely lately; what the chairman of the board had said to the executive vice-president and why he didn't say it to the president; and finally, what kind of grass the mailroom boys were smoking behind the Xerox machines.

This morning he looked as bright and eager as ever, but there was a trace of apprehension on his thin freckled face.

Sally touched the roses. "Hi, Frank. Thanks."

His look of apprehension disappeared.

4

"Come on. What's cookin'?" she asked. "Tell me about him."

Frank sat down across from her. He studied her face. God, he thought, she's a sexy woman. And an intelligent woman, too.

"There's good news and there's bad news," he began cautiously. "The good news is that you have plenty of support and your head is not going to roll. The board was divided right down the middle: four for you and four for Budda. Our dear chairman broke the tie because he fancies himself a bold innovator and also"—Frank lowered his voice conspiratorily—"because Budda has something on him. I couldn't find out what, but give me more time and I will."

"Some good news." Sally shrugged. "Everybody assumed I had it sewed up and then they go hire some hotshot from California. And we're faced with a *fait accompli*. They really kept that secret."

"The bad news," Frank continued evenly, "is that the guy happens to be a genuine genius. Had his own agency in San Francisco when he was twenty. Got every conceivable award. Print, radio, TV, regional accounts, national accounts, public-service ads, you name it. He's tops even by our standards. Knows how to use people, too. Now here's more good news. To him, just being our creative director means nothing. Rumor has it he's being groomed to be the next president of the company. So, you play along and you'll be up where he is now in a year or so."

"I'm thrilled." Sally turned to look down at Park Avenue. Shit, she thought, these past six months. I lost six months working on that damned Chicago bank when I should've been playing politics. Serves me right for being so dedicated. "Anything I can use today?" It sounded almost like a plea.

"Well, genius or not, Budda has a reputation for being pragmatic and a very professional guy. Deal with him on those levels. Otherwise . . ."

"Otherwise, all my people will be swept away?"

"Those without long contracts, I'd say so."

Sally felt herself getting angry. To be outmaneuvered like that by a twenty-four-year-old kid. She knew which four board members had voted against her. Three were personal friends and former lovers. At least one of them could have been persuaded to vote for her. If only she'd known.

At ten-thirty she pushed open the oak door and walked into the once-familiar office. The office of the director of creative services had always been huge, but now there seemed to be no end to it.

5

Along one wall, from ceiling to floor, there was an aquarium stocked with hundreds of tropical fish, all colors and shapes. The other walls were covered by enormous blowups of California landscapes: seashore, mountains, desert. The windows looking over Park Avenue were tinted dark blue, creating the illusion of night outside. There was no furniture, only a deep red carpet and a few pillows. There was soft sitar music and the aroma of incense. On one of the pillows sat a chubby, smiling young man resembling the cheap statues of Buddha in Chinatown souvenir shops.

"Hi, Sally." He smiled even wider, putting away the folder he was reading. "I greatly admire your work. What you did for the Chicago National Bank commercial was simply fantastic. Please sit down."

They studied each other for a few seconds.

I wonder if he's ever been to bed with a woman, Sally thought. A real woman. To him, everything is probably a head trip, a mental exercise. Her anger returned, reminding her that lately her own love life had been pretty dismal and that the men she went to bed with failed to satisfy her, even marginally.

"I have a problem, Sally." Budda unfolded his hands. "I want you on my staff. In fact, I need you. But I would be dishonest with you and with myself if I said I am satisfied with the overall performance of our creative people. Too much dead wood."

"Don't tell me what you're going to do. Let me guess . . . uh, Stanley?" There was open sarcasm in her voice.

"I have to do it, Sally!" Budda stood up. He was perhaps five feet tall. "You'd do the same thing in my place. Smoke? I have some marvelous Colombian grass." He took out a gold cigarette case.

"No, thanks. And listen to me, Stanley." The tone of her voice changed. It was cold, deliberate, and menacing: the delivery that sent shivers down the spines of even the most seasoned writers and producers. "I don't care what the fuck you do, but you leave my group alone. No firings, no transfers, nothing. You understand?"

Budda's hands actually trembled as he lit his joint. He took a deep drag, rubbed his eyes as if he were seeing her for the first time, and sat back on his pillow.

"I can't." He finally sighed, putting away the joint. "You have two writers each pulling close to thirty grand who should've been fired years ago. Your art director is a dinosaur, your producer an alcoholic. And that's why you're so overworked. How long can you go on like this? Another month, two? Look at yourself!"

6

He jumped up with such agility that she was startled. In one hand, he now had a mirror with an antique silver handle and he actually held it in front of her face.

Sally didn't know whether to laugh or to punch him in his fat belly. For a moment she thought she saw no reflection and was almost relieved. But the mirror confirmed once more what she already knew. The long tension-filled days, the one-night stands, the nightmares and the anxiety, the kaleidoscope of faces, each of them demanding something, each of them ugly.

Budda snatched away the mirror. It disappeared magically.

"And very soon, Sally, your work too will be getting mediocre." Budda seemed to have been reading her thoughts. Sally knew the little shit was right. She had already let some sloppy print ads go by. But she wasn't about to give up.

"You just said how you admired my work."

"And I do!" He waved his arms in the air. "What you did for General Foods in 1978 was brilliant. I saw every one of your commercials at least ten times. I'm really looking forward to working with you."

"Then what's your problem?"

He became very serious, though there was a twinkle of compassion behind his hooded, heavily lidded gray eyes. "I've seen good, creative people burn themselves out, Sally. For nothing! I came to the edge myself a couple of times. I believe you're there now. I don't want to see you go over."

She was almost touched by his lecture. "So what do you suggest?"

"Take a month off. Oh, I'd take a month in a second, if I could," he added hurriedly, apparently hoping not to offend her any further. "Only I am stuck, and you're not. How long has it been?"

It was more than a year since she had had a vacation, and it was none of his damned business, but Sally knew that Budda had once again hit it right.

"Okay, Stanley. Let me think about it. I'll let you know." She got up. "First, I want you to promise not to touch my producer. He's a decent man who's having a rough time. And let me tell you something else: he's one of the best in the business."

"He stays." Budda bowed his head and remained seated, his hands folded, a small statue in the huge, strange room.

* * *

7

At the Russian Tea Room, Sally waited for almost half an hour, drank two ice-cold vodkas, and finally ordered their famous hors d'oeuvre, the delicious *zakuska*. Absentmindedly, she tasted the pieces of smoked salmon, pickled herring, eggplant caviar, and a slice of pork in aspic. The *zakuska* was gone. Sally had another vodka. This was ridiculous, she thought. Where the hell was Sandor? It was his stupid idea to meet here instead of having lunch as usual at the Four Seasons. She had suffered through the horrendous midtown traffic getting to the restaurant on time, and now what?

Sandor finally arrived. He walked down the narrow aisle to her small table, wavering slightly, kissed her hand, and sat heavily across from her.

"I am so very sorry to be late," he said. "Please forgive me." Sandor was tall and distinguished-looking, with a strikingly handsome face resembling a young Gary Cooper. Now his gray hair was uncombed; his patrician nose was red at the tip; he could barely keep his eyes open. Sally knew he was drunk. He ordered a double Stolichnaya.

"They used to have waiters who spoke Russian," he mused. "Now, who knows? Well, their Georgian *shashlik* is still good. Shall we order? I am celebrating!"

"I can see that, Sandor. I'll have chicken à la Kiev," she decided. "What's the occasion?"

"The occasion?" He looked around for support, as if wanting someone to remind him. "The occasion, yes, you're looking at a *rich* man. Yes, drink up and, waiter! Bring us a bottle of your *best* champagne. No, not a split . . . hurry!"

"What happened? Horses, numbers . . . cocaine?" Now the boring lunch she had envisioned was turning into something else.

"I am *rich*, Sally. My wife, my kids can have everything they desire and I hope I won't have to deal with them ever again. Oh, I forgot, I no longer work for you. I *resign*." He drank his glass of vodka in one gulp.

"Sandor, you've flipped out, haven't you?"

"Oh, no." He was now serious. "On the contrary. For the first time in my life, I've done something sensible." The champagne arrived: Château Lafite Rothschild, vintage.

"What?" Sally couldn't wait any longer.

Sandor ceremoniously waved the waiter aside, pouring the golden liquid himself. They raised their glasses.

8

"A toast. To you, Sally." He lowered his voice to a whisper. "All you did for me, I am so very grateful."

"Don't be silly." She drank her wine. After four years of working together, the man still knew how to flatter her. She put down the empty glass. He instantly refilled it. Their food arrived.

"What did you manage to do that was so sensible?" she demanded.

She knew the sad truth. Once he lost his job at the agency, he wouldn't be hired anywhere else. He'd be just another one of thousands of embittered middle-aged executives with nothing left to do.

"It's difficult to explain." He fidgeted.

For the first time, she was aware of just how nervous he was. He avoided looking at her. He took a large bite of his meat and almost choked.

"Hey, Sandor, take it easy."

Sandor swallowed hard. He looked at Sally pleadingly. "You will not understand—yet, you were, ah, shall I say, instrumental in making me rich!"

"Come on." Sally laughed. "I know how much I am paying you."

"No, not that!" Again, something came into his eyes. He was *frightened*. "No, my being rich has to do with my background, the old country . . . you know." He drank some more champagne.

"*No, I* don't know." She was totally puzzled. Also, she had a very uneasy feeling that he was more frightened than drunk. And what was even more curious, frightened of *her*.

Sandor concentrated on eating. He seemed to be pulling himself together.

"Do you recall Dr. Faustus?" He was staring directly into her eyes for the first time. She began to get annoyed. He should not invite her for lunch and then arrive in such a condition. And proceed to make an ass of himself. People at other tables were beginning to listen. She ate, trying to ignore him.

"Of course you do, Sally. He's the chap who sold his soul to the devil. Question is, what devil? There's a big devil, a small devil, all sorts of devils. And they're all very powerful. Oh, yes, but you know all that. You should." He actually winked at her.

That did it!

"I don't have to take this shit from you, Sandor," she said very quietly. "You go sober up. I want to see you at ten sharp on Monday

9

morning." She poured the remaining champagne, drank it, and stood up.

"No, don't go," he protested weakly. His shoulders drooped; he looked pathetic. "I shall explain everything."

Outside, having taken a few steps down Fifty-seventh Street, she suddenly felt dizzy. "Champagne," she thought. She walked a few more steps. The dizziness increased. What a day! She stood in front of a Japanese restaurant, looking for a cab. The light was red; no cabs were coming. She walked some more.

I hope he has enough money to pay for the lunch and that champagne, she thought. But he'd seemed sincere when he had said he was rich. And that talk about devils. I didn't realize how bad off he is. Budda was right. I can't rely on Sandor anymore.

She heard a knock on a window and turned. A young Indian woman dressed in a sari was rapping at the storefront window from inside. When she got Sally's attention, she beckoned her with slender fingers. What the hell was this?

It was a tiny cubicle between two stores: READER/ADVISOR. Cards, crudely drawn palms of hands, a cheap poster of the signs of the zodiac. Had it not been for the champagne and the vodka and the crazy day itself, Sally would have kept right on walking.

Instead, she pushed open the small door with a sense of adding another adventure to her day. She had seen these storefronts everywhere, even in the best locations of the city and she often wondered how the gypsies, or whoever these readers/advisors were, could afford it. Now she was going to find out.

The large sign above the filthy couch on which Sally sat down had the words *five dollars* and a crudely drawn palm on it. Sally took out a ten-dollar bill, which the young woman hid immediately somewhere in her sari.

The fortune-teller had large brown eyes. They looked sad. She took Sally's right hand, held it tenderly, looking somewhere past her head. She began reciting in a hoarse voice: Sally was a famous person, she would soon travel a great distance, she very soon would fall in love with a handsome and powerful man.

The young woman paused, turned over Sally's hand, and looked at her.

For the first few seconds, Sally did not realize what was happening. The Indian woman slowly let go of her hand and slid awkwardly to the stained carpet. Her eyes were closed; she lay motionless. She had fainted.

10

A baby began to cry behind the thin plywood partition. Sally jumped up, staring down at the woman with strange fascination. She first thought the woman was dead, but she was breathing heavily.

The baby cried louder and louder. The Indian woman opened her eyes but did not get up. She waved her hands, imploring Sally to get out. Sally took another ten from her purse, dropped it on a small table, turned around, and left.

Confused, she walked in a daze across Sixth Avenue against the traffic light. Tires screeched. Suddenly she was confronted by a cabby who had nearly hit her. He was very young with long blond hair and the beginnings of a goatee. He was saying something excitedly.

She saw that the door of his cab was open; she climbed in. The young man shrugged his shoulders, then climbed behind the wheel.

"Hey, lady, are you stoned?" he asked with some concern.

"Yes, I guess I am." She opened the window.

"Can you tell me where you want to go?"

"Yes, of course. Take me to East Seventy-seventh Street, near Fifth Avenue."

"You got it," he said, sounding relieved.

Sally had a large apartment on the top floor of an elegant brownstone house. It was supposed to be haunted, according to the old super who himself looked like an apparition.

As she got out of the cab, the super was watering the flowers and plants in the large wooden boxes outside the ground-floor apartment. When she went past him he mumbled something that could have been interpreted as a greeting or a curse. He put down his hose.

"Hi, Vlas." She waved her hand as she went into the foyer and up the curving stairway. She still felt a little dizzy, but now she also had a feeling of euphoria, that something exciting and important was about to happen, something that would forever change her life. "I am drunk." She laughed to herself. "I am simply drunk as a skunk. Champagne and vodka—what a lethal combination."

"What's this?" As she was about to unlock her door, she noticed a large white envelope on the mat. One corner of the envelope was stuck under her door.

The envelope had only one word written across it: *Sally*. There were no stamps, no return address. Another mystery.

When she sat down to read the letter, her cat, Sponge, distracted her with loud meows. Evidently Sponge was hungry. He'd been an alley cat when she took him in and was always hungry. Sally put the letter aside and went to her kitchen to open a can of tuna for him.

The meowing stopped. Sally watched in bewilderment as Sponge's back arched. His fur stood up; he made threatening hissing sounds at her from across the room.

Sponge was an unusually friendly animal. Even when she spanked him with newspapers for his transgressions, he never hissed.

"Sponge," she called, "here, kitty, kitty."

Sponge darted past her into the bedroom and hid under the bed. He was still hissing, his eyes gleaming in the darkness. Sally noticed there was still some food in his dish. He must be getting senile, she thought. Either that or I am spoiling him rotten.

She opened her bar cabinet, took out a bottle of Finnish vodka (one of her accounts, and just as good as Russian vodka), poured some in a glass, added two ice cubes, and went back to her couch to read the letter.

It was written in large, old-fashioned and slightly familiar handwriting.

"My Dearest Sally,"

Without even reading any further, she knew who had written it. That knowledge spread a warm, sensual feeling throughout her body. A feeling she had forgotten for nearly a year. She gulped the vodka and read on.

Today is exactly one year since I left New York City and you. I must say I thought of you quite often and yet I have a feeling that to you I was simply another man, one of many who, I am sure, enter and leave your life. I am not certain that you remember our meetings at the United Nations Plaza, our brief, and to me, unforgettable romance, if I may call it an affair. Perhaps a meeting of two different people who for a few days were as one. Forgive me. I am looking right now at the white sand near my cottage and the roses are beginning to bloom. Beyond the sand is the Black Sea so calm today, ah, but it is ever so treacherous. As a wicked witch pretending to be a beautiful princess in one of our Romanian fairy tales.

I am drunk. Forgive me. I am drunk and the moon is high and it is full and bright. I remember the night at your apartment; I remember waking up and looking in your eyes. I was afraid. I was relieved when I received my orders to return to my country. I was afraid. I am not usually afraid. All through the war, I was afraid only once. Not of bullets, not of my enemy. I was afraid of something I did not know. And you, I do not know you and yet I know you so well. I am drunk, but this is my last bottle of cognac. Our Romanian cognac is thick and strong, you cannot buy it in America. Like our blood, our moon, our mountains, it makes us crazy, it makes us want to love a woman. Where are you now? Is another man now kissing your breasts the way I kissed them in New York? If he is, I am going to kill him. I am lonely. You awakened the feeling I had only for my wife, God rest her soul. God? I don't believe in any God; I am a Communist, a high party official, a captain in our Ministry of the Interior. I love my country. I love my people.

Why am I so miserable? Why do I drink and stare at the moon and want you so very much? The bottle is almost empty. I lied. I am not drunk, not completely. I, Nikolai Chernev, wish to invite you to come visit me this summer. I wish to show you my beautiful country. Its beaches, its mountains, its castles, and its cities. I wish to hold you. That is the truth. Please come.

Nikolai

His address in Bucharest, home phone number, work phone number, his address in Mamaia (cottage, no phone) were neatly written at the bottom.

How did the letter get here?

Scribbled on the inside of the envelope: "I am sending this letter with a trusted friend who will deliver it to your house."

At least there's one mystery solved. She looked at her watch: a few minutes to five. How fast time flew today. She dialed her office.

"Frank," she said, now totally sober. "Book me on the next flight to Bucharest. Bucharest, Romania. Yes, my passport is valid."

Today's Friday and my bank stays open late, she thought. I'm so lucky.

"Well, do what you can. At least get me to Vienna. Tonight? Yes, tonight. And, Frank, will you take care of my Sponge? He's sort of weirded out."

She listened for a minute or two.

"Yes, I have an extra set of keys in my desk. And you're certainly welcome to stay in my apartment. I don't know, maybe a month. I'll send you a postcard."

She hung up, then immediately dialed again. The sitar music was still audible in the distance.

"You know what, Stanley?" she said. "I am taking that vacation. Starting tonight. Where am I going? You're so bright, Stanley. I'll give you three guesses."

The sitar music grew louder.

"I hear the Black Sea beaches are lovely this time of year and not very crowded." Budda's voice was unemotional, as if he were reading from a travel brochure. "And the Carpathian Mountains are magnificent, especially at dusk . . ."

two

How very pleasant it feels to daydream with a glass of wine on a late summer afternoon, sitting at a tiny outdoor café in the middle of nowhere. A small village, God only knows its name, thousands of miles from New York City, hundreds of years in the past. To admire the magnificent panorama of the Carpathian Alps at dusk and await . . . await with sweet anticipation the return of your lover. A rendezvous in a most romantic setting—the picturesque Romanian countryside. All her troubles behind her, Sally sighed a great sigh of relief, took another sip of an excellent local wine, so thick and red, and closed her eyes.

A gust of chilly breeze brushed back her chestnut hair. The poplar trees were bending, as if to welcome someone, and an eerie silence descended on the village. It became so quiet, in fact, that Sally opened her eyes and looked around. Everything appeared to be standing still. Almost directly above her the wooden sign showing two moons on a dark blue surface stopped swinging back and forth. The Romanian flag atop the Hotel Red Danube hung limp. A Volkswagen bus, two Fiats, motorcycles, and several bicycles parked around the village square—the only visible signs of modern civilization—looked as if they had suddenly been abandoned. Where are the people, Sally wondered. What had happened to the German tourists sitting at an adjacent table? What had happened to her waitress? Never mind the people; there was not even a dog in sight. The sun was already behind the mountains and a soft gray mist had covered the valleys. Sally took another gulp of wine and

15

smiled; she thought the whole country was taking a break, day-dreaming along with her. She closed her eyes again.

Nikolai is a bit late, she thought, but it doesn't matter. Ever since she'd met him, he'd proved so dependable, so punctual, and, most important of all, by far the best lover she had ever had. And Sally had sampled a few lovers. As associate creative director at a large advertising agency, she often met interesting, creative men: writers, artists, composers—some of them very talented. She remembered so vividly the penthouse party, the colorfully dressed UN diplomats, the East River bridges, the sea of lights. On the balcony had stood a huge Romanian man, staring moodily into the distance. She'd laughed when he invited her to visit his country and look him up. He'd said he was a policeman with his legation and that this was his last evening in America. Tomorrow he would be flying back to Bucharest. She'd thought she would never see him again. Now, this village, only a year later. Oh, well. Sally poured herself another glass of wine and raised it to her lips and—quite suddenly her hand froze in midair, her mouth hung open.

The black carriage, as she looked up, appeared as graceful as a large bird in flight. Rolling silently along the curve of a new asphalt road, past the white houses, the poplar trees, and the neatly kept gardens, it seemed like a ghost out of some distant past. Four gray horses, beautiful and proud; an old coachman, waving his long whip now and then; a soft tinkling of bells. The vision moved closer, closer, in slow motion, toward the center of the village, toward the Two Moons Café with its few outdoor tables, and toward Sally.

I must still be dreaming, she decided, and bit her lower lip. The carriage kept right on rolling. Past the Volkswagen bus and the Fiats, past the Hotel Red Danube and the village fountain. Closer and closer. Sally could almost hear the hoofbeats and the horses breathing, see the face of the coachman—the sad, wrinkled face of an old peasant.

That does it! Sally put down her glass. After all, what she was seeing must be real. For a fraction of a second she imagined herself behind her huge desk in her corner office, calling in her copywriters and art directors and telling them what a great idea she had for a dynamite opener. What commercial? Any commerical. All her accounts from a bank to a skin-care lotion could use it. Too bad the bank had switched to another agency. . . . It must be real!

On and on, inevitably, the carriage approached her table. Perhaps it's come for me. It can't be for me, how silly. I don't know anybody here. Maybe it's Nikolai's idea of a joke? Well, I suppose I will find out in a few seconds. I should've brought along my Nikon, she thought ruefully. Now no one will believe me.

The carriage looked even more impressive up close. It must have once belonged to a prince, possibly a king. Intricate, ancient designs—menacing faces, bats, wolves, and snakes carved out of wood—decorated its exterior walls and framed the outlines of its windows.

In one of the windows, so close to her that she was startled anew, was the face of a young man, the most beautiful, most gorgeous man Sally had ever seen. Better-looking than any model, any actor, anybody! The face of an angel perhaps, a face from some great canvas hanging in a museum. Delacroix? Rembrandt? Velásquez? There was something familiar about his face. But how was that possible?

The curls of his black, shiny hair were falling over his high forehead, almost touching his exceptionally large eyes: two gray universes, gray as the horses that were pulling his carriage, gray as the mist that covered the valleys and was now rising up to the walls of Dubrava castle. In those eyes, a look of utter boredom and despair; and yet, they were also restless, moving, cunning, seeing all, leaving nothing untouched.

Sally saw he was looking directly at her; she felt the blood rushing to her head, a tingling sensation, very sexual, and so powerful that she nearly fainted.

She was uneasy and confused, but she kept looking at the man's face, hoping he was a dream, praying that he and his carriage would disappear, or at least ride past her; that the dream would end the moment she opened her eyes. But her eyes were wide open.

When the carriage and the man's face were just a couple of yards from Sally's table, the man smiled. He smiled with his lips and said something very quietly: "hello" or "how are you?" His smile was friendly, tentative, inviting. There was curiosity more than anything else in his eyes now. There was also an expression of concern, worry. Whatever for? And something else . . . pity.

And, while he was still smiling, the fabulous carriage passed Sally's table and rolled away, with the same slow pace, the same monotonous tinkling of the bells. At the far side of the village it turned off the main road to an unpaved road leading up to Dubrava castle.

Sally drank the wine she had in her glass, poured out the rest of the bottle, and swore softly to herself. Here she was, sitting and waiting for a friend in a tiny Romanian village: good wine, great view, and . . . I can take the carriage, she thought. I can take all of it, except that face. Damn it! Seeing him smile, she had experienced something embarrassingly close to an orgasm. This had never happened before. This whole thing had to be some sort of illusion. Perhaps it was the wine? No, she'd had the same wine yesterday and in Bucharest. True, Sally found Romanian men exceptionally sexy and attractive. And, judging from a few nights with Nikolai, they were the world's greatest lovers. She shook her head. To take one look at a man, one glimpse, really, and to be flustered like that? It was beyond her comprehension and it annoyed her.

Where the hell was Nikolai anyway? My punctual, dependable policeman. She glanced at her watch. He'd promised to meet her over an hour ago. I'll finish this wine, she decided, and go up to my room. It's getting chilly anyway.

She noticed that the village was no longer quiet. Dogs were barking; a group of German tourists were loading their suitcases and their knapsacks into the Volkswagen bus. A young man with his girl friend drove by on a motorcycle, kids yelled, sounds of a radio could be heard. It was getting dark. The castle was almost black against the evening sky. She looked at it thoughtfully.

Was the man in the carriage riding to his own castle? Impossible. Nikolai had told her that the Dubrava castle was now a state museum. Someone touched her shoulder. She jumped up, dropping her glass, ready to scream. Then she saw Nikolai, grinning widely.

"Don't ever do that! Do you want me to have a heart attack? Just look!" An ugly red stain spread over the clean white tablecloth.

"Don't worry, please." He motioned to the waitress, who moved quickly to pick up the glass and to take away the tablecloth.

"Where have you been?"

"My automobile broke down eight kilometers from here. I walked through the forest. I'm sorry to be late."

With Nikolai standing next to her, Sally's usual self-assurance returned. And Nikolai, a tall, handsome bear of a man, did inspire confidence. She was safe now. He sat heavily next to her, took her hand, held it.

"Something frightened you?" His eyes were gray, too, but not as large or as cold.

"Well, it's not that I was frightened, but—" Sally now felt a little ashamed. Maybe she had imagined the whole thing.

"We'll do this," he said crisply, as though issuing an order. "We'll discuss what had frightened you over dinner. I am very hungry. Shall we go inside?"

After the dinner, she told him. To her surprise, he listened attentively, sipping his brandy and pulling on his mustache now and then.

"The man you saw, his name is Michea Basarab," said Nikolai quietly. "He is a very famous man."

"Never heard of him."

"However, he was awarded the Nobel Prize and he is state poet laureate."

"A poet? That explains it. I don't read poetry."

"He is also a famous dramatist—a playwright."

"A Renaissance man?"

"Yes, indeed. But, of course, I don't care at all for his writing."

"Why not?"

"You really never read any of his works?" Nikolai was incredulous.

"They . . . they contain far too much suffering and . . . well, violence."

"This coming from a secret policeman?" Sally laughed. She was now totally relaxed.

"Not too secret. We're not Russians. Yes and also, there's, I might say, sadism; oh, yes. And I also don't like the man personally."

"May I ask why?"

"You see, you are an American, yours is a very rich and powerful country. We are not rich." He paused, wondering how best to present it. "And we're not yet strong enough. Throughout our history, we were dominated by others. Recently, we began building a just and good society—"

"You are a Communist, of course?" Sally interjected.

"Yes . . . and a Romanian. I love my country. Sally, during the war, many Romanians collaborated with the Germans. And many did not. I fought in the underground . . . and this man, Michea Basarab, he was entertaining the Nazis, riding in his carriage even

19

then. He had enough food on his table when our people were starving. He even had his servants. It seems some things never change."

"You said that he was a poet and a very famous man. Could it be that you're simply envious?"

Nikolai leaned toward her, a sad, faraway look in his eyes. Sally thought he hadn't heard a word she was saying.

"Yes, Sally, in 1944 I was only twelve and I belonged to a small partisan unit. For almost a month we were chased by a much larger unit composed of Romanian Nazis. They were most feared and they were relentless in their pursuit. We were exhausted from fighting and running, almost out of ammunition. We had not had any food for over a week. Only twelve of us were left. We had to kill our own wounded to prevent them from falling into enemy hands. Finally, we successfully ambushed the first company of the enemy's unit just outside this very village. We knew they would stop chasing us for at least one night—they had to stop to lick their wounds. They withdrew to the village and we retreated to the castle." Nikolai took a long pull on his brandy, poured himself some more, and continued; so quietly that Sally had to move her chair over so she could listen.

"Michea and his mother greeted us with bread and salt and they also put some cheese, some meat, and a few bottles of wine on the table. We ate, we drank, and we fell asleep right there, in the main hall of the castle. We did post a guard, but he, too, must have fallen asleep. When I woke up, the first thing I saw was a Nazi captain in his black uniform pointing a pistol at my head. I reached for my rifle, but there was nothing. Someone had removed it. The Nazis wanted to hang all of us in the village square as a lesson to others. As they were marching us outside, I saw Michea and his mother standing at the top of the stairs looking down at us and smiling, *smiling!* There was no doubt in our minds that they were our betrayers. When we got outside, there appeared to be some confusion. Several trucks arrived and the Nazis were being hurriedly loaded into them. Their captain ordered five of his men to take us down to the ravine near the castle and to shoot us there. The rest of his unit departed. Only one truck remained. We did not know it at the time, but the Red Army had made a big breakthrough and the Nazis were fleeing for their lives. We were ready to die.

"A miracle saved us. Janco the hunter saw our predicament and killed two of our guards—we are going to meet him tomorrow. He is now a watchman in the castle museum. And we ran in all directions. I picked up a rifle dropped by one of the soldiers and jumped into the bushes. My commander and some of our comrades escaped too; others were killed. The Nazis sitting in the truck joined the battle, but more partisans also appeared. As the fighting continued, we retreated to the castle; even now you can see bullet marks in the main hall. Another new partisan unit joined us; the fighting was fierce, but we were victorious. We killed all the Nazis, even those who surrendered. My commander then took me and another comrade and we walked upstairs to Michea's apartment . . ." Nikolai rubbed his face trying to erase painful memories. He drank some more brandy.

"You know, Sally"—he was almost whispering now—"that bastard was still smiling and . . . and hiding behind his mother. Our commander informed him that he was under arrest for treason; that he would be taken to our regional headquarters near Brasov for interrogation and then shot. But Michea kept right on smiling, as if we were joking. I and my comrade moved to take him. That is when his mother attacked us. She began scratching and biting and screaming like a demon. And she was very strong. I had to hit her twice with the butt of my rifle. She fell down and he stopped smiling. He gave me such a look of hatred . . . I will never forget! My commander should have shot him right on that spot."

Nikolai paused again, absorbed in his thoughts.

"Those were unique times, Sally; people were dying like flies."

"What happened after the war?"

"I was sent first to England, then to America to continue my education. I studied architecture at Columbia University." He smiled for the first time. "But when I returned, I discovered that we already had more architects than were needed. So I visited my former commander, who now holds an important position at the Ministry of the Interior and . . . became a policeman."

"And what happened to Michea?" Sally was not sure she could pronounce his last name, and Michea sounded very sensuous.

"He surfaced, had a brilliant career . . . our government gave him back his old apartment . . . we even gave him a new Mercedes, and, of course, his carriage."

"Why?"

"I suppose our leaders are not as tough as they once were. They

21

are now very sensitive to criticism—they don't want to have another Solzhenitsyn on their hands."

"And you don't approve?"

"Not one bit! You know, Sally"—he now spoke louder; he was excited. "Just last year I went to see one of his plays. And after the play, I saw him on the street as he was about to enter his Mercedes. I said, 'Hello, old friend, remember me?' And he looked at me with that same hatred, perhaps even more intense. I swear, I had the feeling if we were alone, he would have somehow jumped on me and tried to kill me. And this time, I swear, for a moment or two, there was a red glow in his eyes, somewhat like a burning fire. Of course, it was only a reflection from the streetlights. But there was so much hatred. I was actually afraid and I reached for my pistol— by our law, I am required to carry my pistol at all times—and I am not so easily frightened."

"What a mysterious man. We are going to see the castle?"

"Oh, yes, tomorrow morning."

"Perhaps we'll run into him?"

"I rather doubt it. I am told he detests tourists."

"It would be nice to go see a real castle. I've never been in one in my whole life."

"The Dubrava castle is very famous. Steven the Great himself lived there; and Count Dracula, whom you Americans find so fascinating, he lived there, too."

"Dracula, the vampire?" she asked.

"What nonsense! Dracula was a *voevoda*, a military leader, another cruel despot . . . of whom we had more than our share."

"Then you don't believe there are such things as vampires?"

"Of course not. I am a Communist, I believe in socialism, in our people. Not in God or Devil; and most certainly, not in any vurdalaks."

"Vurdalaks?" she asked.

"Vampires, I suppose. According to our superstitions, they, though dead themselves, continue preying on the blood of the living and can turn themselves into wolves or snakes . . . or bats . . . but enough of that!"

You said it, thought Sally. Nikolai, assertive man though he was, never liked to display any affection in public. Sally had even teased him about it. Now she huddled next to him and began stroking his big, muscular hand.

It was getting late. The moon came up over the mountains. There were several lighted windows in the castle. I wonder what Michea is doing right now, she thought. And immediately she decided to forget it. She leaned over to Nikolai as close as she could, kissed him hard on his lips, and whispered, "Let's go to bed."

three

Bright morning sunshine poured through the small window. The aroma of fried sausages, coffee, and freshly baked bread caused Sally to raise her head off her pillow; she couldn't keep her eyes closed any longer. Naked, with long reddish scars running across his hairy chest, Nikolai smiled at her; he was contented, unshaven, sleepy. Half the night they had been making love, sometimes violently, sometimes very gently, very tenderly. The other half, they'd slept as soundly as babies.

What a contradictory man, she thought. He must have had a terrible childhood. He never mentioned whether or not he had a family.

"We should hurry and get dressed." He reluctantly glanced at his watch. "Soon the bus will arrive."

"What bus?"

"The one that will drive us to the castle."

"My God, what time is it?"

"Almost noon."

Outside, the sky was blue and transparent. Dubrava castle seemed like a golden, shimmering bird sitting on top of the mountains, the sun reflecting from its ancient walls and towers. Not at all menacing, just a watercolor cut out of some children's book.

A new red and white bus carrying only six Canadian tourists stopped briefly to pick up Sally and Nikolai at the village fountain. The driver was surprised to see them since he had never picked up any tourists in the village before. Driving fast along the main road, then through the hills on a bumpy country road, the driver chatted to no one in particular about how he had driven a cab in New York City for an entire year, and how the Romanian tourist business depends on books about Dracula published in America. As soon as some book on Dracula comes out, he commented, his bus is filled with tourists, then it's quiet until the next time, like today. At one point, when the bus was climbing almost straight up the bumpy road, the Canadians looked unhappy. The entire ride, however, lasted only ten minutes and no one got carsick. They pulled into a small parking lot in front of the main gates. Only two other cars were parked nearby, an elegant gray Mercedes Benz and an old brown pickup truck. The main gates were closed, but to one side was a small, rather triangular entrance and a frail figure of a man waiting for them, scholarly looking, with a white goatee and thick glasses.

As the tourists got out of the bus, the driver settled back comfortably, put his feet on the wheel, and began leafing through an old issue of *Penthouse*. He wasn't going to any castles, especially Dubrava castle.

Walking across the parking lot, Nikolai took Sally's hand. For the first time since his wife's death, nearly five years ago, he was feeling something for a woman; some strange chemistry was pulling them together much faster than he would have preferred.

"Good day, ladies and gentlemen, welcome to Dubrava castle." The man, his eyes beaming behind his glasses, was ushering everybody into a round reception area with two desks and several display cases filled with souvenirs ranging from delicate Romanian blouses to black Kung Fu slippers made in Hong Kong and, of course, local jewelry, postcards, brochures, and art books.

"As some of you may already know," the goatee continued in excellent English, "Dubrava castle is our national monument as well as a state museum. I am sure you will enjoy your visit and find it most interesting and informative. My name is Dr."—he emphasized the importance of doctor—"Ladislau Tagarū. I am the director and the chief curator of this state museum. At the moment," he smiled apologetically, "we are grossly understaffed, and one of our regular guides has been taken ill. Therefore, I am going to conduct this tour myself. Please follow me."

Everybody followed him up the marble steps into the main hall of the castle. On the way, and continuing into the hall, Tagarū gave a brief historical outline. The Romans had been the first to build an outpost on this site, but the outpost was demolished sometime in the first century. Since then the castle had been destroyed and rebuilt at least two dozen times.

The main hall was impressive: two curving stairways led to a balcony some sixty feet above their heads, the balcony where Michea and his mother had been standing and smiling, according to Nikolai. On the whole, Sally was reminded very much of the Cloisters; there were large tapestries and portraits, and glass-enclosed cases with ancient weapons and manuscripts—almost like an ordinary castle. Almost. When the group stopped by a huge fireplace, Sally, as well as everyone else, became aware that this was not an ordinary castle after all.

Above the fireplace, looming threateningly over them, was an enormous figure of what must have been a devil, screaming in agony and anger, partly consumed by yellowed marble flames. It was a bas-relief, but an incredible one: the devil's eyes were half-closed from pain, and yet the carving conveyed such strength, such power, that Sally became uneasy. The devil may have been burning, but he was far from being defeated. Sally shuddered. The eyes reminded her of another pair, gray and cold and powerful.

"Tremendous," exclaimed one of the Canadians next to her.

"A masterpiece," said a deep voice from behind the group. Heads were turned briefly toward the voice. The speaker was impressive: a very tall, thin, ascetic-looking man, his face and his head clean-shaven; only his large piercing eyes, black as his thick eyebrows, were alive, sparkling and curious. Otherwise he had a robotlike appearance. Another good one for a commercial, Sally couldn't help thinking. The entire place could be cast in some Hammer Films production.

"Early seventeenth century," continued the man. "It was completed by a Romanian master sculptor known only as Anton . . . from original sketches supplied by Leonardo da Vinci."

"Nikodim"—Dr. Tagarū was relieved to see the skull with black eyes—"friend," he whispered to him in Romanian, "I am happy you arrived—Annoushka is sick. I know it's your day off, but please do me a favor and take this group off my hands. I have to finish my report to Bucharest, or it's the end for all of us."

As they were whispering, Sally decided it was the time to see what she had been yearning to see all along—the carriage.

"May we now see the carriage?" she inquired.

They both abruptly stopped whispering and looked at her as though she had said something quite unmentionable.

"What carriage?" Dr. Tagarū asked.

Sally looked at Nikolai, who seemed to be amused at the way both Dr. Tagarū and Nikodim were startled by such a simple question. He winked at her and squeezed her hand, urging her to go on.

"The beautiful black carriage, which I understand belongs to one of your great poets—may we see it?"

"It's not . . ." Tagarū stammered. "We are not allowed, you see, the carriage you are referring to is not part of our museum. . . . Just where, might I ask, did you hear about it?"

"I saw it! Yesterday, as it passed through the village."

"Yes, yes, you're quite right, it belongs to one of our most illustrious citizens."

"This we know," said Nikolai abruptly. "Nevertheless, we wish to see it."

"Impossible." Dr. Tagarū was no longer smiling. "I am sorry."

Nikolai silently produced his identification and shoved it toward Dr. Tagarū.

This was also something the good doctor had not expected. He decided on the maneuver every bureaucrat the world over utilizes when he's caught in the middle: to shift the responsibility.

He smiled politely at Nikolai, took off his glasses, wiped them, put them back on. "Comrade Captain, you must excuse me . . . I have been instructed by my ministry."

"Why not let them see it?" said Nikodim softly, and he smiled, revealing two rows of even white teeth.

"Yes, Dr. Tagarū, why not?" asked Nikolai in Romanian. "Is this carriage our ultimate secret weapon?"

"You don't understand." Dr. Tagarū waved his hands in the air, dismissing the whole problem. Time to shift the responsibility in another direction. If Nikodim wanted to show it, let him be the one to make the decision.

By this time, the Canadians were curious, too. They had politely refrained from entering the exchange until now.

"I would love to see an old carriage," smiled a pretty blond with a slight French accent, and her companion vigorously nodded his head in agreement.

"Ladies and gentlemen," Dr. Tagarū announced. "This is Nikodim

Pavlovic, one of our regular guides. He will continue with you as I must depart to other duties. If he feels there's enough time for you to see the carriage . . ." He shrugged. Dr. Tagarū should have departed a few minutes earlier. As it happened, the third surprise of the day fell suddenly on his scholarly shoulders.

"Nikola!" someone roared, and everybody turned their heads to see another big man, this one with a full black beard and wearing a guard's uniform, running up the stairs toward the little group.

"Nikola!" the man roared again, and gave Nikolai a bear hug, lifting the policeman up in the air as though Nikolai were a child. Then he gently put him back on the ground.

"You swine! Where have you been?" he continued in Romanian, totally ignoring Dr. Tagarū and everyone else. "What are you doing now?"

They kissed three times and Nikolai, in his turn, threw the big man up in the air and caught him gently as he was coming down.

They bounced each other a few more times. The big man finally noticed Sally, with great approval.

"I spunk this boa!" he said proudly.

"Sally," Nikolai said, "this is my friend Janco, our hunter. He saved my life."

Janco showed her two stubby fingers in a V sign. "Moore, tfiz." Sally noticed now that Janco smelled exactly like a brewery she had once visited in California.

"What you do?" he again asked Nikolai.

"I am a policeman."

"Foooi!" said Janco explosively, and spat with great gusto on the immaculately clean marble. He looked at Nikolai again and roared with laughter. Pointing to his uniform, he shouted, "Me, too! I am a police in this cemetery." He switched to Romanian. "Hey, Nikola, this Tagarū and, and Nikodim too, they're mummies!" He leaned toward Sally, trying to show her what a mummy looked like. "Tell her"—he made a frightening face, rolling his eyes—"tell her mummies are nothing here. In this castle, we have things that'll frighten the dead." For the first time, he seemed aware of the tourists. He jumped up, bared his teeth, made a flapping motion with his hands, and advanced toward them.

The Canadians stepped back, astounded.

"I don't believe this guy's for real," muttered one.

"I don't believe any of them are," said the blond with the French accent.

28

"Enough!" Dr. Tagarū regained his composure. "Stop it! Immediately. Drunk again!" The goatee and glasses jumped up at Janco and raised two fists to his face. Janco tried hard to suppress another attack of laughter; he began hiccupping.

"Out! Disgrace." Dr. Tagarū pushed him toward the stairs. Nikodim, the robot, took charge.

"Ladies and gentlemen," he announced gravely, "please disregard this incident and follow me to our library. We will stop and see the carriage later in our tour."

The library was something of a disappointment, even though Nikodim tried his best to explain that it contained priceless manuscripts and documents, some of them from the time of the Mongol invasion.

He then led everyone down to the courtyard, which was round and had a forlorn, unused look about it. Cobwebs hung on the ancient walls. Only the stables were relatively modern. The carriage itself was at the far end of the stables and was being polished vigorously by a little old man. Sally immediately recognized the coachman, who looked at the visitors and screamed at Nikodim in a high falsetto voice, "Have you lost your mind? Take them out of here! The master will be very angry."

"Move over, grandfather." Nikodim was unshaken. "This carriage" he told the visitors, "is another masterpiece, from approximately the same time period as the bas-relief over the fireplace. Our glorious government," he said with palpable sarcasm, "considers it priceless. You will observe these carvings, the excellence of workmanship. This is one of the reasons it is not, at present, shown to foreign visitors. We are simply understaffed."

"What is your other reason?" asked Nikolai. "Are you afraid of Michea the Great?"

The robot ignored him. "It is believed," he continued, "to have been made in Venice; the woodcarvings of the animals were added later, perhaps a century or so."

"Was it made for Count Dracula?" asked Sally. She was pleased to see the carriage again. It was magnificent, even in the dimly lighted stables.

"Dracula?" The big robot looked at her seriously, his square face twitched a little. "No, not the Draculas. We believe it was originally made for the house of Basarab. At one time in our history they were very powerful and evil kings who ruled eastern Romania and all along the Black Sea and what is now Moldavia, Bessarabia."

"Michea Basarab, could he be a descendant of these kings?" Sally asked Nikolai.

"Nonsense. He took Basarab as his pen name, his real name is Michea Adelescu," Nikolai said.

"Basarab may have another meaning." Nikodim's square face was looking at Sally very thoughtfully now, as if seeing her for the first time. "In most Slavic languages *bas* means the devil and *rab* means the slave—it could mean 'devil's servant.' "

As they moved back through the main hall, Sally glanced back for just a second and saw two figures on the balcony. She had her trusty Nikon around her neck, and she raised it and clicked the shutter. Then she wanted to take another, better, shot, but when she looked through her lens, there was nothing to focus on. The figures, if they indeed had stood there, had vanished.

Dr. Tagarū met the group in the reception area and invited everyone to examine the souvenirs, explaining that all proceeds from sales would be used for restoration and maintenance. Sally bought a blouse. The Canadians started toward the bus, but Dr. Tagarū stopped Nikolai and Sally. He seemed in much better spirits.

"Comrade Captain, I took the liberty of informing the person who, mmmm, presently has the use of the carriage . . . you understand?"

"It's quite all right."

"Well, yes, Michea was unusually gracious about it, he didn't mind at all. He even asked me to invite you and Miss . . ."

"Edmondson."

Forgetting that he was in a socialist country, Dr. Tagarū bent down and kissed Sally's hand, doing it so swiftly that she didn't have time to pull back.

"And, of course, you, Miss Edmondson. Tonight we are having a small celebration here at the castle. Actually, Michea, whom your companion happens to know, is entertaining a few friends . . . literary people, and he invited our small staff and you."

"Me?" Nikolai asked.

"Oh, yes, specifically you, Comrade Captain, and your friend, Miss Edmondson. Babulescu is due to arrive from Bucharest," he added importantly.

"Babulescu?" Nikolai was now interested.

"Babulescu?" repeated Sally, though the name meant nothing to her.

"He is sort of our Hemingway," Nikolai explained. "I loved his novels when I was much younger."

"Let's come." Sally squeezed his arm.

"I don't know." Nikolai felt uneasy.

"Do come," insisted Dr. Tagarū.

"When? What time?"

"About eight. Oh, and there will be dinner served as well."

Outside, Nikolai turned briefly to Dr. Tagarū, who, along with Nikodim, stood in the triangular doorway.

"It's kind of you. And, oh, one more thing, Dr. Tagarū. Do not be too hard on Janco; he is a good man." They moved out toward the waiting bus.

Nikolai was thinking about Michea's invitation. Was Michea laying some sort of trap? Or maybe he actually wanted to make peace. No, that last thought wasn't realistic, not with so much hatred still in Michea. But it would be good to see Babulescu anyway. The last time he'd heard Babulescu read his stories was a very long time ago, in a different world.

They climbed into the bus and the driver didn't waste any time moving out of the small parking lot.

Dr. Tagarū and Nikodim stood in the doorway until the bus had disappeared into the dark green forest that surrounded the castle.

"Must we go tonight?" Nikodim asked very quietly.

"We must, my friend, we must," sighed Dr. Tagarū and they both went inside.

In his tiny room in the castle's dormitory, Janco the guard sat on his cot. Let them believe I am a fool and a drunkard, he thought. Looking at the forest, toward his little cottage hidden so well that no one except his friend Nikolai knew how to find it, he thought of his new still. For a few years now he had made a very comfortable living on the side, making and selling homemade alcohol; he called it vodka, but actually it tasted more like gin.

Janco had been astounded to see Nikolai, but the woman with Nikolai had made him uneasy. She reminded Janco of someone. What a striking woman, and so sexy! He approved, and yet he couldn't shake the feeling that he might have seen her before. Only where? Under what circumstances? And these people upstairs . . . Janco sighed. It would be so good to break a few bottles with Nikolai once again as they used to do years and years ago, he

31

thought. I hope he is not too preoccupied with this woman. This woman? Oh, what the hell do I care?

Janco lay on his cot and closed his eyes.

The bus driver didn't bother to chat on the way back. He sat grasping the large wheel with one hand, whistling a tune and watching the trees and the flowers roll by on both sides of the road as the bus crept down the steep incline. Suddenly he slammed on his brakes. The Canadian tourists were piled up on top of one another, and Nikolai and Sally were jarred from their seats.

The cause of the sudden stop was a small girl walking in the middle of the road, her long blond ponytail swinging back and forth. She was carrying a bunch of flowers and singing.

"Get off the road, you stupid!" the driver yelled, honking as he drove slowly behind her. Then he had to slam on his brakes again as the girl suddenly fell down on the dusty road, dropping her flowers.

Nikolai was the first one to jump out. He felt her pulse. It was weak but steady, and she was breathing evenly; her eyes were wide open. Nikolai picked her up and carried her to the bus.

"Stop in the village and wait for me," he ordered the driver. "We may have to take her to Brasov."

"I can't wait," the driver protested. Nikolai showed him his identification card and the driver shut up.

At the Two Moons Café the girl's identity was quickly established. She was Marinca, the daughter of a Forest Ministry employee living in a state compound three kilometers north of the village. An emergency call was placed, but by that time, the girl had come out of shock, perked up, and was clearly apprehensive about what her parents would do to her once they came to pick her up. Otherwise, there didn't seem to be anything wrong with her, not a scratch. She said she had been picking flowers along the lower road when she'd met a lady, a very nice lady who looked a little like Sally, except her hair was longer and she was wearing a black dress. The lady showed Marinca a beautiful secret garden—a magic garden, full of flowers and wonderful animals. Then she gave Marinca some flowers and told her to go home.

"If you are a policeman," she said very seriously to Nikolai, "you should go to the crossroads, walk farther—half a kilometer—and right under the old walls you'll find two men sleeping. You should go and wake them up because they have been asleep for a long time now."

"I will go," Nikolai promised. "The lady who was with you, do you know her name?"

Marinca wrinkled her forehead trying to remember. "No . . . but I believe she had wings," she whispered. "Yes, I am sure she did."

"Why are you so sure?"

"Because I was all alone," she confided, "and then, the lady was standing next to me. She must have flown down from the castle."

"But you did not see her wings?"

Marinca concentrated again. "No," and with the stubbornness of a child who knows that she is telling the truth, the truth that grown-ups are not going to believe, she said, "SHE DID HAVE THEM!"

Nikolai did not wish to pursue this further. The waitress brought Marinca some hot chocolate and then her parents arrived in an old Fiat. They did not appear to be overly concerned about their daughter, although her mother admonished her briefly about wandering off too far.

"She has this habit," her father explained. "Sometimes she wakes up very early, even before sunrise, to pick her flowers. I am afraid that she lives in a dream world; she is seeing a child psychologist."

"I'd have her checked out by a physician anyway," suggested Nikolai. "She seemed to be in some kind of shock."

"Of course, we will certainly do that."

"Comrade Captain," pleaded the driver. "May I go now? My tourists are getting angry."

"Yes, and be sure to notify the district militia of the incident." Nikolai could not erase from his mind a nasty feeling about the two men Marinca said were sleeping under the old walls. Sleeping a long time, eh? Perhaps he should go take a look? He was so absorbed that he almost forgot about Sally, waiting patiently at the table. After a few moments, he walked over.

"What did the girl say? Everything OK?"

"I suppose so. She must have had quite a time. She said she saw a magic garden and a lady with wings who looked somewhat like you, Sally." He ordered some wine and quickly drank two glasses.

"Like me?" Sally was surprised.

"That is what she said." He thought of telling Sally about the two sleeping men but decided to forget it. Perhaps they both should leave this very afternoon and forget the invitation. Michea would never make peace. How very convenient—here I am in the village, after all these years, and he just happens to throw a party. But if all seventeen years as a policeman taught me one thing, it's not to believe in coincidences. My automobile should be repaired by now. I have four more vacation days. To the devil with all of them and their castle. Someday later, I'd like to find out what kind of a whorehouse they are running up there. But for now, I should take Sally to the Black Sea, away from this nonsense. Life is too short to make it complicated.

"Everyone wishes to find happiness," the gypsy had sung in his favorite nightclub in Bucharest. "To love and to be loved . . . and happiness always lies in our paths and we always walk around it." Nikolai realized that he was happy with this American woman. For the first time since his wife had died, he felt happy with a woman.

Throwing his usual caution to the winds, he embraced Sally and kissed her.

"To us." He lifted his glass. "May we always be happy."

"We will," Sally quietly replied. She, too, wanted to get away now, to forget the castle and everyone in it, even to pass up the generous invitation and what promised to be a most exciting evening. She felt that something was not quite right in the castle, something no one on the strange staff was mentioning. Except for Janco, with his funny vampire imitation. Did I really see anyone on that balcony? She still felt curious and wanted to meet Michea. But . . . there was a nagging *but,* a doubt which put her subconscious on the alert. She drank some more wine and smiled. How foolish of me. What am I worried about? Nikolai will be there with me.

A few minutes and a few glasses of wine later, Nikolai's car, a Romanian version of a Toyota Land Rover, was delivered. The mechanic noted sadly that the glorious Romanian Land Rovers have a habit of breaking down shortly after the first fifty thousand kilometers. And once they start breaking down, they keep on breaking down. The mechanic left with his helper, who had followed the Land Rover in a tiny sardine-can-like contraption. Nikolai could only hope his car wouldn't break down during the next few days. And we're trying to export this junk as being virtually indestructible, he thought. Yes, indeed, I should've kept my old Volkswagen.

Still, it was a beautiful afternoon, not a cloud in sight. Someone was singing in one of the houses, about happiness, of course. Somebody was listening to a radio. With his Rover parked near the Red Danube Hotel, Nikolai felt as if his trusty old friend was back. Now if he wanted to, he could simply take off and never see the village and the castle again. He could do anything. No wonder the Americans were all car-crazy. The little girl must have been dreaming it all up, he decided, and that was why her parents were so unperturbed. That's why she is seeing a psychologist. What an imagination! Perhaps we should take a drive to see the old ruins anyway? They were impressive, and he hadn't seen them since after the war.

"Do you want to see some more of our countryside? There are some very interesting ruins and tunnels near where the girl saw those men."

"What men?"

"Marinca said she had seen two men sleeping under the old wall."

"I'm game. Why don't we drive out and see? What else is there to do?" She said it with emphasis, dropping a hint that they could be occupied with something better, possibly in their hotel room. Nikolai missed it entirely.

It was nice driving for a change: only five minutes, and they were on a very narrow road overgrown with tall grass and underbrush. Then the road disappeared altogether into a field, a small valley between two very high mountains. At the end of the valley stood an ancient wall. Once, that wall must have been an enormous engineering achievement. Even now, it was at least fifty meters tall and very thick. Parts of it were hidden under bushes of wild roses; other sections jutted into the air like parts of some sunken battleship sticking up out of the water. The Dubrava castle loomed high above it to the north; some smaller ruins were scattered on the opposite side. Nikolai parked next to the wall near a patch of pine trees.

"Over there, the Nazis were going to shoot us," he said, pointing to a field covered with flowers. They walked along the wall. There were no sleeping people in sight, which was just what he had expected. Not only was this a desolate place, but the superstitious villagers would never have ventured near it. This was the Valley of

35

Blood, said to be a mass grave for thousands of people: conquerers and victims alike, who had perished in battle or had been put to death right in front of the massive wall.

"The Valley of Blood," he said loudly. "At night, the old people tell us, one can still hear the cries and groans of the dead and wounded who were killed in many battles near this wall. When we camped here during the war, it was frightening. Down there—you see those holes—that is a honeycomb of ancient tunnels. We had our arsenal and a radio in one of the tunnels. One night two of our comrades went to explore further and they never came back. And we never found them."

Sally looked at the wall with fascination, as if she had seen it before.

"Maybe it's human nature, always building walls and always trying to scale them."

"I wouldn't know. . . . What's up on the slope?" she asked.

"Some more ruins. Perhaps some fortress used to stand there."

He wasn't quite sure himself. Perhaps another castle. Sally tugged at his sleeve. "There was something moving by the rose-bushes, near the tunnels. Someone's watching us."

"Let them watch." Something else had caught his eye. Something that certainly didn't belong among the ruins: a bright blue pup tent.

She saw it too. "Tourists?"

"Here? At the Valley of Blood? I rather doubt it. Let's go investigate." Holding on to the bushes and the branches, they climbed up the old walls. Just below the bright blue pup tent, they saw another tent, a much larger green army tent and a very small canvas hut, evidently used for storage.

"Anyone here?" shouted Nikolai. A swarm of startled little birds flew out from under the rosebushes. Silence. He shouted again; and again, nothing.

The large tent seemed to be the field office for an archeological expedition. It held a big table with charts, tools, even a portable gas stove and canned foods. The blue tent contained two cots with sleeping bags and personal belongings of the archeologists, including cameras and knapsacks. Nikolai looked in one of the shoulder bags hanging loosely near the entrance. Along with a wallet, it contained a folder with permits and specifications for a two-man expedition from Leipzig University in East Germany. The permits

36

were in order. Nikolai was annoyed that the men were leaving their equipment unprotected. Anyone could come and steal it.

And another thing, too. Why wasn't a local guide attached to them? This is rugged country.

"Shmitt! Landau!" He shouted their names. Nothing.

"They must be busy digging somewhere." Sally now wanted to get back. It was positively creepy around here. Creepy even with Nikolai around. And she still felt that somebody was in the bushes, watching their every movement.

"You're right. There's nothing we can do here. I will ask Dr. Tagarū tonight what it's all about."

"Whoever is watching us, he might know."

"Perhaps." Nikolai was getting mad. "This is more than a whorehouse up here; it is some insane circus. Somebody must be responsible. Perhaps tonight, at the dinner, there will be some answers.

"You know, Sally." He stopped climbing and slapped his forehead. "Now I know what Marinca meant when she said two men were sleeping. She meant the archeologists. What an imagination."

"Maybe, but who was the mysterious lady with wings who looked like me?"

"Hmm, indeed, who?" Nikolai left her by the Rover and walked quickly toward the bushes where Sally thought she had seen someone.

"Come out!" he ordered. "Come out, immediately!"

A little elderly man, drunk and frightened, came out with his hands shaking, holding a basket.

"Who are you?"

"I am Rusai, the caretaker at the castle."

"And what are you doing here?"

"I am delivering some food . . . for the Germans."

"Why were you hiding?"

"I was afraid . . . I couldn't find them."

Nikolai looked at him thoughtfully. He looked harmless, not like a thief, but one couldn't be sure.

"Listen, old man. Go leave your food in their tent. They don't seem to be around—unless you happen to know where they are?"

"No, no, I don't." From his tone, Nikolai was sure that the little man was lying, but he didn't want to pursue the point any longer. The archeologists were bound to be found sooner or later. They seemed like a neat and well-organized crew, typically German. Not the kind to explore the tunnels on the spur of the moment. "You may go." Nikolai thought he could always question the old man later if need be.

"Well, have you seen enough?" he asked Sally.

"More than enough. This place is creepy. Let's get out of here."

"All right . . . no, wait one goddamned minute!" Nikolai suddenly felt as if someone had poured two or three buckets of ice-cold water on his head. His heart was thumping. Dark clouds were scudding very fast over the Valley of Blood. The old man, Rusai, stood staring at what Nikolai had noticed. On the north side of the big wall, there was a neat square hole in the ground, right under the wall. A human foot was sticking awkwardly out of the hole.

Automatically, Nikolai felt for the handle of his Skoda revolver. He pulled out the gun, as he had hundreds of times before, looked briefly at Sally, then ran toward the foot.

At the bottom of the hole, about half a meter down in the freshly dug brown soil, two men were sleeping, one sprawled on top of the other, as if some giant had thrown them down there. The men were wearing green overalls and had their shovels and picks right next to them. They both had contented expressions on their faces, as if they indeed were sleeping and having pleasant dreams. The older man, probably Dr. Landau, was smiling under his white mustache. The younger man had a puzzled expression in his wide-open, baby-blue eyes, an expression of totally unexpected but welcome surprise. Everything was so peaceful. A large orange butterfly flew over them and settled on a rosebush.

Nikolai wiped away the sweat pouring down his mustache and climbed into the hole. They were dead, all right; had been dead for some time now. Both bodies were cold. He briefly examined them for any marks of violence. No marks of any kind. Perhaps a poisonous snake? There were several varieties in these mountains. No, it must have been something else. No snake was large enough to kill both men at once. Besides, he had seen the expressions on men and women bitten by snakes. This was different. Murder? Perhaps some form of suicide? In any event, that was for someone else to solve. He walked to his Land Rover. One of the things he had been forced to install in the car was an emergency radio-telephone. He'd laughed once with his superior about its value: should the

Russians decide to invade, there would be no need for any radio-telephone.

Today was the first time he had actually used it. There were surprised squawks and clicks at the Ministry of the Interior switchboard. Someone whispered excitedly, "Comrades, we're on the radio." Nikolai couldn't help smiling. It was an open secret that both the Russians and the Americans, and even the Yugoslavs, were tuned to the Romanian airwaves.

The voice of Colonel Bugash, his former partisan commander, came through cold as steel: "Nikolai, good to hear from you . . . are you drunk?"

"I am not. We have a situation here."

"Why call me?"

"Two archeologists . . . two faces." Colonel Bugash would remember that during the war they used to refer to the corpses as "faces."

"I understand." The voice was concerned now. "Where are you?"

"Just below Dubrava."

"How's your vacation, you lucky man?" Bugash laughed, but it did not sound sincere. Nikolai knew that assistants had already been called into the radio room.

"How's your beautiful American woman?"

"I am returning to the village." Nikolai tried laughing too, but couldn't make it.

"Understood," said Bugash softly as he put down the receiver.

"You, grandfather." Nikolai addressed Rusai, who was still standing nearby with his mouth hanging open. "Stay here and guard the bodies until the militia arrive from Brasov." He showed the old man his badge.

"I am not staying," Rusai protested. "What if it is dark before they arrive?"

"Are you afraid of the dark?"

"Around here, I sure am. I may be old, but I am not an old idiot. The devil himself walks in this godforsaken valley."

"There is no devil, old man, but if you are not going to stay, if you disobey me, you'll wish you were dead—you'll see ten devils before I am through with you. Stay!"

Rusai silently dug into his basket of fruits and vegetables, took out a half-empty bottle of vodka, and drank some of it.

"We will be back here before dark, don't worry," Nikolai reassured him. The old man grunted and drank from the bottle again. Nikolai and Sally rode back in silence. In the village, a telegram was waiting for Nikolai, and a telephone was reserved for him at the hotel.

"Please, Sally"—he was at a loss for what to say—"I have to take charge until the militia team from Brasov arrives. They don't have a single policeman in this village."

"No policeman?" She now felt very tired. Everything was moving so fast. She didn't care whether she ever saw the castle again. I should have dragged him to bed instead of going for a drive, she thought.

"Perhaps you'd like to take a nap." He seemed to have read her thoughts. "I'll wake you up when this business is over." He kissed her again, held her. So utterly stupid . . . and frightening, he thought. We must get out of here; the sooner the better. Bugash can send somebody else to handle this mess. I am on vacation.

The telegram was to the point: "Important you keep all information confidential. The militia team will be there at four. Call me as soon as possible. No radio."

"Yes, Colonel, we're on the regular telephone. Yes, anyone can listen, so I shall be as brief as possible. No, I don't know what killed them . . . maybe it was a suicide pact. Perhaps they were homosexuals—they did have a happy kind of expression on their faces. You know, all Germans are homosexuals. Yes, snakes, it occurred to me, too. Listen, Colonel, who's in charge of the castle? Are they running some sort of a whorehouse there, in a manner of speaking? All of them are weird except Janco. And Janco is dead drunk, as usual. Actually, Michea invited us; he is having some kind of celebration tonight."

"He invited you?" Bugash was incredulous. "Go, by all means! Perhaps there's a connection."

"I'd rather not."

Bugash thought it over. "I don't care what you'd rather do; you will go and you will enjoy yourselves and you will not mention the dead archeologists. Understood?"

"Comrade Colonel, may I remind you that I am here on my vacation. All I ever wanted to do was to show Sally one of our castles. I have no intention of doing anything after your team arrives."

"I have news for you," said Bugash coldly. "As of now, you are no

40

longer on vacation. We are dealing with an international situation. I can't let Brasov's idiots handle it and, right now, I can't spare anyone else—had you been reading the papers, you'd know that the French prime minister is visiting us next week."

"I must protest . . . I don't like it."

"To hell with *you* and what you like or dislike. You and me, we're policemen and we do our job. What else is there? Listen to me good, Nikolai. From the time the autopsy is finished"—an ominous note crept into Bugash's voice—"you have forty-eight hours, and not an hour more, to complete your investigation and to make an arrest. Have your report and the prisoner here in my office. And that, Captain, is an order."

Nikolai glumly put down the receiver. He went over to the small bar, ordered a double cognac, drank it, ordered another. Drank that one, too.

To the great relief of Rusai, who by now had finished all his vodka, the team from Brasov—a closed green van and a Russian-made jeep with four policemen and a physician—arrived at the wall just before dusk. The bodies were gathered up and packed away in the van, the grounds were searched, and two men were left behind to guard the tents.

There was nothing left for Nikolai to do until after the autopsy was completed, which would be sometime in the morning. He fortified himself with another double cognac and went upstairs to wake Sally. She was already awake, dressed, and combing her lovely hair. It was dark. An almost full moon hung directly over the castle. All the windows on the upper floors were brightly lighted.

"Are you sure you want to go?" he asked and embraced her. "You don't have to. We don't have to," he added firmly. "To hell with Bugash and Michea."

"I would like to go," Sally replied, much to his surprise. "I had the strangest dream just before you came back. . . . Yes, I'd like very much to go. We don't have to stay long, do we?"

"Of course not, Sally." He hesitated for a moment. "May I ask that you . . . could you not mention the archeologists?"

"All right."

On the way to the castle, Nikolai turned on his radio: soft, romantic music. Sally sat very close to him; she was trembling. Now she wanted to see the castle again . . . and to see the garden. She was sure there was a garden. She must walk through it.

The same door where I thought I saw two figures this afternoon,

41

thought Sally. It seemed like two centuries ago. The hidden meaning, the longing, the feelings of love and hatred, of eternity and of distance which could not be measured. And time. Suddenly time did not matter at all.

Sally thought for a few minutes that time really had stopped dead in its tracks. How many days had passed since she'd come to the tiny Romanian village, to the Two Moons Café, and the castle, to the fairy tale that was unfolding and becoming more real with each passing hour?

At the castle Nikolai knocked hard: once, twice.

Michea Basarab, wearing a red velvet suit, opened the door. His face was the one Sally had seen in the carriage window, but the changes were unbelievable. Sally could only whisper, "Oh, my God."

Michea bowed his head and said in a deep, resounding baritone, "Please enter freely. I bid you welcome."

four

Michea led them quickly across his very large living room; the white wall-to-wall carpet was so luxuriously thick it felt as if they were walking on a cushion of air. A Steinway grand piano, black and gleaming, reflected a crystal vase filled with poppies. The paintings and the sculpture, all mystical and majestic, seemed immortal, the work of great masters. In the equally large dining room, the feast was already in progress. Indeed, it was a medieval feast. On the long table the food and wines competed with one another, and the guests were filling their plates and their glasses again and again. Michea ushered Sally and Nikolai to two empty chairs.

"This is a very happy occasion for me." His English was faultless. "Let us set aside our feelings this evening." He again bowed to Nikolai. "Please enjoy our time together."

They found themselves seated across from the suckling pig, an apple still in its mouth, and just to the left of two pheasants under glass which were in the middle of the table. About a dozen people were busily gorging themselves. Aside from the museum's staff—Dr. Tagarū, Nikodim, and a pretty, rather shabbily dressed young woman who introduced herself to Sally as Annoushka—the rest of the guests were definitely the cream of Romanian society. There was one other non-Romanian at the table: a bony English lady wearing a green silk dress, who was sitting next to Michea.

Sally noted with some amusement that Michea's chair at the head of the table was twice the size of the other chairs and was upholstered in the same red velvet as his suit.

"He must have a thing for red velvet," she whispered to Nikolai, who was busily filling his plate.

"He also thinks he's sitting on a throne," Nikolai said, smiling.

Michea *was* sitting much higher than the rest. He was sipping some of the wine in front of him, but his plate was empty.

Aside from the pheasants and the suckling pig, there were large platters of garnished veal, the traditional Romanian spicy beef rolls, a huge baked sturgeon, a variety of pickled and fried mushrooms, salads, vegetables, and at least three kinds of caviar. A steaming pot of delicious *mamālyga*, a corn mush, was standing on a round table next to the kitchen door. The *mamālyga* was served in saucerlike containers by the wrinkled coachman, now dressed in white and acting as waiter. The wines were mostly French, but there was one bottle of the Romanian red that Sally had been drinking in the village and one bottle of California Almaden Chablis. Sally saw the familiar bottle of the local Romanian wine. The little servant, as though reading her mind, quickly filled her glass. Nikolai finished his beef roll and dug into the sturgeon.

Sally found the pheasant delightful. There was little conversation as yet; the guests were too busy filling their stomachs, though Michea was quietly talking to the English lady on his right. She did not appear to be interested in food either. Michea filled another glass for himself and rose from his throne.

"A toast, my dear friends."

Everyone stopped eating.

"To each and every one of you, my wishes for health and for happiness. I am touched, Comrade Deputy Minister"—he pointed his glass toward a fat middle-aged man sitting to his left—"that you choose to honor us by your presence. To my dear friend and colleague, the great Babulescu," he said, pointing to a round man wearing thick glasses and sitting next to the English lady. "To the representative of our glorious Ministry of the Interior." He nodded toward Nikolai, his eyes suddenly flashing. "All of you, thank you from the bottom of my heart!" He sat down. Some people applauded weakly and drank to his toast. Others, including the deputy minister, were already preoccupied with what remained on their plates.

"He singled me out, Sally," Nikolai explained, "as a warning, so that other guests would be on guard not to say anything stupid against our party and the government. Very clever." He cut himself and Sally two big slices of suckling pig.

"I have never had so much to eat in my life," Annoushka confided to Sally. "I know I will probably be sick, but I can't stop eating. Everything is so delicious."

"It certainly is," Sally agreed. "Who cooked it?"

"His mother, I think."

"What a fantastic cook! It must have taken her a week to prepare all this."

"To our illustrious host." Babulescu rose to his feet. He was very much under the influence and tried hard to find just the right words. "Our greatest poet . . . to hell with it, the greatest living poet in the world today! . . . Michea, my friend, will read tonight some of his poems . . . to you." He stopped just before burping, evidently deciding it was time to sit down. Again, some weak applause. Then the feast continued.

Nikolai finished his pork and wine, and settled back in his chair, looking over the guests. There were two or three familiar faces. He thought he had met the deputy minister somewhere before. Babulescu looked exactly as he had ten years earlier. The lady in green also looked vaguely familiar.

"His face." Sally tugged at Nikolai's sleeve. "I just can't understand the change in Michea's face. All the lines. The face I saw in the carriage belonged to a much younger man."

"Perhaps it was not Michea's face you saw?"

"Oh, it's the same face, all right." She stopped. Michea was looking directly at her. The same gray eyes were studying her. His face looked bloated. It was still handsome, but not nearly as handsome as it had seemed in the carriage. Somehow she had imagined him as tall and slender. The Michea she was looking at now was small and stocky.

"He . . . perhaps he has a hangover," Nikolai observed as Michea downed another glass of red wine.

"Michea"—Babulescu was getting louder and louder—"how can you keep yourself away from this food of the gods?" He laughed. "My friend, you never eat."

Michea smiled, put some veal on his plate, and ate a little of it without enthusiasm.

"I am trying to diet."

The little coachman took the plates into the kitchen and brought back desserts: an assortment of pastries and fresh fruits with pots of black coffee and tea.

The guests were then ushered into a spacious living room with comfortable red leather armchairs, sofas, bookcases, and statues. Behind an oak desk, Rusai set up a podium. Michea was leafing through the papers from which he was planning to read. The guests relaxed with their drinks and talked. Nikolai and Sally found themselves sitting next to Babulescu, who kept staring at both of them as if they were carriers of a horribly contagious disease.

"Ministry of the Interior?" he finally grunted. "I think I've met you before. You people are *everywhere*." He poured himself a shot of cognac and turned away.

"Yes, Comrade," Nikolai replied evenly. "We met once at a lecture you gave in Bucharest. I was one of your admirers. I have read your trilogy, *The Sons of the Forest*."

Babulescu did not reply. He was falling asleep. And not only Babulescu. The deputy minister slumped in his armchair. Many other guests were yawning openly. After that substantial meal, Nikolai himself felt drowsy. Now was a good moment to exit, he thought. Michea went back to the dining room.

"Sally." Nikolai shook her. She, too, was falling asleep. "I think that now is a good time to leave."

"Please," she begged. "Not right now. I am so comfortable."

Nikolai poured himself some more cognac. The lights went out. For a moment or two, the room was in total darkness. Then a reddish glow appeared over the desk and the podium. Another red spotlight bounced off the ceiling, and a bluish light went on behind the piano. At the piano, a dark figure was sitting: evidently old and evidently female. She touched the keys in a sad, lonely melody—a melody that was so familiar to Sally that she held onto Nikolai's hand. She couldn't remember where she had heard it, but she instinctively knew every note. Michea appeared by the podium. He put the typewritten pages down, gazed at the dark room, at his guests, who were beginning to wake up. Now his face was beautiful—not the bloated face of a middle-aged man but the face of a young angel. He began very softly, speaking in Romanian. Sally couldn't understand the words, but somehow she knew what he was talking about.

At night,

Michea's voice grew louder and louder,

he came out on a cliff overlooking a small fishing village. He had eyes that knew no laughter.

46

For him it was strange hearing mothers sing and
rock their children to sleep . . . the
old men pray . . . the younger men drink and
shout and fight in the village tavern.
He knew, early in the morning, as the mist
covers the waves, the seagulls will cry,
the boats will set out in search of fish . . .
the women will do their usual chores,
and the children will play . . .
The sea . . . the mist and the small fishing
village.
He came to the cliff every night, year after
year, century after century.

Michea's eyes began to sparkle eerily. The music was soft and
haunting. He licked his lips and continued.

The wars and the fires will ravage the village.
The houses and the fishing boats will be destroyed
only to be rebuilt again.
The fishermen's children and their children's
children will set out to sea, again and again . . .
and again . . .
The sea and the mist and the small fishing village.
Almost eternal.
He would listen carefully to the sounds of life.
The barking of a dog. The ringing of the church
bells on Sunday morning. The sounds of the
mandolins and the words of the songs in the
tavern.
He would listen to all, and try to understand.
He would envy the sounds of life and would
secretly wish to be a part of them, of
every sound: the seagulls and the creaking
of a mast.
He would wish very much to set the sails in
search of the fish, to fight in the tavern's
brawl . . . to have a woman wait for him
and kiss him when he returns to his house . . .
to have children of his own.
Sadly he looks at the village at night.
Every night from the beginning of time.

Every night listening to something new . . .
   and not understanding it . . . every night,
   the sea, and the mist and the small fishing
   village!
He knew he would come to the cliff until the earth
   is no more.
For he was Death, and he was lonely.

Michea stopped. The lights went out again.
Someone said, "Not bad." A few people applauded. The lights
went on; the portable bar was still there, with the wrinkled little
man behind it. There was no one at the piano.
   "Could you recite another one?" Sally leaned forward, filled her
glass, and added, "Something historical?" Why did I say that? she
thought. Because this castle, everything here is historical, that's
why.
   "Historical?" Michea seemed amused. "I shall try, dear lady." He
smiled slyly. "After all, I am a somewhat unwilling student of
history."
   "His historical knowledge and expertise are simply amazing,"
whispered Babulescu.
   Michea turned slightly away from his guests, gazing at the east
wall, his eyes widening as if he were in a trance.
   "Imagine yourselves," he began in English, "high above the
beautiful city of Samarkand in central Asia, seven centuries ago. You
are standing in a large, lavishly decorated room, the private cham-
bers of Bibi Khanum . . . an exquisite beauty, the daughter of the
emperor of China who is beloved by Timur the Lame, known as the
Conqueror. Timur is by her bedside along with the bodyguards, the
mullahs and the prophets, the doctors and the maids and . . . an old
Tartar sorcerer, standing alone by a round window.
   "Bibi Khanum is quite ill; her face is pale; she is unconscious.
There are two red marks at the base of her neck and everyone in the
room is aware that these marks were made by a vampire.
   " 'Leave!' Timur cries out. He has recently conquered India; the
world is his, yet his beloved is dying.
   "The mullahs, the maids, and the doctors scurry outside. Only
the bodyguards and the Tartar sorcerer remain.
   " 'Sit, shaman!' Timur speaks again. 'Throw your bones and look
at your skull. Tell me who is responsible for this outrage and how it
was accomplished.'

"The sorcerer does as he is told. He meditates on the skull of his dead father until the knowledge of the dead is passed on to the living and he can see and understand things unknown to mortals. He is frightened by the vision.

" 'Tell me,' Timur commands.

" 'It was done, oh Master of the Earth, in your palace,' the old man replies. 'Among the Khans of the Golden Horde stood one who was not a Tartar, a nobleman from the distant country of Moldavia . . . his eyes met the eyes of your beloved wife . . .' The sorcerer pushes aside the skull; he can concentrate no longer.

" 'Tell me,' Timur insists, 'how could this be done? One thousand warriors are guarding my harem. Not even a mouse can run past them.'

" 'Vampires take many forms.' The sorcerer is now tired.

" 'Impossible!' Timur shouted. 'My harem is protected against all witchcraft. You told me so yourself.'

" 'Ordinary witchcraft, my Lord, ordinary vampires, my Master.'

" 'Explain your yapping, dog!' Timur was losing all patience.

"The sorcerer, shaking from fear, dropped onto the floor. Timur motioned one of his guards to cut off the old man's head, but changed his mind.

" 'Rise, old man, don't be frightened. Will my wife herself become a vampire?' he asked gently.

" 'I do not know, my Lord,' the shaman stammered, 'perhaps, if she dies.'

" 'And if she becomes a vampire, will she be immortal?'

" 'No, my Lord, an ordinary vampire lives but two or three centuries.'

" 'Two or three centuries? Not bad.' Timur was thoughtful. 'You are saying *ordinary?*'

" 'Yes, my Lord, there is one among them: a prince born during the time of the total eclipse of the sun . . . my father knows, he lives in a secret magical garden.' "

Michea paused and screamed, startling everyone:

" 'Enough!' Timur shouted. 'Sit down, old man, and look at your skull once more; look carefully. Tell me where this prince might be found. I want to see his head.' "

Michea shook himself, turned to face his guests, and smiled broadly. "Ah, my friends, you are thinking, what does this have to do with our history? Well, the following morning, a small unit composed of Tamerlane's best soldiers left Samarkand on a long and dangerous expedition. Why, here, to this town, of course, to this very famous Dubrava castle!"

"And did they find that prince and his secret garden?" Sally asked.

Michea ignored her; something else had caught his attention.

"Stephen!" Michea suddenly yelled out at the small coachman, who was trying to maneuver the bar between Michea's podium and the deputy minister, and had stumbled on someone's foot so that a bottle of cognac fell off the bar wagon, spilling some of the liquor over Michea's red slacks and his highly polished black shoes.

"You clumsy goat!" Michea slapped his servant on the back of his neck—not a weak slap, but hard and vicious. Everyone in the room heard it and the little man fell down on his knees. He got up quickly though, and bowed to Michea.

"Next time, watch yourself." The dark lines on Michea's face were moving up and down; his eyes were shining. He was still angry, but now, aware that his guests found the slap unpleasant, he tried smiling.

"Disgusting!" said someone loudly. Annoushka stood up and, looking directly at Michea's smiling face, threw down her glass, turned around, and walked out of the room.

"I am sorry to have lost my temper. Stephen, forgive me." Michea embraced the servant, which seemed to terrify the old man far more than the slap. My friends, please refill your drinks. We will have a brief intermission."

"This is the best time to leave . . . Sally, Sally?" Nikolai touched her arm. She was staring moodily at the vase with the poppies.

"Yes, you're right. Time to leave." She stood up. "I am so tired anyway. I'm not used to dinners like this one." Michea did not protest. He walked them to the door, apparently preoccupied.

"I would like to see you again." He smiled. "Nikolai, please forgive me . . ." Michea said this so matter-of-factly it sounded patently false. "I know what you must think of me and you are wrong, my friend, terribly wrong."

"I am not your friend, Michea," Nikolai replied evenly. "But we both thank you for the dinner."

"Nikolai!" Michea's eyes flashed again, an expression of pain on his face. "If you only knew." He said it imploringly.

But Nikolai was already walking down the steps, his arm around Sally's slender waist.

"If he only knew," Michea murmured to himself, his face becoming quite vicious, the eyes growing red and menacing. "If you only knew!" He quickly shut the door.

The main hall was lighted by only one bulb now; the shadows were long and eerie. There was a guard on duty at the entrance: an alert, middle-aged man, Ivan.

"Do you like working here?" Nikolai couldn't resist asking him.

"No, Comrade, this is a queer place. I am quitting the moment I receive my salary for this month."

Outside, everything was quiet. Two chauffeurs were standing near the limousines, smoking, talking quietly, and looking at the lighted windows. Nikolai helped Sally into his Land Rover. Riding back, he thought how easily he had let himself be trapped. If only I hadn't found the bodies . . . if only I were not a policeman . . . if only I had driven with Sally to Mamaia, to my little cabin and miles and miles of soft white sand and the sea . . . if only. Tomorrow, he knew, the results of the autopsy would be known and he'd have to drive back to the castle. Tomorrow. Tonight he had Sally. He looked at her; she was asleep. He parked quietly by the hotel and carried her inside.

Annoushka couldn't sleep after the party. She knew she shouldn't have eaten or drunk so much. Many thoughts were running through her mind. Two more months of working for the state museum and then she would be married and living in Bucharest. She hated the Dubrava castle job. She had taken it only to save some money: the state museum provided her with room and board, and the salary was better than when she had worked for the national tourist agency. Everything had been so nice until a month ago, when Michea began riding in his carriage and odd things started to happen. She thought of going to Nikolai and telling him about one or two of the incidents. As one Communist to another, just as one decent human being to another. Nikolai seemed to be an honest man. It was very fortunate that he was also a policeman. This nightmare had to end. Tomorrow! I must get to talk to him tomorrow. She closed her eyes and thought about her family and her lover, Pavlo. The moon was just rising over the mountains.

Annoushka's room was in a semibasement of the castle and her only window faced the forest. She loved to look out in the mornings when the birds sang their songs and two gray rabbits came up

51

almost to the level of her window to snatch the bits of carrot and cabbage leaves she left for them. At night, she could see a patch of the star-filled sky over the forest and the snow-covered peaks of the Carpathian Alps. And when she was really bored, she would listen to her radio or play her guitar and sing. Once, she had thought seriously of singing professionally in some resort hotel on the Black Sea. But now, all her thoughts were with her Pavlo, who would be getting out of the army in exactly two months; of their life together, marriage, children. To begin with, Annoushka wanted two children, a boy and a girl. And a good apartment in one of the new high-rise buildings, possibly even with a balcony. And oh, yes, instead of Pavlo's silly green motorcycle, an automobile, a sky blue Volkswagen. Two more months.

She opened the window and gazed at the dark forest. The mountain peaks were glowing white. There must be a full moon tonight, she decided. Such a blinding reflection.

Something rustled at the edge of the forest. Probably some cow was lost again. Annoushka looked more closely: there was, indeed, a darker outline among the trees. Whatever it may have been, the object was not standing still. It was moving toward her.

Uneasy, she started to close her window. But the dark mass was moving toward her now with superhuman speed. It flew past her into her room with a gust of icy cold air. And everything became unreal. For the first few moments, Annoushka felt she was in paradise. The walls of her room opened up, stars and planets, some orange and red, others shining like emeralds, whirled around her: endless strings of beads, as she slowly floated toward a castle made entirely of tiny crystals, twinkling and whistling and calling her name. The castle was surprisingly small. Annoushka had to bend down to enter the narrow round gate. As she entered, she felt she was in mortal danger. Her entire being was suddenly shocked by the realization that she could die, at any moment, on any step of the curving, treacherous stairway she was now descending.

The stairway led into a round windowless room with a mud-covered floor. A black table stood in the middle, on which a black candle was burning.

I must get out immediately, Annoushka thought.

"Help!" she cried out when a hand touched her shoulder. She wanted to run, but she couldn't move a muscle. *I must still be in my room,* she thought. *This cannot be happening. This is some form of illusion.*

She tried convincing herself that no one was holding her by the shoulder; that it must have been the food she had indulged in so freely. She must call the doctor.

Unfortunately, the grip on her shoulder was growing stronger. She was now in pain.

"Let me go, whoever you are," Annoushka whispered, desperately. She did not dare to look around.

"Silence, you fool!" That voice was so familiar and yet so totally different from any voice she had ever heard. Forceful, sensual, coming at her as a bolt of lightning, penetrating her every nerve.

Annoushka closed her eyes, pulled together the few ounces of strength she had, grabbed the hand holding her shoulder and struggled to shake it loose. After what felt like an eternity of combat, she managed to tear the hand away. Encouraged by her success, she turned around to face her tormentor.

"You fool!" The face staring at her was contorted with rage. Annoushka was pushed back across the room as if she were a mere feather. And the woman, whom Annoushka recognized, to her horror, as the happy American lady who had sat next to her at the banquet, slowly advanced toward her.

Annoushka prepared to defend herself. She grabbed the candle with its heavy candle-holder and held it as a weapon in front of her.

It wasn't the candle itself, but the flame, as it grew larger, that startled the woman, the creature, the female vurdalak. She tried grabbing the candle away from Annoushka, but her movements were now very slow, groping. She couldn't even control her hands. Something else seemed to stop her; not Annoushka's feeble defense. Something that she must have heard or seen. She stood still for a few moments, listening like a forest animal to some distant noises.

"You must obey me now!" she suddenly shrieked. No longer a command, but a cry of desperation, of loneliness, and . . . fear.

Annoushka knew that she must faint now, that only by fainting did she have any hope of surviving. The half-human being would advance again, and would do whatever it wished with Annoushka's body and her soul. With knowledge came the will. Annoushka's whole body collapsed and she sank to the musty floor.

The last thing she heard was the crowing of the cock.

five

_____

It was a disturbing night for Nikolai, too. Exhausted as he was, he kept waking up, tossing and turning. In his dreams, the events of the past few days were assuming fantastic significance. He was a child of five. His mother appeared to him behind their peasant hut. She was frightened. She kept waving at him and shouting, but he couldn't hear or understand what she wanted. Then, he was a much older boy wearing a white peasant shirt and new boots, and walking importantly to his communion. In the church, incense smoke and soft, sad singing engulfed him. "Confess your sins," the priest told the boy. "Confess and you will be free." Nikolai looked up; that wasn't the voice of the priest.

"Confess and you will have Maria or any girl," the priest whispered, bending closer to his ear. "And they will all like you. I will make sure that they do."

How did he know? Who had told him? Nikolai felt frightened. He wanted to get up and run. Above the priest's robe, Michea's face was staring at him: black circles under his huge eyes, mouth twisted and open, ready to bite.

"No!" the boy screamed, and ran. Again, his mother appeared. Singing. What was that song? About a little shepherd boy who must die. And later that day, eerie quiet descended on the village and the first German tanks rolled on along the road to Bucharest.

Nikolai was hidden in a field of corn, watching. He imagined that these tanks and trucks were giant beetles coming to devour the land. These beetles made a terrible noise, the earth shook, and he ran home.

The tanks were gone; the fields were now peaceful. A long stretch of white beach. He was walking with his wife to their cottage, hand in hand. Some wonderful moments, sensual and tender. The nightmare was clearly over.

And then Sally screamed.

He reluctantly opened his eyes. No, this wasn't a dream. Sally was standing naked by the open window. She was staring at the mountains, cold wind brushing back her hair.

Nikolai jumped up, embraced her, walked her back to bed. He noticed that through half-closed eyes, she was smiling, but it wasn't her usual smile. A wicked, hungry, gleeful smile, the smile of the Nazi lieutenant leading Nikolai to the execution.

"What is it?" he asked.

She did not answer. Instead she kissed him very hard and then sank her teeth into his lower lip.

"Stop it!" he cried out and tried to push her away, but she kept on biting and licking away the blood while her hands, her fingernails, were scratching and pinching his nipples.

It hurt so much, but it was also pleasurable. Either he did not want her to stop or he was unable to push her away.

"Lie down," she whispered. Again he was startled, even slightly frightened. She whispered in pure, old-fashioned Romanian.

What the hell? I am imagining things, he decided. Must be all that drinking at the castle. He sighed and leaned back.

She lowered her head and bit his already sore nipples, biting and kissing and licking the blood all at the same time. Her hands were now lower. He had never been so aroused in his entire life. When her mouth came down on him, hard and soft, he closed his eyes. Her head was coming down faster and ever harder; her hands were probing deep into him.

Sensations such as he had never experienced flashed through his body, the pain she was inflicting turned to pleasure. When he came, it was as if she had managed to suck in his entire being: body and soul, everything, leaving him with a spasm of delight, a limp, large body drained of all feelings and thoughts.

But she was far from finished.

She slid next to him and whispered things only a whore whispers to arouse her customer—again, he thought, in pure old Romanian—and turned on her stomach.

Finally, it was light outside and the roosters were crowing. She lay asleep. Nikolai got up, his legs shaky. He felt groggy. His whole body was moving in slow motion. He lit a cigarette, inhaled deeply. What have I got here? he thought. A liberated woman? Oh, no! A whore? Not even a whore can please a man in such a way. The things we did through the night! He shook his head and inhaled again.

And every time, she seemed to predict his most intimate, deep-felt, and long-suppressed desires.

And the language, that part really bothered him. Perhaps he had only dreamed it in the heat of passion? Perhaps. What other explanation could there be? He watched her closely: she looked very tired too, breathing heavily. What stamina! What power! And they say American women are never good in bed. American! Well, let me find out.

He shook her gently, insistently, until she opened her eyes. He spoke to her in Romanian: "Wake up, my dearest, it is time to wake up."

"Oh, Nikolai." She smiled and gently hugged his hand. Her usual lovely smile. "I am so tired, I . . . I need . . ." Her eyes were closing. He let her go back to sleep. He sat quietly by the bed, finished his cigarette, lit another. "Sleep, my love." He watched the sun come up over the mountains. "Sleep."

He then began dressing. He had quite a day ahead of him and not a moment to lose.

six

The sun came out and transformed the landscape into a beautiful fairyland. Not one cloud, and the mist was rapidly dissolving. The morning seemed to be whispering to Nikolai, it's another beautiful day, look around, at the poppies in the fields, at the forest, so peaceful and green, at the wild roses and the golden fields; it's a day to relax, you must relax, everyone must relax. Rest, that's what I need, thought Nikolai: to swim in the Black Sea, to sleep on the beach. I wonder how the roses around my beach house are doing?

The car screeched to a stop. He got out, walked a few steps into a field, and took a deep breath of fresh air. The sergeant, too, climbed out.

"It's a wonderful morning." Nikolai sighed. "Hate interrogating people on a day like this."

"I agree." The sergeant's official mask of eagerness was gone; his eyes were wistful; he sighed deeply.

Nikolai looked at him: a young man around twenty. He probably has a woman somewhere. He should be with her. Everyone should be with a woman today. He wanted to hold Sally very much, to make love to her in this field amid the tall green grass and the red poppies.

At the castle, everything was more or less arranged. Another militia sergeant led Nikolai to Dr. Tagarū's study.

"I've set up the tape recorder here." He opened the top drawer of Dr. Tagarū's massive desk. "Everyone whom you wished to see has been notified. Anything else, Comrade Captain?"

"Yes, I'd like a thermos of coffee, some sweet rolls, butter, jam, cream, everything—I am going to use the soft approach, understood?"

"Certainly, Comrade Captain." The sergeant saluted and softly closed the door.

Nikolai reached for the telephone. He started dialing Bucharest, but then thought better of it and put the receiver down. After the sergeant brought him the laden tray, Nikolai asked to see the first man, old Rusai, the caretaker.

"Slept well, grandfather?" Nikolai turned on the recorder and invited Rusai to sample the food. The old man did so with unusual gusto. Three rolls, one after another, disappeared within a few seconds, followed by a cup of milky coffee. Nikolai stopped him as Rusai was ready to grab three more rolls off the tray.

"Tell me something first," he insisted. "These Germans, did they pay you well?"

Rusai shook his head.

"Did they give you any tips?"

"No."

"Have another roll, grandfather . . . did you ever observe them arguing, fighting, angry?"

"No."

This is getting me exactly nowhere, decided Nikolai. And I'll also run out of rolls very fast.

"You may go, grandfather. If you see or hear anything suspicious, notify me immediately."

"Mmmgh." Rusai slammed the door so hard that a diploma hanging behind Dr. Tagarū's desk fell on the floor and the glass broke. The militia man poked his head inside.

"Never mind," said Nikolai, picking up the pieces. "Call Ivan."

The night guard ate and drank slowly. He spoke only when he had finished. "Comrade, this castle is a very bad place."

"Why?"

Ivan thought for a few minutes. "I am quitting anyhow, so it's nothing to me, but the poor people who are staying—" He shuddered.

"Come on, Ivan, tell me what's on your mind."

"There are such things going on at night, the devil's own teeth would be chattering from fear."

Nikolai poured Ivan and himself some more coffee. This was interesting.

"One night, oh, two weeks ago, I was standing guard in the great hall . . . I don't know how to put it, Comrade . . ."

"Were you drinking?"

"No, God knows, only maybe a glass of vodka with my supper . . . no more than two. But I was sober, just as I am now. Well, I heard something . . . singing, a woman was singing a lullaby, so softly that my eyes began to close. I thought I was hearing things. I thought, wake up, Ivan. I look around, don't see anybody . . . only there's this singing again. I listen, this time, and my hair begins to stand up. This was the same song my mother used to sing when I was a small boy . . . I listen closely and it *is* my mother, God rest her soul, singing to me. I am not lying, it was her voice; we came from Carpatho Russia . . ." Ivan stopped, licked his lips.

"So you had another glass of vodka?"

"No, Comrade, not then. I was so frightened, I ran outside."

"You left your post, you left our museum unattended?"

"I couldn't help it."

"Aha, how often did that singing . . . happen, and are you sure it was your mother?"

"Positive. In the song, she calls me 'Lichoi.' Only she called me . . ." Tears filled Ivan's eyes. Nikolai also noticed a faint odor of alcohol.

"This singing, does it happen now?"

"Yes, almost every night."

"And every night, you leave your post and run outside?"

"I . . . yes," Ivan whispered.

Now here was something concrete.

"What time does this usually happen?"

Ivan thought hard. "I think, just a few minutes after midnight."

"And when you get outside, you don't hear this song?"

"No, Comrade."

"How long do you stay outside?"

"Oh, ten, fifteen minutes."

"When you go back, do you hear that song again?"

"No." Ivan lowered his head in shame.

So, every night, at a certain time, the museum is left totally unattended? Nikolai thought some more.

"Tell me, Ivan, do you realize that some of our priceless national treasures are in this museum? And instead of guarding it diligently, you come to work drunk and then you hear voices. I can arrest you now—sabotage, dereliction of duty."

59

"No, please."

"And believe me, in our jails you won't hear any mothers singing lullabies."

Ivan jumped up.

"Sit down." Nikolai saw no point in arresting or even frightening a poor drunk. He was after much bigger fish. "It is not my duty to detain you, and nothing was reported stolen. Have you observed anything . . . unusual?"

"Yes, I did, but you are not going to believe me again."

"Talk."

"There are these lights . . ."

"What lights?"

"Hmm, they are both lights and not lights." Ivan was uncertain.

"What do you mean?"

"Well, they *look* like lights, green and sort of yellow . . . but they go right through the walls and the floor . . . and real lights, they don't go through the walls, do they?"

"I hope not."

Ivan sat silent.

"Ivan, I am going to recommend to Dr. Targarū that you be suspended and sent to a treatment facility. Two, three months and you'll feel as good as new. Alcoholism is a disease and it can be cured. You need not be ashamed to admit it. You may go now." Nikolai lit a cigarette, inhaled deeply, and swore to himself. All this time wasted.

He got up to open the door and welcomed Janco, who had been waiting glumly in the reception area. Janco already reeked of alcohol, ten times stronger than Ivan.

"Sit down, my friend." Nikolai embraced him, led him to his chair. "Have something to eat, to drink."

Janco looked with contempt at the coffee and the rolls. He pulled out a metal flask from his pocket, took a long pull on it, coughed, and handed the flask to Nikolai.

Nikolai's first reaction was to push the flask away. What the hell, he quickly decided. With the day going as badly as this, I'll need some reinforcement. He took a gulp and choked. This was not ordinary vodka: it was home-distilled and tasted a little like wood alcohol.

"Are you sure this is safe to drink?"

"Only tastes bad when you first swallow."

True, Nikolai didn't taste the second swallow at all. His taste buds were dead.

"I don't like to do this," he began, "but I have two corpses on my hands . . ."

"Shut up, Nikola, and ask what you have to ask." Janco used his flask again.

"I don't even know what to ask . . . did you notice anything unusual recently?"

Janco's eyes grew round and he pulled his lips away from the flask and smacked them.

"Only don't tell me any fairy tales. I've heard enough gibberish about witches, vurdalaks, and strange lights. I am not interested in anything supernatural."

"That's too bad," Janco said seriously. "Because right here, in this castle, we have a witch, a vurdalak, and we have plenty of strange lights." He calmly watched Nikolai, and Nikolai felt uneasy. Certainly Janco would not lie to him. And yet?

"Damn you," he almost shouted. "I am just interested in finding the murderer, the person who killed those two Germans."

"Why? Between the two of us, we must have killed at least a hundred of them in '44 . . ."

"This is not '44, but '81, and killing them is illegal now."

Janco thought for a minute or two.

"So, you are asking me whether I noticed anything unusual? That's a very good question. Up until about a month ago, the only unusual occurrence I can remember was when a big boar wandered across the parking lot and terrified a busload of Japanese tourists."

It was Nikolai's turn to put his lips to the flask.

"Then, a month ago, Michea came back."

Nikolai jumped up in his chair. "Wasn't he living here all along?"

"Nooo." Janco was choosing his words carefully now. "He came back. The next day, his old creep of a mother and his servant arrived with that carriage. Well, his highness wishes to go for a ride every day, but just before sunrise and just after sunset."

"What's wrong with that?"

"Nothing, except that his highness happens to be a vurdalak."

"Stop it, Janco!" Nikolai shouted and leaned across the table. "Stop this nonsense. Michea is a bastard, I admit. I should have killed him back in '44 . . . but a vurdalak?"

"You asked me, and I am telling you."

Nikolai lit another cigarette, threw the pack to Janco. This was going to be worse than he'd expected. He visualized Sally waking up, washing her beautiful face. Shit!

"Let's get back to the Germans. You met them, talked with them?"

"I don't associate with garbage."

"When did they arrive here?"

Janco's eyes suddenly lit up with interest. "Nikola, that is another good question. They arrived a month ago. What a coincidence!"

"Yes, isn't it?"

"Well, they're dead." Janco made a mocking sign of the cross. "Bury them and forget about them."

"I can't."

Janco suddenly roared with laughter. He looked at Nikolai's long face and stopped.

"What's so funny?"

"You're right, you can't bury them."

"What are you talking about?"

"If you bury them, they'll rise from their graves, like Lazarus . . . and they'll be very, very hungry." Janco made sucking sounds with his flask and wiped his lips. "For human blood!"

"You're out of your fucking mind!"

"I am, I am," Janco readily agreed, "if you say so."

"Besides, we are shipping them back to Germany right after the postmortem."

"Good, good, very good. Let them suck the blood of their own people."

"You don't really believe this?"

"Why not? There are, after all, things we know nothing about. Who'd have believed in '44 that a man would walk on the moon?"

"This is different."

"I agree." Janco took the last swig from his flask and put it back in his pocket. He was serious again. "And that is why I want to be fired."

Nikolai still wasn't sure whether Janco was playing with him, whether it was a put-on, whether Janco would suddenly jump up and grab him and laugh at the joke. But Janco now looked sad.

"That bad?" Nikolai asked.

"Not very good."

"I can arrange a transfer to Bucharest."

"I'd be really grateful."

Nikolai remembered the recorder, ran the tape back to the latter part of their conversation. "I have to do this, for official records." He felt himself getting red, ashamed of being a policeman again.

"I understand."

"I don't. What is it that can frighten you, of all people?"

"When you find out what it is, you'll need this." He slapped his pocket.

The militia sergeant knocked. The autopsy report had arrived.

For the next few hours, Nikolai was absorbed in rather lengthy and contradictory medical explanations. Twice he called the chief examiner and questioned him at length. Only when the sergeant brought him a bowl of tasty lamb stew did he push away the thick blue folder.

"There's a young woman waiting to see you, Comrade Captain. She says it's of utmost importance . . . she's a member of the party."

"Invite her in." Nikolai dug into the stew.

Annoushka came in, hesitated, then sat down across from him.

"Excuse me, Comrade, I am almost finished," Nikolai swallowed a piece of lamb and pushed the plate aside. "May I see your card?"

Annoushka gave it to him. Nikolai smiled, "You know, Comrade, I was afraid we did not have a single member of the party in this . . . investigation. Would you like some coffee, some food?"

"Thank you, I've had my lunch."

"You said it was important?"

"Terribly important . . . I feel my life is in danger."

"One question first . . . your predicament, does it relate in any way to the unfortunate incident?" Nikolai was sure by now everyone in the castle knew about the Germans' mysterious demise. "I am speaking about the German archeologists . . ."

"Yes, yes, that too."

"In that case, Comrade, I must turn on my tape recorder."

"I don't mind." She paused, gathering her strength.

Nikolai suddenly noticed the dark circles under her eyes, her haggard appearance. At least I am going to hear an intelligent story, he thought.

"Comrade," she rapidly blurted out. "You may not believe what I am going to tell you. It's so, well, unreal . . . I am not a superstitious woman. I don't believe either in God or the devil; I believe there are only people: good and bad. When that monster, Michea, arrived, many queer things began to happen. You can ask Dr. Tagarū . . ."

"Realistically, what happened?"

"That's just it. What happened was not entirely real. It was as though we were hypnotized . . . or possibly poisoned by some hallucinogenic drug. Am I making any sense?"

"Yes, you are!" Nikolai exclaimed. That would account for lights and sounds, and much more.

"I would not be surprised if Michea were the mastermind of some kind of conspiracy: he is a reactionary; to hear him talk, you'd think he was a prince of old Romania."

"I, too, would not be surprised. I had an encounter with him some time ago. Can you give me some clue? Something . . ."

"I believe I can." Annoushka interrupted him. "I'd like to report one instance. I was conferring with Dr. Tagarū two weeks ago about a priceless thirteenth-century manuscript in our collection, a chronology of historical events from 1073 all the way through 1240 or 1250. Evidently, it was compiled by some obscure Bessarabian monastic order and preserved by their followers when their monastery was burned by the advancing Tartar horde. We, Dr. Tagarū and myself, feel the manuscript should be placed in the archives of our National Historical Society. For one thing, they have adequate security and we don't. There are a number of other reasons. We had just finished writing a letter to the Ministry of Culture when the door flew wide open—we were at this office—and Michea appeared, asking us to lend him the manuscript." She paused, poured herself some coffee, and drank quickly. Her hands were trembling.

"We explained to him," she continued, "that he had to obtain an official permit even to read it, never mind taking it out of our custody. He simply picked up the phone, this phone, dialed the minister of culture himself, told the minister what he wanted, and then handed the phone to Dr. Tagarū. The minister said that Michea could have any manuscript and an order of verification would be sent by the courier."

"Michea has the manuscript?"

"No, he returned it."

"Then, what's the problem?"

"Several pages in it are *now* clever forgeries."

"Are you sure?" For the first time today, Nikolai was getting excited. Now he had something concrete to go on—if she was right. And she sounded truthful.

"Are you sure?"

"I am absolutely sure. What's more, Dr. Tagarū knows it too."

"This is very serious . . . although frankly I don't know how it relates to the two German archeologists."

"There is a connection. Two or three days after Michea got the manuscript, I witnessed a commotion. After supper, I went to my office next door to finish a thesis I was working on at the time. I stopped in the great hall. There was an angry argument going on on the balcony between the two Germans and Michea. They did not see me. Michea accused the older German of being a thief. They were shouting at each other, mixing German and Romanian, and I understand some German. The old German screamed at Michea, 'You have no power now, you have no power.' He just kept repeating it."

"No power?"

"That's exactly what he said."

"Anything else? Please try to remember."

She frowned. "Possibly. They were talking about the war . . . just before the great Soviet breakthrough in 1944."

"Oh?" Now there was something, an inkling of a motive. Nikolai was very much interested.

"The older man said, 'You were on our side, but yet you did not help us.' " She continued. "Something also about gold and precious stones. A treasure of some kind. I am really not making any sense, am I?"

"When the older archeologist screamed, 'You have no power,' what was Michea's reaction?"

"He just laughed."

"Anything else?"

"Yes, both Germans were terrified. They did not see me as they walked down. They were speaking so rapidly I couldn't understand what they were saying, though they repeated the word 'death' several times."

"Did Michea see you?"

"No."

"Are you absolutely certain?"

"I was pretty sure. I left right away, but after what happened to me last night, I don't know."

"Last night? After supper?"

Annoushka told Nikolai what had happened. The only part she omitted was her recognition of Nikolai's friend, the American woman. Since this was clearly a hallucination, she thought it made no sense to drag in an innocent tourist.

"I don't know what to believe." Nikolai was touched by her story and fully shared her apprehension. "When you did regain consciousness—on the floor in your room—there was mud on your nightgown?"

"Yes."

"How can you explain it?"

"I can't . . . Comrade, it is possible . . . whoever drugged me . . . could have entered my room after I was asleep and rubbed the mud on my nightgown."

"That means, if you are correct, and I have no doubt that you are . . . you'd best pack your belongings and leave. Do you have relatives?"

"Yes, but my work . . ."

"Forget about your work for the time being. I'll talk to Dr. Tagarū. I have the authority. My main concern is to get you out of here. If Michea wants to kill you, I am not sure I can protect you. Not here."

"And why not? You are a policeman . . ."

"I am a good policeman. This is why I am telling you, not just that, *ordering* you, to leave the castle. Do you understand?"

"No, I don't!" Annoushka was defiant. To her, it was like fleeing under fire.

"Just do it," barked Nikolai. "Sergeant!" he yelled, and the alert head immediately popped in the door. "Take this woman to her room, make sure she packs her belongings, then drive her . . . where are your relatives?"

"In Brasov."

"Drive her to Brasov in your car."

"But, Comrade Captain, I've been assigned here, my duty . . ."

"This, Sergeant, is an order." He stood up, shook Annoushka's hand, and wished her good luck. The day was not entirely lost, after all. Whatever game Michea was playing, at least he was in on it. Nikolai felt like a hunter, hot on the trail. His left ear began to twitch, as it had hundreds of times during previous investigations. He was definitely tracking the beast. The old feeling of confidence surged through his body; once on the track, he never lost his prey.

"Another thing, Sergeant, send two of our men to bring me Janco, the guard. If he's drunk, revive him; if he refuses, tie him up and carry him here. Right here!" Nikolai pointed to the chair. He then called the Two Moons Café to leave a message for Sally that he'd be working late. This won't take long, my love, he thought. By tomorrow afternoon, we'll be driving down to the sea.

A knocking sounded on his door again. Had they got Janco so soon? No, it was another militia man. Apparently there was an odd-looking, tall man who wished to see the captain.

"Not now." It was getting late in the afternoon and he had one more task to accomplish. He waited until the militia man brought him Janco, who was very angry and not entirely sober.

"Your flask full?" asked Nikolai.

"Half full. Why are you doing this to me?"

"Good enough." Nikolai cut him off.

"We, my friend," Nikolai said softly, "are going to take a little drive . . . to the Valley of Blood."

"Not me." Janco backed away. "You are crazy, Nikola."

Nikolai pulled out his pistol, checked it, and said to the militia man accompanying Janco, "Please issue this man a rifle."

"You are crazy, Nikola." Janco was grinning from ear to ear. "But, by God, you have courage."

seven

Sally woke up, glanced at her watch, and couldn't believe it: half-past one. Her head was throbbing; she felt groggy. Must be that wine from last night. All those nightmares, too. She remembered waking up in a cold sweat. Michea had appeared a few times and frightened the hell out of her, then some ugly peasants were chasing her with giant flaming torches while she was running with someone's baby in her arms. Ugh! She got up, splashed some cold water on her face, looked in the mirror. What a mess.

An hour later, however, after applying heavier makeup than usual, combing her hair, and putting on her new Romanian blouse, the usual happy, neat, and confident Sally walked into the Two Moons Café and ordered herself a good lunch.

"How long does it take to walk over to the castle?" she asked the waitress after being informed that Nikolai was there on business.

"Do you want to walk up there?" The waitress was surprised.

"Why not? It's such a wonderful day." Oh, I must not forget my Nikon; I must take at least a few shots before we drive to Nikolai's cabin.

The waitress gave her directions and warned that the last kilometer was all uphill. Sally returned to her room, loaded a new roll of film into her camera, put on her walking shoes, and was soon in the forest on the way to the castle.

Passing the last house in the village, Sally decided to take a shot of a perfect village scene: an old woman hanging out the wash and singing quietly. Sally stopped, raised her Nikon. And . . .

something unexpected happened. The old woman saw her, grabbed up her wash, and ran into the house, slamming and locking the door after her. As if she were afraid of Sally. Well, perhaps she was shy and didn't want her picture taken.

An odd thought ran briefly through Sally's mind. She had seen that very house and the crumbling walls of the church and the boarded-up house next to the church some time before. Another curious thought: there was an orthodox priest in that house, near that upper window. A handsome, robust young man. And everything was bathed in moonlight, sinister and bright. Then, too, the women were terrified and the children cried. What possible harm could she bring to them? She forced the morbid thoughts—residue, no doubt, from her nightmare—out! She smiled and continued walking.

Half a mile from the village, an old truck passed her and stopped. A handsome young man, no more than eighteen, jumped out, brushed his curly dark hair with his hand, and, smiling widely, invited Sally to share his ride. He didn't speak any English and Sally didn't speak Romanian, but it wasn't hard to guess what he wanted. Sally refused, with some regret: if it weren't for Nikolai, she'd have taken the kid's offer. He sped away and she continued in the direction of a brand-new sign proclaiming: DUBRAVA CASTLE, NATIONAL HISTORIC MUSEUM, 2.8 KM.

The narrow road climbed up and up and the countryside became more wild. Several rabbits hopped across the road, stopping to look at her for a moment as if to ask what she was doing there, then dashing madly into the thick underbrush. A large brown snake was curled up in the sun in the middle of the road. It didn't even move as Sally cautiously walked around it. About halfway up the hill, Sally decided to rest a bit. There were a couple of large stones on the side of the road—a perfect place to sit down. The birds were chirping all around her and a beautiful small deer walked importantly across the road. Sally waited for a few more minutes. When another deer crossed the road, she took a good close-up. The click startled the deer for a second, but then he continued calmly on his way. Sally finally got up.

A few hundred steps farther, the road abruptly turned and went almost straight up the hill. That's what the waitress meant about the last kilometer. Sally paused and took a deep breath. A little brown-and red-colored bird jumped directly in front of her from one of the bushes. Sally walked toward it. The bird seemed to be injured; it chirped loudly and dragged one of its wings on the ground. Sally bent down to pick it up, but the bird flew a couple of steps and then dropped to the ground.

"I won't hurt you; let me see what's wrong." Sally advanced toward it again, and again the bird flew off and landed, this time in the grass near the road. Sally followed it. The bird repeated its maneuver again and again, once almost letting Sally touch it. And each time the bird flew deeper and deeper into the forest. I'm not going to chase you anymore, Sally decided. The road was already out of sight. The bird was sitting on a tree stump in a small clearing, chirping as if daring Sally to come near. Exasperated, Sally took a few steps toward the clearing. The bird flew off effortlessly, high into the blue, blue sky, and out of sight. Sally stopped. She realized that the bird had led her away from its nest. Sally turned back and started walking toward the road. Within a few minutes, she stopped. What the hell? The trees and bushes now looked unfamiliar. They were much larger and darker. She kept walking. I should've been back on the road by now, she thought, and stopped again. Here and there, the rays of sunshine came through tall trees, but the forest looked even darker and more foreboding. I can't get lost on a day like this. I know I'm walking in the right direction. Sooner or later, I am bound to cross the road. She slowly looked around. In the general direction of the road, she noticed a bright sunny spot, a clearing. She walked toward it. She breathed easier as the forest finally ended and she entered a large field, on the other end of which stood some old ruins. On closer inspection, she saw that these were the ruins of a church: Byzantine frescos of stern-looking saints were glaring from the crumbling walls. Behind the church was a cemetery, unkempt and long-forgotten. There were wooden Orthodox crosses that had turned gray and were tangled with ivy, tall grass, and various wild flowers, which grew in abundance.

Sally started taking pictures almost immediately. Close-ups, long shots, all kinds of angles. The photographer in her took over. She noticed that some of the graves had gravestones made out of granite or something similar; some had very elaborate carvings. All had Orthodox crosses and writing that resembled ancient Hebrew underneath; some even had profiles on them. Deeper into the cemetery, Sally stopped. Here was a curious sight: a spot of barren earth, about ten feet by ten feet, with a large tombstone in the middle.

The curious part was that wild flowers and grass were growing in every other part of the cemetery; bright green vines covered the church's ruins; but here, nothing at all, not a single blade of grass. And it wasn't fresh ground either. It looked as if it hadn't been disturbed for centuries. Sally stepped cautiously on the brown earth and bent down to take a close-up of the tombstone. This one was very different from the rest: there were no crosses on it; there was a star and a crescent just above two crossed swords, some writing underneath, also quite different from the rest and, painted in color, portraits of a man and a woman. They were both wearing pointed fur hats and, although most of the paint was chipped and most of their faces were indistinguishable, they were of Oriental origin, with slanting eyes, square, savage features.

What a find!

As she was finishing her roll of film, she thought for a few seconds that the place was familiar to her, that if she tried hard enough, she could read the ancient inscriptions. The man and the woman in the portrait had, at one time or another, possessed some influence on her life; somehow it was all connected with Michea. What a fascinating man. She thought for a moment that she knew him, too, knew him intimately. . . . The thought faded; she finished her roll of film.

The sun was already going down on the other side of the mountains and the mist was creeping into the valleys. Now was the time to shoot the panoramic view, thought Sally. But she had no more film.

When she came out of the woods, there was a young militia man sitting in a gray car. He jumped up in surprise when he saw her. Sally couldn't wait to tell Nikolai about her adventures. Near the museum shop, she almost ran head-on into Dr. Tagarū, who was walking deep in thought. He told her that both Nikolai and Janco had left just a few minutes ago. That was a disappointment. Dr. Tagarū smiled. "Would you please do us the honor of having an early dinner with the staff? It will be a farewell dinner." His face turned sad. "My very able assistant has taken an indefinite leave of absence; her aunt is quite ill." He ushered Sally into a small dining room, where dinner had already been served. Annoushka, Nikodim, and Ivan were getting ready to begin eating aromatic soup, which an old woman had poured directly into their plates from a large steaming pot.

"Another plate, Olga, we have another guest." Dr. Tagarū seated

Sally at the head of the table and sat to her right. Sally thought that Annoushka was startled by her appearance. She kept looking at Sally as if she were seeing a ghost; her face bore the same expression of fear as had that old peasant woman hanging out wash in the village. Sally smiled, said hello to everybody, and started eating. Annoushka still kept staring at her.

"Anything wrong?" Sally asked.

"No, no, please excuse me." Annoushka got hold of herself and put the spoon in her bowl.

The soup was followed by an exceptionally tasty cutlet in mushroom sauce, homemade ice cream and coffee for dessert. After the dinner, Dr. Tagarū opened a bottle of wine and proposed a toast: "To the best assistant I have ever had, lovely Annoushka, may she return very soon."

Annoushka raised her glass. Her hand trembled as her glass touched Sally's. She drank her wine fast and excused herself. Sally felt sleepy after her little adventure. She remembered seeing a large overstuffed couch in the museum's library. Would Dr. Tagarū mind if she took a short nap until Nikolai came back? Not at all.

The couch felt comfortable and warm. Sally closed her eyes and, within a few moments, was fast asleep.

eight

Aside from Sally's breathing, there was no movement in the library. No windows opened or closed; the spring activating the secret panel behind the bookcases remained untouched, and the mosquito that had been buzzing over Sally's head stopped buzzing.

Michea stood silently by the side of the couch, his hands crossed on his chest, his huge liquid eyes looking somewhere in the distance. He stood, frozen as a statue, dressed in black: wide trousers stuck carelessly into the narrow, pointed boots; a ceremonial dagger, its handle encrusted with shiny jewels, hung on a wide, gold, embroidered belt. He looked young again, with his black hair falling on both sides of his face. On his head was a small golden crown with a tear-shaped ruby in the middle.

Michea lowered his eyes for a moment to study Sally. She was the only being dear to him, this elegant lady sleeping on the couch. So elusive was her soul and so infrequent was her appearance. He seemed to gaze inward. "Why, my Lord," he whispered, "must I be tormented so much? Why can she not travel with me through the eternal mist? Why does she have such need for human lovers?" He stood in silence for a few minutes, then he looked directly at the massive leather-bound books, his eyes cutting through the castle walls, past the mountains and forests and the river guarded by stern Russian soldiers with their submachine guns, to his native Bessarabian earth and the steppes, to another sunrise and sunset, and the stars and the moon, spinning before him in a never-ending circle.

He saw smoke across the vast horizon and the advancing Tartars devouring everything in their path, like a giant swarm of locusts. He saw himself being born, at the moment of the total eclipse of the sun; the earth standing still and the green grass drying up in the fields. He saw another Michea: a little boy, surrounded by women and monks. He saw Tartars screaming and howling as they climbed the walls of his ancestral castle. His father was slowly advancing toward him, blood running through his heavy armor. He saw his father raising a dagger and plunging it deep into the boy's heart. Michea's hand slipped down to feel the dagger, the very same dagger. The very different heart.

Michea saw even further; in the wild Ural Mountains, in a shaman's yurt, he saw a pale youth drinking his first cup of blood. He saw the old sorcerer throw himself on the ground at his feet, and the Tartar women huddled near the fire. He saw . . . until he could look no more. He turned slightly and looked out the window, to the Valley of Blood. He watched Nikolai and Janco searching the Germans' tent. Something resembling a smile crossed Michea's face. Imbeciles, he thought contemptuously, you will never succeed against me. You'll live and die, and for me, it will be just another second. He saw Nikolai examining the pages of the manuscript. He'd found it! A frown of annoyance appeared on the thick eyebrows. It did not matter, nothing mattered.

Michea pulled out his dagger, raised it high over his head. "My Lord," he whispered, "accept my humble offering." The walls and the floor of the castle shook as if touched by an earth tremor; the windows rattled. And Michea swiftly lowered the dagger.

This time, the secret panel behind the bookcases slid open. Two shrouded figures entered the room and fell prostrate before him.

"Take her away," he ordered. "She is not yet ready. Prepare her."

The secret panel slid back in place and the figures were gone. His dagger back in its sheath, Michea looked again at the Valley of Blood. This time he saw long columns of Turkish janissaries hurrying into battle, thousands of arrows in the darkened sky. High on the hill, he saw Stephen the Great surrounded by his Catholic priests and German knights, walking confidently to his white horse. Again, a slight smile appeared on Michea's face. He closed his eyes.

When he opened them, he saw an early morning, and a young blond girl picking flowers. He blinked. Nikolai and Janco were now sitting in the car, drinking and laughing. Nikolai started the car's engine. Michea's hands trembled for a very brief moment. He closed his eyes once again. When he opened them, Nikolai and Janco were gone. All the trees and the grass were gone as well. The Valley of Blood was covered with iridescent sand. A shiny triangular object flew fast over the sands. Michea watched it disappear, a spark of curiosity in his expressionless eyes. He turned and walked toward the closed door. Something must be done, he thought; they must not understand the manuscript. But first, Annoushka is becoming dangerous. He left.

Everything in the library remained exactly the same. The door and the windows remained shut. The secret passage remained hidden behind the ancient tomes. And on the couch, Sally slept peacefully, breathing evenly.

In the great hall of the castle, the young militia man standing guard yawned as the clock struck a dozen times.

nine

After three hours of methodical searching, Nikolai had found what he wanted. Wrapped in plastic and carefully sewn inside the lining of one of the knapsacks was a leather pouch, crumbling with age. Inside the pouch were thick yellow pages, still in good condition, from what appeared to be a thirteenth-century manuscript. He placed the pages under the lamp—no doubt, they were authentic.

"This," he said with great relief, "will put our friend Michea away for a very long time."

"What are they?" Janco wasn't sure just what was going on. They both looked at the first page.

"Old Slavonic." Janco was disappointed. "The devil himself couldn't read it."

"You're wrong. A long time ago, before joining our partisan unit, I actually studied to be an altar boy and, believe it or not, we did study Old Slavonic . . . let me see what I remember . . . umm, this isn't like any Old Slavonic I knew." He looked more closely at the page, flipped it over, looked at the second page.

"In any event, Janco my friend, we do have specialists who will decipher it . . . I am just curious. Let me see, Old Slavonic has undergone many changes through the ages, and in every country it was printed differently. This, it seems to me, is closest to the Russian style. Anyway, we have a good cause to celebrate . . ."

"We've already finished my flask," Janco interrupted.

"Go to my car: under the back seat, I have a bottle of our good

76

Romanian cognac . . ." He saw Janco hesitate. "Go on, I'll try and see if I can't learn something more."

Janco left, taking his semiautomatic rifle, while Nikolai concentrated on the first page. It was difficult. The historian who described the events had not bothered to separate the words from one another, nor the sentences. Only the paragraphs were set slightly apart from one another. There were a few small drawings, though, which helped make some sense of an otherwise senseless tale describing the victories of Batu Khan and his warriors "whose numbers were as vast as the blades of grass in the fields near the river." That's as far as he got on that first page.

Janco returned with the cognac. They both drank, looking sadly at the manuscript.

"Eh!" Nikolai banged his fist on the flimsy table. "What I wouldn't give to be able to understand it now . . . wait," he exclaimed. "Old Slavonic was meant to be read aloud . . . now, I know Russian, how's your Russian?"

"A little rusty." Janco smiled. "And, to tell the truth, I hope I won't have to use it."

"Listen then . . . from here: 's *vostoka priishla velika orda sojigaya nishi zemli moldovanskie zabiraja nashih zin i ditok.*" Nikolai stopped, drank a bit, smiled. "Now we are getting somewhere. Listen to this: *moria krovi zaliv . . . gore ludam pravoslavnim . . .* I can't read this: *krepost?*"

"Fortress." Janco was getting interested.

They were silent for a few moments. From the edge of the forest came the lonely howling of a wolf.

"Maybe he knows what we are doing." Janco listened closely. "That's a big one."

"The sooner we get through it, the sooner we leave." As Nikolai turned the page, one of the brown canvas ropes hanging at the entrance of the tent came to life, suddenly dropped to the ground, and began slithering toward them.

Nikolai continued reading in a monotone: "*nash slaven voevoda Setozar pal v boyu i vladika Georgiu ranen v serdzu tatari vzali stenu i lezli v gorod . . .* What the hell! Are you crazy?"

Janco pushed Nikolai to the side with such a force that he fell, scattering the papers on the ground. Horrified, he watched as Janco pounded the big brown snake with the butt of his rifle. When the snake was clearly dead, Janco calmly picked it up and threw it outside.

"That was close," he said somberly. "Too close. I am a hunter, I should know . . . maybe Michea doesn't want you to read this manuscript?"

Nikolai picked up the papers. "When I am through with him, he'll *wish* he were a vurdalak. Nothing is going to help him."

"Snake . . . do you know what that means?"

"Of course," Nikolai interrupted. "I was born here too." He arranged the pages and took another swallow. Miraculously, the bottle had remained standing during the commotion.

"It means"—Janco was serious—"that when a vurdalak can't kill someone himself, for one reason or another, he sends a snake or a wolf, or a bat . . ."

"I know, I know. But don't you think there are hundreds of snakes living in this valley? And don't you know that snakes are attracted by warmth?"

"I know we should be getting back, that I know. Maybe Tagarū can help you translate tomorrow?"

"You're right. Only wait a few more minutes. I want to scan the rest; it won't take long."

"You are a dangerous man to be with, Nikola." Janco sighed and sat down.

"Here, the historian says . . ." Nikolai shivered and fell silent, but continued to read to himself—he understood one prominently mentioned word well enough—"vurdalak, vurdalak." The ancient chronicler had underscored his point in several instances by inserting the word "vampire" right under the word "vurdalak" and connecting the two with a red emblem shaped like a tear.

"Let's get out of here." Nikolai raised his hand. It dawned on him that they had been gone for nearly five hours. Sally would be frantic by now.

They put out the lamp, walked silently to the Land Rover. Nikolai made a wide U-turn in the field and they headed for the castle.

"I'd feel much safer with the top up." Janco looked uneasily at the stars and the moon.

"On such a beautiful night?"

"I remember bats and wolves."

"Shut up, you're crazy! Tomorrow afternoon Michea will be sitting in custody; no bats, no wolves are going to help him. Even a real vurdalak won't escape from our jails."

"I hope you are right." Janco took a sip and handed the half-empty bottle to Nikolai.

The narrow road ran through the forest. Nikolai felt the cognac burn in his mouth. He gave the bottle back to Janco, and pushed down the accelerator.

Suddenly, a huge furry object lunged at them from the darkness of the trees. The wolf's onslaught was so ferocious that Janco and the rifle fell out of the car and Nikolai had no chance to pull out his pistol. The animal was tearing at his shoulder, its sharp white fangs getting closer and closer to his throat. He couldn't hold it away much longer. So this is the end, Nikolai thought, just when I was getting somewhere. No, my friend, I am not finished yet! He let go of the wheel and, with all his strength, pushed the wolf out and jumped out himself. The Land Rover rolled down the shoulder of the road and slammed into an old pinetree. Nikolai landed on top of the wolf. He tried to strangle the animal from behind, but the creature was too strong. Within a few seconds, it wrestled away and jumped on Nikolai again, tearing his leather jacket to shreds. Nikolai had his pistol ready now. He shot twice, but missed, the echo of his shots ringing through the forest. Again, the wolf was right on top of him, biting the hand holding the gun: Nikolai realized he was almost helpless. The wolf now jumped for his throat. Suddenly the animal fell, limp. Nikolai climbed out from under it. Janco was holding his rifle.

"Shoot him again, shoot him!" Nikolai yelled. Janco raised his rifle and fired at the animal's head. The wolf's hind legs jerked a couple of times. It was all over.

"I've never seen a wolf that big," said Janco quietly, leaning over him and examining the huge head. "Not in these parts of the country."

Nikolai gazed at his crippled Land Rover. A quick thought flashed through his mind: will the insurance cover the repairs? Ridiculous! The bottle of cognac had smashed as well; not a drop could be salvaged.

"Let's drag him off the road, into my car," he suggested. "That way people will know he belongs to us."

Both of them silently dragged the body down and dumped it on the back seat.

"You are bleeding badly." Janco noticed Nikolai's hand. His own face was bleeding, cut in several places by the sharp claws. "Here." He tore a piece of his shirt and bandaged Nikolai's hand. "Anything else?"

"My ear."

Janco bandaged Nikolai's ear.

"My leather jacket saved me, you know."

"I know. I thought you were finished."

"Well, we might as well start hiking to the castle . . . it's only a couple of kilometers."

"Now, I hope that the bat isn't sitting somewhere up there, waiting for us."

"Let him wait." For the first time, Nikolai was aware of the pain, especially in his shoulder. "Let him wait," he repeated grimly and fired his pistol in the air.

"Why waste your bullets?"

"Because, if they hear shots at the castle, the sergeant just might have enough brains to investigate."

"I doubt if they'll hear you; sounds don't travel very far in these parts."

They both continued walking, watchful and ready for just about anything. They walked silently for another kilometer. The road turned sharply and went straight up. They both sat down to rest on a large stone by the side of the road.

"That wolf, he'd never attack on his own," Nikolai finally blurted out, revealing what bothered him the most. "The wolf is a very shy animal; he'd never attack two men in a car, not even if he was starving."

"This one was not starving."

"Unless he was sick."

Janco didn't answer. He was listening to some rustling.

"In any event," Nikolai continued, "we'll have to undergo a series of rabies shots. That's very painful."

"Shut up, Nikola, you're lucky to be alive and you're worried about some shots . . . how's your bleeding?"

"I think it's stopped."

"Good, now listen very carefully. Act normal, light a cigarette, and give me one."

Nikolai gave him one, glanced around and didn't hear or see anything. But he knew Janco was an experienced hunter, and he relied on him completely.

Janco smoked, put out his cigarette, and commented softly, "We've been followed . . . for a couple of minutes."

"Where?"

"Look to your right, to that clearing. You see that tiny speck of light, see how it moves?"

80

"What's up there?"

"Ruins of some old church and an abandoned cemetery."

"Maybe somebody is visiting a dead relative." Nikolai grinned. "What a ridiculous situation. In my own country, somebody might actually be trying to kill me."

"If that's a visitor, he's a little too late. Nobody's been buried up there for the past six or seven hundred years."

The light moved up and down in an uneven pattern, as if someone was walking with a flashlight.

"Be still." Janco's finger was on the trigger and he raised the rifle. "When I touch you, Nikola, drop to the ground." Nikolai thought Janco was exaggerating the danger; the light was at least a hundred meters away, perhaps more . . . but . . .

"Now!" Janco gave Nikolai a light push and Nikolai dove into the roadside grass. As he fell, he noticed a tall, dark object, resembling a man's figure, darting past him at an incredible speed and waving something like a sword. Simultaneously, he heard a volley of shots: Janco emptying his rifle. If I were a religious man, this would be the time to cross myself, thought Nikolai. Instead he raised his head a little.

"What the hell was *that?*"

"You can relax, Nikola." Janco was calmly reloading his rifle. "Whatever it was is either dead or far, far away by now."

"What could it be?"

"Damned if I know." Janco scratched his head. "It really is dangerous to be with you, Nikola." He kept on scratching. "One thing I am sure of—it wasn't anything human."

Nikolai stood up, lit another cigarette. His hands were trembling.

"Janco, did you see him . . . it, swinging some sort of sword . . . or am I going insane?"

"Maybe we are both going insane. I saw it, too . . . in fact, if you'd been sitting, instead of hitting the grass, he'd have chopped your head clean off."

"How did you hear him?"

"I didn't, and that's very strange . . . it was my instinct."

"Maybe we are both imagining all this; maybe it's your home-made vodka?"

"I hope so. Come on, it's not far now."

They didn't have to walk; the bright lights of an automobile were now rolling down the hill. The car stopped about fifty meters from them and a young halting voice shouted, "Please do identify yourselves . . . this is the People's Militia . . . this is a wildlife refuge. All shoot . . . hunting is prohibited . . ." The boy was evidently reluctant to drive any farther. Nikolai shouted back, explaining who he was and that he needed assistance.

Within minutes, Nikolai and Janco were sitting in Dr. Tagarū's office, sipping hot tea, while Dr. Tagarū, who was also a doctor of medicine, was examining and washing out their wounds.

"Both of you will have to appear tomorrow morning, as early as possible at Brasov's Clinic Number 3."

"Rabies shots?" Nikolai was feeling the pain now.

"Don't worry, Comrade, the old and painful series is no longer in use. You are lucky, though; another centimeter and your artery would have been severed."

Nikolai looked at the torn left side of his jacket. It was also lucky he had put the manuscript pages in his right pocket. They were unharmed. He took them out, noticed how Dr. Tagarū's eyes widened under his thick glasses. This is not the right time to ask him, Nikolai decided, and put the pages in the pocket of his trousers, beside his pistol. So much to do, and his eyes were finally beginning to close. He asked Dr. Tagarū to prescribe something to keep him awake.

After the examination, Janco returned to his cottage. Nikolai leaned back in Dr. Tagarū's comfortable armchair. Now he had to think; he had to put all events in their proper perspective. Including the sergeant, he had only five militia men on hand. Two were at their posts, one guarding the great hall, the other at the entrance. One militia man was sleeping and the sergeant was checking on some noise in the stables. Dr. Tagarū informed Nikolai that Sally was sleeping in the library; there was no sense waking her up now. Aside from Janco, the museum's personnel and presumably Michea, his mother, and his servants were all asleep in their rooms—except for Dr. Tagarū, who was sitting across from him, looking rather nervous.

"Annoushka?"

"You see, Comrade, after dinner, the other militia sergeant had to drive back to Brasov . . ."

"Wait a second, is she still here?"

"Yes, she's in her room."

This was bad news, thought Nikolai. Doesn't the old goat realize she's in danger here? No, how could he?

82

"Dr. Tagarū, please wake up the militia man and ask him to stand guard in the vicinity of her room."

He watched Dr. Tagarū leave, reached for the phone, and dialed the ministry. Did he know what time it was? No, he noticed his wristwatch was smashed. It had stopped at eight. Yes, this was definitely an emergency. Yes, he would wait at this number.

The sergeant entered, sleepy and angry. There was nothing wrong with the horses and it wasn't his job to look after them anyway. Nikolai asked the sergeant to check on Annoushka and report back to him; after that, the sergeant could get some sleep. He felt uneasy about Annoushka—that young fool, he thought, she should've left right after our conversation.

The telephone finally rang. Nikolai summarized to a sleepy Bugash the events leading up to his finding the missing pages. What had happened afterward, he decided to omit for the time being.

"With your permission," Nikolai concluded, "I'll arrest Michea in the morning on the suspicion of double homicide."

"You're mad," Bugash roared. "You'll do no such thing. Permission denied. I forbid you to even question him."

"Why?"

"You are blowing this case out of all proportion. You have five pages of an old manuscript and what else? Come on, you couldn't convict a flea on such evidence."

"I'll go over your head."

"You can go to hell, as far as I am concerned. But Michea is not to be touched. At least not now." He added in a conciliatory tone, "Nikolai, are you all right?"

"I need more men."

"You will have them in, oh, two, three hours . . . listen, Madame Radū and I had a conference about your case this afternoon. We decided it was a mistake to assign it to you in the first place. After all, you were on your vacation . . . so, we have decided to send your friend Startz over, to help you . . ."

"I don't need Startz now," Nikolai almost shouted. "I tell you, I have it in my hands—"

"Nevertheless," Bugash continued evenly, "upon his arrival, Startz will be in charge. This is mine, as well as the minister's decision, so you can't go over anyone's head. As soon as Inspector Startz is familiarized with the situation, I suggest you take your richly deserved vacation with your lovely American friend."

Here Nikolai lost his self-control and yelled back that he had almost been killed, first by a snake, then by a wolf, then by something which came at him with an object like a sword, and, Startz or no Startz, he was going to find out who was responsible. Bugash listened until Nikolai was out of breath.

"Now I *am* convinced you need rest. And when you return to your desk, I suggest you stop by and see our section's psychiatrist . . . only a suggestion."

Nikolai was so angry, he hung up on his superior. "Bastard!" he swore, and added a score of choice obscenities. What is taking that sergeant so long? Nikolai stood up, put on a jacket lent him by Dr. Tagarū, and went to check out the guards. The one guarding the entrance was sleeping peacefully in the car. The one posted to guard the great hall was also asleep on top of one of the exhibit cases. Nikolai was too tired to bother with them and let them off with a warning.

The entrance and the museum secured, Nikolai stepped into the courtyard and lit a cigarette, his last Marlboro. He crumpled the pack and threw it away. He thought momentarily of America—what a strange country, so full of contradictions. He wanted to visit there again, at least once. Perhaps he should marry Sally; at least he should ask her what her views were regarding marriage and family. He inhaled deeply. So quiet, at last everyone's asleep. His job was finished in any event. Knowing Startz as he did, he knew the small, efficient inspector with the German name was already on his way. Only a matter of hours, perhaps less, before he would arrive. And Startz was probably the best . . . I sure would love to read his conclusions and recommendations . . . Nikolai's thoughts turned back to the insane chain of events. He wondered again if he had been hallucinating, part of the time, at least. It didn't matter anymore. Tomorrow morning, actually today, after a brief stopover in Brasov to get his shot, he'd be driving Sally to his cabin. And then . . . damn! He remembered his Land Rover. Now it'll take me a whole day just to find a good mechanic. And what am I going to do with the wolf's carcass? Let Janco skin him and keep the fur? But then how can we explain killing him in a wildlife refuge? Hell, how can we explain his attack? How can we explain anything? Maybe the carcass won't be in my car anyway. Nikolai felt he'd almost be better off if it had disappeared. He finished smoking.

Where *was* that stupid sergeant? He should be back by now. A few more hours and it will all be forgotten. Bugash and Radū probably think I'm crazy, he thought. Why should an internationally renowned poet kill two archeologists? Why? Why, indeed, do people murder other people, people from all walks of life? Basic motives: love, hate, greed, power; it could be almost anything. Why should even great poets be any different? And Michea was certainly not a great poet. His concentration wandered. Sally must leave this place. He could stay behind and wait for the Land Rover to be repaired, then follow her.

Nikolai sighed, rubbed his aching hand, and walked back into the castle. So quiet here, too. Like a tomb. He walked up to the great hall; the militia man was asleep.

Nikolai rudely kicked him off the display case. "Stand at attention," he yelled and slapped the soldier's face. Two big tears fell down the kid's thin cheeks. He was no more than eighteen, and he was trembling.

"Listen, kid, you fall asleep again and I'll send you to a place where they'll wake you up at four in the morning, every morning. Do you understand?"

"I don't know how it happened, Comrade Captain," he stammered. "It will not happen again."

Nikolai left him and started walking to Dr. Tagarū's office. Where was that sergeant? How dare he disobey my direct order? He decided to check on Annoushka himself. He did not know exactly where her room was, just the general direction of the staff's dormitory. As he walked downstairs, he was suddenly aware that something very unpleasant was about to occur. He pulled out his pistol and stopped. From the corridor below he could hear some whimpering. He advanced cautiously. Someone was clearly vomiting and choking. The sergeant, his face white, was leaning against the wall, throwing up. The door to the room next to him was open and the light was on. Nikolai put away his pistol and tried to help the sergeant.

"I am sorry, Comrade," he sobbed; he was also very young. "I am very sorry . . . only I have never seen anything so . . . horrible."

Nikolai rushed past him into the chamber. The room was in a shambles—the bed was overturned, the chest of drawers was open, and clothing was scattered everywhere. Dr. Tagarū sat on the corner of a large suitcase, holding his head with both hands, not moving. On the floor, in a large pool of blood, lay the body of Annoushka, her throat ripped wide open.

Nikola turned away, fighting for control. "Sergeant," he called. "Please get hold of yourself and come here." He turned to Tagarū. "Doctor, you must try to help me. Please."

Dr. Tagarū looked up at him as if seeing him for the first time. "Dr. Tagarū, you must help me," Nikolai repeated.

A spark of recognition; Dr. Tagarū stood up. "Yes, of course, I will help you in any way I can."

"Stay here for a few minutes." Nikolai knew he had to get to the telephone immediately. "Sergeant, you come with me." He ran up the stairs and turned to Dr. Tagarū's office, almost knocking over a small, conservatively dressed man with a neat, gray mustache and green Tyrolean hat.

"Startz," Nikolai exclaimed. "I never thought I'd be so glad to see you. We have a vicious murder on our hands . . . party member . . . you go, Sergeant, take Inspector Startz downstairs. I have to call our medical team."

The sky outside was almost blue, another beautiful day was coming. A gray bus stopped at the edge of the parking lot and the militia men spilled out, like green beans, into a small formation.

ten

Back at his cottage after the night's ordeal, Janco drank steadily, but he couldn't fall asleep. He desperately tried to remember where he had seen Sally before. Something sinister was connected with her. He watched the sun rise, the forest awaken.

Finally, just as his eyes began to close, he jumped up, erect and alert, as if from an ice cold shower. Of course! He had been a boy of about eleven when his village priest had committed suicide. Janco, along with two of his friends, had climbed into the priest's room after the burial, partly to test each other's courage, partly out of curiosity. The house was locked, but the priest's window, on the second floor, remained open.

They were all scared, but wouldn't show it. The moon was high; they'd all heard stories of vurdalaks and witches, and they had talked quietly about calling it a night and going home.

Then all three of them saw a face appear at the window: the face of a beautiful woman, smiling and friendly—the American lady. She had asked where the handsome priest was buried, asked without saying the words. She had very sharp teeth, glowing in the moonlight, and her smile was strange. The three boys had screamed and run out of the house, not stopping for anything until they got to their respective homes.

It was her face! Nikolai must be warned. I must go up to the castle and warn him. But Janco was feeling very sleepy now. He couldn't even move. *I'll tell Nikolai later this evening,* he thought, and immediately fell asleep.

eleven

Driving to the castle, Startz had
thought that he was once again being brought into a case on the
horns of the usual bureaucratic dilemma. Nikolai's leads, however
contradictory and bizarre, seemed to point to Michea. On the other
hand, Bugash had expressly forbidden any kind of intrusion on "the
great man." Political considerations.

Now, badly shaken, Startz kept looking at Annoushka's body.
Political considerations? A huge gash in her neck, down and across
her left breast, so small and delicate, blood on the floor, overturned
furniture! The murderer must have used something as sharp as a
straight razor, probably twisting it a few times to ensure her death.
He noticed dried blood under Annoushka's fingernails: that was
something to go on. The window was open: something else to check
out.

"Comrade, please leave this room. I wish to be alone for a few
minutes."

Dr. Tagarū stood up. He wanted to explain why he was here:
Nikolai had asked him to stay; he was a doctor of medicine; and . . .
he saw hardness and determination in the small man's eyes. Once
the order was given, it must be obeyed. Tagarū shrugged and left.

Startz cautiously sat down on the edge of Annoushka's bed. He
took out his silver cigarette case and lighter, a gift from his late wife.
He inhaled deeply and studied the room intently.

Startz remembered visiting the castle with his parents when he
was a boy, in another lifetime, long before the war. His father had

been a prominent physician and their family, the descendants of the German colonists who had populated Transwald over two hundred years previously, was one of the very few in Brasov to own an automobile, and a Mercedes Benz at that. Startz's older brothers went on to uphold the family tradition and had both become doctors. Startz, always a black sheep, had flunked out of the university and, to his parents' dismay, had joined the Communist party. He was the only one of his family to survive the holocaust of the Second World War and subsequent purges. Like Nikolai, Startz was a widower without children. A thoughtful, fastidious, and low-key man, he was almost an anachronism in his neatly pressed blue suit, polished shoes, and his well-known Tyrolean green hat with a red feather. He looked like a middle-aged German shopkeeper; only those who worked with him knew that he was a brilliant investigator. He had solved every case assigned him—and he was assigned to the most difficult cases, when all else failed. His most recent promotion, to the rank of inspector—which was equivalent to lieutenant colonel—had come a few years ago when he had uncovered and eliminated a rather subtle KGB plot to assassinate Chauchesku and other independent members of the Romanian politbureau. Startz knew that this was the highest he'd ever get in the ministry, considering his German name and nonproletarian background. He loved his work; it was the only thing he had left. It was a continuing and exciting education, an intricate chess game with an opponent unknown to him until the inevitable checkmate.

There was one case, however, which he still hadn't solved, though it had been officially closed years ago, along with the usual letters of praise from his superiors. But Startz knew that the wrong man had faced a firing squad. A young man's throat had been torn open and several young children had disappeared. Startz thought about that case often, but after all these years, he could not arrive at any rational conclusion. And now this.

Startz finished his cigarette, collected the ashes in the palm of his hand, threw them out the window, and put the butt in his pocket. Then he bent down over Annoushka.

A party member? This altered everything. Now Startz had a free hand, no more "political considerations."

A knock on the door and the militia lieutenant reported that the detachment was assembled and awaiting his instructions. Startz evenly recited the usual: fingerprints, guards around the walls, a search team, communications team, deployment inside the castle; the list continued. The lieutenant saluted and left. Startz stood by the door. All murders are unique, and yet . . . strange, he thought, this particular murderer evidently did not care whether he got caught or not. She must have screamed; there were all the signs of a terrible struggle; and the museum was guarded. Strange. Startz waited for the fingerprint team, then went upstairs to Dr. Tagarū's office. Nikolai was looking out the window. Startz offered him one of his cigarettes.

"Look down, Startz." Nikolai pulled him over to the window. "That fucking bastard!" Startz saw an old man hooking a team of horses to a black carriage.

"Nikola," he said patiently, "tell me—"

"Quiet," Nikolai interrupted. "Watch."

The carriage rolled a few yards and stopped. A figure clad in a dark suit jumped gracefully into it and the carriage began rolling again toward the old gate.

"You see, you see?" Nikolai shouted excitedly and turned around. Startz was already gone, running down the stairs with the agility of a much younger man, and ordering the militia men to stop the carriage.

"Excuse me, Comrade," Startz said when he reached the carriage. He watched Michea's face turn livid, contorted with rage. "I cannot permit you to leave the castle."

"What?" Michea roared. "What is this outrage! *Who* are you? Do you know who *I* am? I have an official permit."

"I do indeed know who you are, and you're right . . . only this morning a vicious murder was committed on these premises, and I am afraid—"

"What are you talking about? What murder?" There was now mock concern in Michea's voice. "Are you sure? In this castle?"

"Quite sure, Comrade."

"Then, of course, I shall do my best . . . to cooperate with authorities."

"I am delighted." Startz had always thought he was an excellent actor: in his business, this ability solved quite a few cases.

"Perhaps you won't mind accompanying me to Dr. Tagarū's office. I have one or two questions . . . purely routine."

"I am not sure how I can help." Michea reluctantly climbed out of his carriage. "I don't even know who was murdered."

"Inspector Startz, at your service." Startz showed him his identification and pointed the way.

Michea examined the identification, then the curious little man who was smiling so hard. No threat there, he decided.

"My old comrade." Michea nodded to Nikolai when they'd entered Dr. Tagarū's office.

Startz said, "Please leave us, Nikola. We shall speak later." Then he turned to Michea, still smiling. "Please sit down, Comrade. Before we speak, I must tell you that I have been an admirer of one Michea Basarab for a very long time; and my daughter, too. She is now seventeen," he lied. "May I have your autograph?"

"Of course," Michea looked incredulously at a small paperbound volume which Startz fished out of his pocket along with a fountain pen.

"Olga Startz is her name."

Michea expressed his best wishes in the corner of the flyleaf. He had a large signature, forming his letters with almost calligraphic precision. Startz was satisfied: he also thought himself an advanced student of handwriting.

"Thank you so very much, very much indeed." He noticed that Michea was looking past him at the window. What now? Startz discreetly looked out, too. The yard was empty, the horses and the carriage gone, an ordinary morning. Startz put on his most disarming smile. "Now, Comrade Adelescu, where were you last night?"

"I . . . I was working rather late . . . I always work at night. On a new play. I went to my bedroom, I believe, at two, possibly three."

"And fell asleep, no doubt?"

"Yes."

"You did not hear any screams, noises?"

"None at all. Now may I ask you something?"

"Certainly."

"Who was murdered?"

"Annoushka . . . such a tragedy."

"I am grieved to hear it."

"We will find the guilty party, rest assured. I have one or two more questions. You are familiar, of course, with a certain thirteenth-century manuscript?" Startz wasn't sure just how relevant this manuscript was to the investigation. Colonel Bugash, who had told him about it, wasn't sure either.

Michea didn't answer right away. When he did, he chose his

words carefully. "Comrade Inspector, I presume the manuscript you are referring to is the Old Slavonic letopis compiled by Bessarabian monks of the Order of St. Elia the Prophet?"

"Hmm, can you tell me about it?"

Michea laughed lightly. "Comrade, you must be joking. The manuscript contains over seven thousand pages. Actually, there are two manuscripts; I used one for my research, that one is small, only some fifteen hundred pages."

"Your research?"

"Yes, I am writing a new play, as I've mentioned, set at the time of the Tartar invasion, the thirteenth century. You remember your history?"

"Very interesting." Startz felt sure he'd hit a dead end. "There seems to be some question of five missing pages?"

"Nonsense." Michea was adamant. "The manuscript is authentic, and not one page of it is missing!"

"Thank you again, I have no more inquiries for the present."

Michea's face showed some relief. He stood up, bowed courteously, and left the room.

Nikolai walked in almost immediately afterward. Smiling as he sat down, he reached into his pocket and spread out the pages.

"Now we both know he's lying. Shut off the tape recorder."

Startz shut it off, looked at the old pages. "What do you want me to do? How can I use them, those goddamned Tartars?"

"And even vurdalaks."

"Stop it, stop it right here." Startz blew up. "We've been friends a long time, but you say 'vurdalak' once more and I'm going to take it as a personal insult."

"See for yourself." Nikolai pushed two pages toward him. "Can you read it?"

"Of course not, not the Old Slavonic."

"Startz, listen, I can't read most of it either, but . . ."

"I have a feeling I don't want to know it."

"It describes some kind of a ritual, more or less how to get rid of a vampire."

"Get out of here!"

"It does . . . ask yourself why should Michea substitute these particular pages?"

"Get out of here and leave these pages for analysis. If you do find a vampire, let me know. We'll both arm ourselves with wooden stakes and have a grand time. Until then, get out and stay out of my way. I don't need you . . . go have your rabies shot and I hope you don't meet any more wolves."

"I am not giving these pages to anybody."

"Keep them then, by all means, only please go and do not interfere. I have thousands of things to do."

"Can I borrow one of your jeeps and two men? I have to get my Land Rover out of that ditch."

Startz thought about it. "For how long?"

"One or two hours."

"Go ahead. Nikola, I am serious, stay out. *I'll* know how to get in touch with you if I need you. Enjoy yourself."

There was so much Nikolai wanted to say to him. Forget it, he thought, forget it and get out. Startz is right. He'll get Michea eventually. It was a good time to get back to his own life, to Sally. He thought, she has probably finished breakfast by now and is wondering whether she'll see me today. Nikolai stretched out his hand and Startz shook it hard.

"I will get him, Nikola." He was serious. "Not for you, for justice, I will get him." He watched Nikolai leave, and lit another cigarette.

Startz had developed a theory while driving up. Whoever was responsible for the death of the archeologists—and that same person or persons could well be responsible for this morning's outrage—is trying to have it appear as though some supernatural forces, some vurdalaks are at work. How very convenient! Unfortunately, that sort of thing had been done before. Startz recalled again another village and another castle. And a man whose throat had been torn open. Undoubtedly the work of a vurdalak, he'd been told. And he'd almost bought it.

Nikolai is a good policeman, Startz thought, only this time he seems to have wandered into the forest without bothering first to examine the trees. I'll have to keep my ear to the ground, do the basic work. Something will develop. A polite knock and a young militia sergeant brought him a pot of coffee and a breakfast tray.

"Anything else?" Startz noticed the boy hesitate before leaving.

"There's this odd-looking comrade sitting outside. He says he works in the museum and has important information."

"Invite him in." What do I have to lose? I'll give him five or ten minutes. The medical team is late anyway.

Nikodim walked in.

This comrade is certainly a strange-looking individual, Startz thought. Also very familiar. Where have I seen him? No matter. "Sit down, Comrade. A cup of coffee, tea?"

"I asked to see . . . where is that other policeman? That captain?"

"I am in charge now," Startz said gravely and placed his identification card on the table. Nikodim examined it carefully.

"Comrade, you said you have important information. Does it relate to this morning's tragedy?"

"Annoushka's murder? Yes, yes, and many more." Nikodim's eyes were burning under his bushy eyebrows. Beads of perspiration appeared on his bald pate.

Startz felt uncomfortable. Not another maniac! Smile, he told himself, smile. Give him five minutes instead of ten.

"Please go on, Comrade, I am rather busy."

"My name is Nikodim Pavlovic. I am employed by the Ministry of Culture as a guide . . ."

Of course, he's the Orthodox priest! Startz remembered.

twelve

The first few steps were difficult. The massive iron gates shut behind her. It was dark and cold; the wind howled. The ground was hard, covered with thorny bushes. Sally felt her feet getting numb, felt the blood, the cuts and the bruises. She sat down, totally exhausted.

Slowly, a giant screen of bright whiteness opened up directly in front of her, engulfing her in a fine silver mist. She closed her eyes.

The pain was now excruciating, every muscle, every nerve in her body was on fire. I can't take another second, she thought. Somebody touched her shoulder, firmly and gently. She opened her eyes: an old woman shrouded in dark garments held out a round golden chalice.

"Drink this, child," the woman whispered in Romanian. But Sally understood. Thirstily she snatched the chalice away, greedily drank the sour, pleasantly scented liquid. A surge of energy ran through her body. She stood up.

The hag was watching her, a crafty look on her wrinkled face. "You will not feel any pain now," she said, taking the chalice from Sally. "You shall never feel any pain." Her voice rose to a high pitch. "Go, child. Your master is waiting."

My master? "I have no master and never will," Sally protested, but the old woman was gone. The wind subsided. Sally took a step; the grass felt like velvet. What had been ugly, desolate ground was now a thick lawn sprinkled with exquisite flowers, each more beautiful than the next. Birds were singing and two white swans were swimming in a placid lake.

Where am I? she wondered. If I'm dreaming, I don't want this dream to end. She walked some more, feeling stronger now, almost omnipotent. The beauty of the place reminded Sally of some Chinese paintings. She walked by the water's edge and the two swans followed her. There was a small wooden bridge across the lake and Sally walked over it. "Sit down, rest a while and listen to the song of the nightingale," a voice seemed to implore her.

I can't, she thought, somebody is waiting. Master?

"Stay with us for a few more minutes," another voice persisted.

Sally sat down in the lush, soft grass. Instead of pain, she now felt euphoric, pervaded by sensations of warmth and well-being, of fulfillment. She listened to the birds singing. I can't stay very long; I must continue. Continue where? Toward the mansion, of course, where else? She thought about New York and, to her amazement, she had total recall of all the recent events, as if she could flick on some three-dimensional movie. What happened to me today? That was harder. First there was a funny little man in a green hat, one of Nikolai's friends. Nikolai, yes, he was her lover. Driving in a jeep with two other policemen. And the carcass, the carcass of a large wolf. The room in the village, the lovemaking, hours and hours . . . so far away. The Two Moons Café, empty at dusk. Sally saw herself sitting alone at the table, sipping red wine and waiting for Nikolai. There were no German tourists in the Hotel Red Danube; the mist was rolling in the valley below. Stillness. Then the hoofbeats, the monotonous bell. Again! Where was Nikolai? What was taking him so long? This time, the black carriage stopped alongside her table. A voice she could not disobey invited her in.

The nightingale stopped singing and the swans gracefully swam away. I must continue, she thought, standing up. Something strange was happening: large, white statues appeared around the mansion. Not in any order, just here and there, statues of men in long fur capes, pointing their swords and their lances toward the mansion as if getting ready to storm it. As she came closer, she realized that these warriors were Orientals with wide angry faces, slanting eyes—incredibly realistic work. If only I had my camera, she thought. I did have it when I entered Michea's carriage. Whatever happened to it? And what possible exposure? The moon is so bright, my eyes hurt. How can I photograph something that probably does not exist?

She stopped again. Several thoughts raced in her mind, all

somehow connected with New York. Her last presentation for a new cereal: totally wrong! Her bank commercial; she should have shot it in Canada. How stupid can you get? The new creative director. So simple: he bribed one of the board members to break the tie vote, and got himself elected. She could have had that job so easily. She could almost see the new creative director sitting in his corner office: a smiling, fat pig.

"Revenge!" she screamed. "I must have my revenge!"

Somewhere in the back of her mind, the sound of reason whispered, "What are you screaming about? Why kill the stupid man?" Revenge was all that mattered. Revenge! Her lover, too; the strange and melancholy poet. They had had no right to reject his book. . . . Sally bent down, tore off a flower, chewed on it, sweet, intoxicating. Her lover had said he knew something about Sally that she herself did not know. What was it? It did not matter; nothing mattered exept revenge. She walked past the statues toward the mansion. The ground shook under her feet and a cacophony of voices pierced her ears. Frozen with horror, she saw the grinning statue of a young warrior, his dagger high in the air, holding a severed head in his other hand. Black blood dripped, disappearing into the ground.

Sally screamed. The head was Michea's, his eyes closed, his skin as white as the statues! Sally kept staring as Michea's eyes began to open. The triumph on the face of the young warrior turned to fear. The ground shook again and the statues began falling down and breaking apart. A curved sword fell next to her, almost touching her breasts. She realized that she was stark naked. She ran her hands over her body and gasped at the almost electric sense of pleasure.

The last statue toppled from its pedestal and fell. Silence.

The moon now hung directly over the mansion and, in its unusually bright light, Michea was standing, dressed in black, wearing his crown.

He looked thoughtfully at the scattered pieces of white marble: a hand there, a face crying in the grass, a raised lance, a broken sword.

"Tartars," he said derisively, almost to himself. His eyes then rested on Sally, his sad, enormous, all-seeing eyes.

"Zerkal," he said. "Welcome once again into our timeless kingdom."

Without realizing what she was doing, Sally dropped to her knees, lowered her head, and waited.

Slowly, very slowly, Michea came toward her, lifted her, embraced her.

Early morning mist covers the high grass and the rolling, peaceful hills in central Russia, many centuries ago. Out of the mist, like ghosts, two Tartar warriors emerge. They listen carefully to every sound. Nothing unusual, but one of the Tartars is excited. A birdcall in the distance, behind the nearest hill. Both Tartars fall to the ground and crawl like two serpents down the slope where, by a small clear stream amidst some trees and bushes, their horses are hidden.

The Tartars stand up near a tree. They whisper to each other. Two, three more steps to their horses. The Great Khan must be warned. They stop, take out their swords, stand back to back. They know now that their mission has failed.

With shrill whistles, like a swarm of startled sparrows, gray Russian arrows fly out of the underbrush. One Tartar is killed instantly. The other slashes his sword desperately, cutting the thin air. Then he, too, falls facedown on the ground.

The archers stand up. Their bearded commander walks slowly toward the bodies and looks thoughtfully at the dead Tartar soldiers. They are not the soldiers of the Golden Horde. He is puzzled. He calls his second in command, a young man with a long blond mustache.

"Ride swiftly," he orders. "Prince Dimitri must be forewarned."

"Mamaii Khan?" asks the young man.

"I believe so." The commander crosses himself and the young man.

The red sun comes up over the barren landscape. The fog is lifting. Only a few miles away, at the edge of a forest, the Russian army is waiting patiently among the trees and in the clearings.

"Hide their bodies," the commander orders. "No, wait . . ." He changes his mind. "Drain them of all blood, as they did to our brothers and leave them where their horsemen can find them." He looks at the sky: not one cloud, a fine day for the battle.

What's this? His right hand touches a poison-tipped arrow while his left tightens his bow.

A large black eagle is circling above them.

The commander takes careful aim and releases the arrow. There is nothing in the sky now. It is blue and empty.

The Russian listens, waiting for the eagle to fall on the grass. Silence. His archers stand motionless.

The commander crosses himself three times, raises his hand. Seconds later, a dozen horsemen ride out of the trees racing toward the Russian lines.

Behind them, raising clouds of dust across the entire horizon, the hordes of Mamaii Khan begin advancing toward the river.

BOOK TWO

one

The Georghe Gheorghiu-Dej Boulevard looked like a gray river, a mass of humanity during the early morning rush hour. Everyone was hurrying, hurrying. Seven stories above, in his small, neat office at the Ministry of the Interior, Nikolai moodily watched the crowds crossing the wide boulevard and the narrow streets, disappearing into tall new office buildings. He remembered Bucharest as it had been right after the war: a silent, frightened city with Russian tanks guarding every intersection. This morning he is wearing his dress uniform with the Order of the Red Star prominently displayed just above his left pocket. Today is the day of judgment: he is to meet the minister and . . . what will happen is as yet unclear. He could well be fired; that is to be expected. It doesn't matter.

Almost a full month had passed since that fateful night when he and Janco had found the missing manuscript pages. The next day had been even worse. After retrieving the car and driving to get his shots he had returned to discover that Sally had left him—without even leaving a note, without even taking her suitcase. Startz had alerted all airports and every border crossing, but Sally must have picked up a ride with some tourists and passed on to Hungary before the dragnet fell. Nikolai had written, without success. He now felt lonely and depressed.

Nikolai's pretty secretary, Sonya, came in to change the water for the roses, which came from his garden. Sonya was surprised to see him in uniform; it had been years since he'd worn it.

"You should wear it more often, Nikola." She smiled approvingly. "It makes you so handsome . . . two messages."

One was a call from Colonel Bugash, reminding him to be on time—the minister does not tolerate tardiness. The other message was from Startz. He was back in Bucharest and wanted to meet Nikolai that night at Café Lido. Another mystery. Why not just stop by here? Startz's office was only one flight up.

Nikolai opened his desk and took out his unusually long report. The label was simple: *Castle Dubrava*, Murder of Two German Nationals, Age 57 and 24, Male. Profession: Archeologists. Names, permit numbers. Investigating officer: Captain Nikolai Chernev, Ministry of the Interior.

Nikolai had rewritten the report three times. These were the facts as he saw them. This was the end of his career. The day of judgment. It was now almost nine o'clock. He pushed his report back, locked up his desk, combed his hair, and walked out.

A very slow elevator took him to the top floor: the infamous thirteenth floor. There were the same guards at the reception area, the same thick red carpet, installed partly to drown out the sounds from the interrogation rooms behind the steel doors. Two more guards, TV monitors, a brown door at the end of the corridor, a brass sign: M. Radū, Minister of the Interior.

Nikolai knocked. During his nearly twenty years of service, he'd had only one occasion to enter this office: to receive the Order of the Red Star. At least they can't take *that* away, he thought as he stepped inside.

Bright sunshine was pouring through the large windows. Behind an oak desk sat an elderly woman, tiny and alert, smoking a cigarette. By the table stood Nikolai's superior, Colonel Bugash, a tall, white-haired man, livid with anger. Nikolai saluted, remaining by the door.

"Come over, Nikola," the woman cackled. "Sit on the couch." Nikolai sat. The minister stood up, walked around the table toward him. She was even smaller standing up, and stopped to look at him appraisingly for a few seconds. Then she sat next to him.

"I have ordered some coffee and pastries. I hope you'll have some."

Not bad for a beginning, thought Nikolai; at least she's not screaming and throwing one of her famous fits.

A young man in a dark suit entered quietly and set down the tray. He poured three cups of coffee and departed.

"Would you like some cream?" asked the minister.

"No."

She drank some of her coffee. "I read a copy of your report last night. Not bad." She smiled. Smiling, she looked like a wise, mischievous pixie. "Let us do this, Nikola; why don't we form a company? We'll rewrite your report somewhat, expand it, and then sell it to some big capitalist smut publisher in America. And we'll each buy a Mercedes Benz and a dacha and live happily ever after. Your report is so . . . so lurid!" She sipped some more coffee.

This is taking a bad turn, thought Nikolai. "Comrade Minister," he responded with dignity, "I just compiled the facts and drew conclusions."

"Nikola." She softly patted his knee. "How can you do this to me? I admit, throughout our history, we have been plagued by vampires: Sultans' Beys, Greek hospodars, Magyar landowners. And worst of all, our own boyars and priests and princes and kings— these were all vampires in a very real sense: they drank the blood of our people for countless centuries. *They are all dead, Nikola!* And our people are alive. Our homeland is no longer ruled by dark superstitions, tortures, and dungeons. And our people are happier now than ever before. Come on . . ." She dragged Nikolai to her picture window. "Look down, can you tell Bucharest from other cities of Europe or America? Everyone is working, earning good wages. There's plenty of food on the tables, free medical care. And look at that forest of new apartment buildings." She walked him back to the couch. "I am proud of the positive role our ministry played in bringing stability to our country without repression."

"I am proud as well." Nikolai swallowed some coffee. What was she getting at?

Bugash, who was getting redder and redder, finally roared, "How dare you write in an official document that a vurdalak, no less, must sleep undisturbed in a lead casket filled with human blood, that his whole body must be immersed in blood so that he can survive through the centuries?"

"It's only from that Slavonic letopis."

"Why translate it at all?"

"Because, as I have stated, I was suspicious about Michea's eagerness to substitute the missing pages."

"Maybe you also think that Michea sleeps in a casket full of blood?"

105

"I know he doesn't. Startz determined it. He sleeps in his bed. You should see—such a bed!"

"That's something, at least. And hopefully no one has seen him fly?"

"No."

"I had planned to promote you, Nikola," said Bugash ruefully. "You deserved to be a major . . . but after this miserable performance . . ." Bugash picked up a copy of Nikolai's report, then dropped it. "You deserve to be transferred to the traffic department."

"Enough said," interceded the minister. Her voice was dry and emotionless as she walked back to her desk. "You are implying that one of our better known poets, a man with an international reputation, is not only a murderer but some kind of supernatural monster?"

"But—"

"I don't wish to be interrupted. Let me give you a different interpretation of this case. I, too, was in a partisan unit during the war. My unit operated near the Yugoslavian border and we had contact with Tito's men. One of them told me something you might find interesting.

"The German and Chetnik units began spreading rumors among the superstitious Montenegrins that there were vampires with the Communists and that the Communists were nothing more than ruthless haiduks. To make it even more plausible, the Germans would frequently kidnap a few villagers, kill them, drain their blood, puncture their necks to make it look like an act of vampirism, and leave the bodies in areas where they would be easily found. Clever, simple, and it worked . . . to some extent."

"I never said that a vampire was responsible."

"But you certainly implied it," said Bugash. "You even mention the date when this Prince Vurdalak was supposed to have been born: year of 1201? That makes him 780 years old? And he was a Bessarabian, well, Moldavian prince? And you think Michea took the pen name Basarab for some sinister reason . . . maybe you also think Michea is this vurdalak?"

"I told you, this was from the translation."

"Another thing, Nikola. The wolf, I understand, and the snake—but what kind of shit was your assertion that something was trying to cut off your head, some apparition?"

"I wrote it the way it happened."

"Comrade Minister"—Bugash was as red as a beet now—"I know Janco, and I know what they both had been drinking at the time. Believe me, that homemade brew is potent enough to kill an elephant. I just wish that whatever was trying to chop off your head had succeeded."

"In any event, Comrade Captain," Madame Radū said sternly, "I am very disappointed. Your report is sloppy, contradictory, full of legends, erroneous conclusions, and innuendos. I realize the conditions under which we gave you this assignment, and I realize that you were in an automobile accident . . . did you see the doctor as ordered?"

"Not yet."

"Do so at your earliest convenience. I am going to destroy your report: it was never written! Moreover, I am going to suspend you from your duties for one month, without pay. At the end of the month, you'll report to our archive section for reassignment. Understood?"

"Yes, understood," said Nikolai wearily. So they did not have the guts to fire me after all. I am safer somewhere behind a desk.

"And another thing," added Bugash. "You're not to discuss your report or this interview with anyone." He suddenly switched to a conciliatory tone. "Just think how we'd look if the western press gets hold of this: the Romanian secret police accuse the world-famous Romanian playwright of being a vampire."

"Yes, Colonel."

"That is all, Comrade," said Minister Radū.

Nikolai saluted, turned around, and left. In the corridor, walking back to his office, he felt so angry that he spat on the immaculately clean red carpet.

At his office, a young blond lieutenant was waiting for him.

"I must apologize, Comrade Captain, but you are no longer assigned to this office. Here are my orders."

"Can I at least clean out my desk?"

"I am very sorry, your personal belongings will be temporarily kept in the Number Four storage area."

Nikolai knew exactly what that meant. Good-bye report: it had never existed. For a moment, he felt relieved. There was another, unauthorized, copy at his apartment. His relief was shortlived, however. They had probably searched his apartment already. Niko-

107

lai reached into the wastebasket to retrieve the framed photograph of his late wife that he had always kept on his desk.

"What are you gaping at?" he asked the blond man. "You are only following orders!" He turned abruptly and slammed the door.

His apartment, a two-room studio on Republic Square, was in shambles. The report, of course, was gone, along with some other papers. Nikolai poured himself a glass of cognac and sat in his favorite armchair. He sat there, sipping cognac and staring out the window until it was time to meet Startz. He took off his uniform, put on a pair of slacks and a sports jacket. So they are trying to ease me out slowly, quietly, without a bang? And that's the price I have to pay for simply being honest.

The telephone rang just when he was ready to leave. Bugash was apologetic. "Nothing personal, Nikola . . . I hope you'll use your free time wisely. Meanwhile, I'll speak to Radū; I think she will change her mind and you'll get your check."

"Thank you very much, Comrade Colonel."

"Stop it. I am still your friend. I am also sorry about that young idiot who threw all your belongings into the wastebasket. He had no right."

"Come on, Bugash. Just what is it you want?"

"I don't want you to be mad at us. You know there was an arrest in Annoushka's case?"

"Who was it?" Nikolai was suddenly interested.

"A man named Pavlovic, a former priest."

"You arrested him? That man is innocent."

"No priest is ever innocent. Besides, it was Startz who arrested him."

"Why?"

"I was thinking about what you said regarding the old manuscript. Do you still have the original five pages?"

"So that's what you want? You have most of the translation and the synopsis. Why do you want the original pages?"

"Don't play games with me. Those five pages are part of a priceless historical document. They belong to our government."

"And you are the government? If they belong anywhere, they belong in our national archives."

"I am asking you to give me those five pages."

"No."

"I am ordering you to deliver those five pages."

"Ordering me, Comrade Colonel? How can you? My report does not exist. And, according to both Michea and Doctor Tagarū, not one page of the Dubrava letopis is missing."

A long pause. "At least tell me what was on the last two pages."

"And be picked up and driven to some insane asylum? No, thank you."

"I promise this is off the record."

"I don't believe you. However, inasmuch as this is only what's written in an ancient manuscript, and you know how superstitious the Bessarabians are, even now . . ."

"Please, no introductions."

"Well, it's the description of a rather complicated ritual for killing a vampire."

"I knew I shouldn't have asked. What's so complicated? Isn't the stake through the heart enough?"

"Apparently not. There are lots of prayers involved. And invocations."

"Spare me."

"That's providing you've found your vampire. They're very difficult to find, you know."

"Yes, I know. What am I saying?" Bugash swore angrily. "It was a mistake talking to you. Tell me straight, are you going to give me those pages or not?"

"I am not going to give them to you and you are not going to find them either. Tell that to those idiots who wrecked my apartment."

"Continue, Nikola." Bugash was resigned. "Tomorrow I'll send a woman to clean up your place."

"Now, say you found a vurdalak—" Nikolai said, beginning to enjoy this: it was so absurd that the fourth highest ranking officer in the Ministry of the Interior was now interested in vampires. "And you say all these prayers and chant all these chants, then you take out a bottle of holy water. Oh, yes! Because, you see, the vampire is lying submerged in blood, only his face is exposed . . ." Nikolai let that sink in.

"So, you pour the holy water over his eyes . . . and the holy water is supposed to burn through his eyes, so that he can't hypnotize you. Then you take a sharp knife and cut off his head. Are you with me? And that's just the beginning. You have to burn the head on a specially constructed fire, in a very special place, where the grass does not grow."

"I think I've heard enough. It might interest you that Radū and I had a long talk after you were gone. And we found ourselves in agreement that a certain citizen of our Republic named Michea Adelescu, better known as Basarab, is indeed a very mysterious person. Further investigation into his background and his activities is necessary. If he is the killer, Nikola, we will find out. He will be brought to justice. Trust me."

Nikolai smiled and hung up the phone. It was Bugash himself, some fifteen years ago, who had told him that whenever people start telling you, "trust me, trust me," that's when to be careful. He took another sip of cognac. Startz must be waiting for him by now.

Nikolai did not think he would be followed, but he took no chances. He crisscrossed the busy boulevards and the empty side streets. Café Lido was one of his favorite restaurants; he used to visit it at least once a week when his wife was alive. The headwaiter recognized him immediately and ushered him to a small table near the stage. It was quarter-past eight and the punctual Startz was late. Nikolai ordered a cognac and waited.

The restaurant was filled with happy, carefree people, not one tourist in sight. Nikolai thought, finally, we Romanians, too, can afford to go out. Radū was right; the people probably never had it so good. The entertainer, a striking dark-haired woman, sang a lovely Romanian ballad, one that Nikolai hadn't heard recently:

> The sheep will gather over me
> and shed blood tears,
> But you shouldn't tell them about my death,
> tell them that I got married,
> to a beautiful empress:
> The world's bride,
> at my wedding, a star fell,
> the sun and the moon held my crown,
> fir trees and maple trees were my
> dear wedding guests . . .

"I am glad you could come, Nikola." Startz sat down. "My friend," he said with some sadness in his voice, "we have to go back to the castle."

"I am not going. Why should I?" He finished his cognac.

"To help me." Startz ordered a glass of wine. "I need your help, Nikola, and I believe you need mine."

> . . . the wind brought my presents,
> the birds brought us song . . .

the woman continued the ballad.

"I don't see how I can help you. I don't see how you can help me, and I don't need your help anyway. I am suspended; my career is over. I have lost a woman for whom I had very deep feelings."

"Have you forgotten her so soon?"

"I only wish I could forget her. Doesn't matter, she's back in America, probably happy with another man . . . after her Romanian interlude. I was simply foolish to think it could end otherwise."

"You talk as if you still care for her." Startz sighed.

"I do not care for anybody, least of all myself. But, to leave in such a way—no explanation, without bothering to take her belongings." He thought for a moment. "Perhaps she was more infatuated with our great celebrity than I had realized. There's a liberated woman for you, Startz."

"Perhaps she is not so liberated; perhaps she did not leave of her own free will . . ."

"Somebody kidnapped her here in Romania?"

"What if somebody did?"

"For what possible purpose? She is not very rich. Stop talking nonsense, Startz. We both checked and rechecked every possibility, as you very well remember."

"Every possibility except one . . . that she still might be living in the Dubrava castle."

"Michea kidnapped her?"

"Why not? You've mentioned how he looked at her."

"And where is he keeping her? Under his huge bed?"

"I wish I knew."

"Now, you've searched the castle top to bottom, and you personally searched Michea's apartment thoroughly?"

"I certainly did . . . but I did not tell you at the time what we found."

"Something exotic? Perhaps a casket full of blood?"

"Actually something more exotic . . . and gruesome."

Nikolai motioned for the waiter. "Speaking of gruesome, let us order something to eat." He remembered he had had nothing to eat all day and the cognac, and the mention of Sally, and the dark-haired woman singing his favorite ballad, and Bugash and Radū, and Startz looking at him with such sympathy, and Michea glaring at

111

him at the door of his apartment, and Annoushka's pathetic body, and the wolf's white fangs . . . all became so remote, a part of some bad dream, a film without any beginning or any ending.

"Nikola, Nikola, are you all right?" Startz poured ice cold water through Nikolai's half-closed lips and he greedily drank it.

"I don't know, Startz. I am better now."

"Perhaps we could meet another time?"

"No, no, I am fine. Once I eat something." He smiled weakly. "The tremendous tension of these past few weeks must have gotten to me. Now, tell me about this gruesome discovery of yours."

"There will be plenty of time for that after we've eaten."

After the dinner, Nikolai felt much better.

"You must know, Startz, that talking to me right now might be bad for your career. Bugash and Radū might find out. They still have eyes and ears everywhere."

"I couldn't care less. Tell me something; they've suspended you? For how long?"

"Only one month. But try to figure this out. Just before leaving to meet you, I got a call from Bugash. He wanted to find out about a certain manuscript and hinted that I may get my check anyway, that Michea might be a bad comrade, after all . . ."

Startz put down his coffee. "Their position is very shaky, Nikola. Radū's only real claim to fame, as you know, was that when she was a little girl, she sat on Lenin's knee and when she got older, she sat on Georghe's knee: our equivalent of King Carol and Magda Lupescu. There was a rumor going around the ministry a few years ago that she comes from an ancient boyar family, our dear proletarian lady. Perhaps there is a tie with Michea? In any case, the new leadership is trying to kick them both out."

"I don't see how this can help me."

"You handed them your report?"

"Yes, and I offered the two theories. One of them was yours: that someone is trying to make it appear that supernatural forces are at work. Alternatively, well, supernatural forces just *might* be at work at Dubrava. So many events seem to elude rational explanation."

"You idiot."

"I was only being honest."

"I can't believe it! Of all people, you must realize that honesty has nothing to do with our work. So three weeks later, they summon you and yell at you, and threaten you, and tell you they'll forget all about your report, that it was never written?"

"They did not yell at me. Not much anyway. Radū, in fact, patted my knee, treated me like a long-lost son."

"Ha! And after she read you the sentence, Bugash calls you and tells you to be good and to wait for your check?"

"Something like that, yes."

"You could take your case to the central committee."

"What's the use?"

"You astound me sometimes, Nikola. The committee would be very interested. Michea has stuck in their throats like a proverbial bone; they'd be happy to have him embroiled in any scandal, even if he were innocent. And they would also be happy to pounce on Radū."

"Even if he *were* innocent?"

"I have good reason to believe he is the killer." Startz was now very serious. "I believe he killed at least three people. And he will kill again. But he is also an extremely clever man. Touching him may prove as disastrous as touching a land mine."

"Let's say I go up there with you, what do we do, kill him?"

"That idea appeals to me . . . however, *we* may not have to do that. Michea has other enemies."

"Mad enough to kill him? Some critic perhaps?"

"A dedicated fanatic . . . hmmm." Startz cleared his throat. "A professional vampire hunter."

"And you accused me of insulting *your* intelligence?"

"Nikola, that man is a former priest . . ."

"I saw him, too. Startz, wait! Bugash said that you arrested him."

"Only as a decoy, and partly for his own protection. He is free now. He is convinced"—Startz lit a cigarette, offered one to Nikolai—"that Michea is a vampire . . . actually, a king vampire. Strange man. We gave him ten years in the first postwar purge. I suppose it snapped his mind."

"So that's your 'professional'?"

"His family had a running war with vampires through the centuries, according to Nikodim's statement. Sometimes they kill a few vurdalaks; sometimes it's the other way around. But Michea himself has always eluded them. Nikodim is convinced that Michea is virtually indestructible. . . ."

"Excuse me, Startz, but if I were to bet on who kills who, all my money would be on Michea, vampire or not."

"And that is exactly why we must return to the castle."

"You have a plan?"

113

"I do indeed."

They smoked in silence, finished their coffee. Startz picked up the check, studied it, and paid.

"You mentioned," Nikolai said slowly, "that Sally might be at the castle, and that you found something gruesome."

"Yes." Startz cleared his throat again. "I have two new accounts which might concern you. One from a village youngster who saw a foreign woman get into Michea's carriage. Another from a truck driver who saw a naked young woman running into the woods. Both reports came at about the time of her disappearance, when you were in Brasov."

"Did you question Michea about it?"

"Of course. He claims that no one is ever allowed to share the carriage with him."

"I thought you impounded that damned thing?"

"Unfortunately, in the afternoon, I had a call from the ministry: he can ride his carriage; it gives him inspiration. Right now, I'd say he needs it. His writing is getting worse and worse."

They left Café Lido and walked to Startz's unobtrusive blue Volkswagen.

Sally running naked into the forest? Nikolai couldn't believe it. Still, if she were held captive, that would explain everything.

"Can I drive you home?" Startz offered.

"What about your gruesome find?" Nikolai could barely fit into the tiny car. For a second, he felt a tingling sensation of danger, but he dismissed it. What could happen here in Bucharest?

"I found a dungeon, a most interesting dungeon . . . complete with a torture chamber." Startz drove slowly, carefully. "Apparently still being used. Are you coming with me?"

"Yes, as you said, I am an idiot."

"Good, we shall leave tomorrow night . . . in my car."

"Let me off right here. I'll go through the alley."

After Startz drove away, Nikolai was so absorbed in his thoughts that he did not see the sleek gray Mercedes that had followed them for some time.

two

In his apartment, Startz made a pot of very strong black coffee and picked up a manila folder. He decided to reread the contents more carefully, these fantastic journals written with some flair by priests and children and one account by a German knight, no less, in the service of the great John Hunyadi. There was a long, rambling letter of a distant relative of Nikodim's too, a priest named Stephen Pavlovic who had lived in the village until his suicide or murder just after the Great Peasant Uprising of 1908.

Every force creates a counterforce. This theory had always intrigued Startz. And here, before him, written with great aplomb, was a most unusual and intriguing dossier of events, a document of sorts, a record of "good" (priests) against "evil" (vurdalaks). But there was also a third category of a much more mysterious force, on the side of good: the historian/priest, possibly a saint, Setozar, who appeared in different centuries and whose powers were almost as strong as those of force number four: the indestructible and equally mysterious Prince of the Night. Startz drank his coffee slowly.

In his folder, he had a neatly typed translation—the original journals were in Latin, Old Slavonic, and Russian. He smiled. The translator must have been greatly amused, if amused was the right word, to get this little gem of a job instead of the usual dull official documents. He turned the first page.

THE DOSSIER OF NIKODIM PAVLOVIC

115

Early spring, the year of our Saviour 1231, I was twelve years of age. The following I saw with my own eyes while hiding in the woods near our church . . .

The account itself was written by an Orthodox monk named Simeon who belonged to the Order of St. Elia the Prophet. It had been changed to fit the style of the time and elaborated upon, which was also the custom of that age.

The Dubrava castle is a smoldering ruin; fires break out amidst its crumbling walls. In the forest church, an Orthodox priest conducts the evening service. Only his twelve-year-old son and six of the parishioners are present. The rest are either dead or have fled in horror, deep into our Carpathian mountains and forests. The Tartar bands roam the Romanian countryside, plundering and killing at random. The priest prays for all those who perished, for those who are starving in the forests, for the refugees, and for the prisoners. He asks the Almighty to give strength to his suffering flock, to help them overcome the evil and merciless enemy. The priest's voice is calm; his son assists him solemnly.

A slight movement in the church and several of his parishioners leave hurriedly. The priest nods to his son and he, too, leaves through a small side door into the forest.

Later, the priest is alone in his church, praying quietly. Hoof-beats are heard approaching. Guttural sounds can be heard. The church doors are flung wide open and a group of Tartars bursts in. Two of them throw the priest to the ground. The priest crosses himself, fully expecting to enter a better world. Not yet.

"Stop it."

The priest looks up and sees a young nobleman in a black Moldavian attire standing proudly among the Tartars.

"Do not be frightened, Servant of God." The nobleman smiles. His smile is strange; his face is stark white; his eyes are unusually large and burning red, like the Tartars' torches. He terrifies the priest much more than the Tartars.

"You must help us, priest," the nobleman continues. He moves his white hand to one side and the priest sees two bodies wrapped in sheepskins. He can only see the faces, two Mongols, a man and a woman. "You must bury these two souls in your cemetery, so that they shall know eternal peace. Come closer."

116

Tartars push the priest closer: the wide-eyed corpses stare blankly, their faces infused with evil.

"I can't . . ." the priest stammers. "I cannot bury infidels in sacred ground . . . I can bury them in the forest."

"You will do as I say. Bury them in the middle of your cemetery." The nobleman shrieks, his face distorted with rage. He throws a large wooden shovel toward the priest. "You will bury them or these people will die."

The priest notices that the Tartars have rounded up most of his flock, have tied ropes around their necks. He also notices, with great satisfaction, that his son is not among the prisoners. The priest sighs, picks up the shovel, and puts it on his shoulder. He is a tall, powerfully built man. "Release my people," he tells the nobleman, "and I shall do as you say."

The nobleman speaks and the Tartars reluctantly comply.

The priest walks out toward the cemetery, followed by the strange nobleman and the Tartars carrying the bodies and torches.

The priest puts on his cassock and is ready to walk away when the Tartar carrying the female corpse stumbles over some freshly dug earth and lets go of his bundle. The woman's head, which is severed from her body and has been held together by the sheepskin, rolls to a halt at the priest's feet. He bends over it in horror, touches the dark blood which is dripping from her neck, his heart sinking. Suddenly he runs back toward the church. Tartars are shrieking behind him, running after him, equally terrified. The priest feels a sword's edge cut his shoulder, but he continues to run. As he enters the church, two arrows pierce his back. He can hardly breathe. Another arrow tears into his leg. He staggers toward the altar, toward his holiest of holy.

The Tartars stand uncertainly in the chapel. Another arrow lands between the priest's shoulder blades. Without effect. The arrows and the sword do not hurt the priest. His hand, however, where he had touched the black blood, is on fire: the skin is burning; the fire is spreading. The priest reaches for the vial of holy water.

"No, stop it!" the nobleman shouts imploringly. As the holy water spills over the priest's infected hand, the burning stops. His hand is normal again; he can even move his fingers. He thinks about his son, now safely in the forest, of his freed parishioners.

He quickly crosses himself and the Tartars' swords are upon him. He feels nothing.

The nobleman stands watching the priest die. "Did we find his son?" he asks.

The warrior shakes his head.

"We must find him." The Tartar nods.

The nobleman remains standing watchfully, as the Tartars destroy the holy objects and set fire to the altar. He smiles: they are children, mere children. When the church is engulfed in flames, the nobleman rides away. He is thoughtful now; he knows that the drama that took place in this small church will affect human history. It is getting light; the nobleman jumps on his horse and rides hurriedly toward the valley.

Startz picked up another translation. An Orthodox priest with the Serbian contingent wrote meticulously about the great battle of Nicopolis in 1396. He attributed his miraculous escape from the horrible tortures devised for all Orthodox priests by the Moldavian prince and traitor Mircea, actually a servant of Satan, to divine intervention. This appeared in the form of a shepherd boy who led the priest into the mountains.

Startz sighed, drank some more coffee, and leafed lazily through the priest's tale:

NICOPOLIS, 1396

On a wide plain below the fortress city of Nicopolis, besieged for nearly a month by the Christian Crusaders, two great opposing armies prepare for a decisive battle.

In his tent of sky-blue silk, the Sultan of the Ottoman Empire, Bayezid the Thunderbolt, dressed in white, is praying to the almighty Allah to give his sword the power to defeat the accursed infidel once and for all. Nearby, in a magnificent and much larger tent, under the tapestries of saints and martyrs, and surrounded by Catholic bishops and priests, Sigismund, the King of Hungary, is praying to Jesus, his Father, and the Holy Ghost, to grant him essentially the same thing: the power to rid Europe of the dreaded Turk once and for all.

The knights, answering the call from Pope Boniface IX, had come from all parts of France, England, Germany, the Netherlands, and even as far as Sweden. They had brought with them their serfs and attendants, their priests, doctors, courtesans, and their political advisors. They had answered the call to restore the glory of Christendom and to drive the Turkish infidel out of Europe.

But they behaved most disgracefully along the way. Even in Catholic Germany and Hungary, they looted and plundered. When they entered the Balkans, the noble knights outdid even the Turks in their brutalization of the Orthodox peasant. They burned entire villages, raped the women, killed the children and the infirm, and took the able-bodied men into slavery.

King Sigismund, an able strategist, divided his Hungarian army in two. One-half accompanied the knights, and the other half was sent across the Carpathian Mountains to force the fierce Wallachians and Moldavians under Prince Mircea to join in an alliance against the Turks. This was accomplished and Sigismund's entire army, supported by the greatest crusade force ever assembled, joined together outside Nicopolis.

Both Christian and Ottoman forces were about evenly matched. However, the crusading knights, despite appeals from their own clergy, continued their looting and killing and debauches, with the result that instead of a strong force they were now little more than a large, disorganized, bloodthirsty mob. They also refused to accept orders from King Sigismund. They wanted all the glory of defeating the Turks for themselves. Sigismund pleaded in vain for them to wait and attack the Turks together, but the knights would not heed his advice. They charged Bayezid's army. It was indeed an awesome and terrifying sight: thousands of them in heavy armor galloping across the plain, cutting into Bayezid's infantry.

That was their undoing. They penetrated the first Turkish lines of defense, but the troops they managed to scatter were young Anatolian irregulars. By the time the knights reached Bayezid's second line, they encountered the battle-hardened and disciplined Ottoman soldiers. The knights' energy was gone; their horses were tired and dropping to the ground. They charged the Turks by the thousands, and by the thousands they perished. Some escaped; the rest were forced to surrender.

The Hungarians, who were mainly the infantry, fought bravely, even though they were now outnumbered. With the aid of the Wallachians, Sigismund still hoped to defeat the Turks. But the Wallachians withdrew at the critical moment without getting into the battle. And Bayezid's janissaries were pushing the Hungarians on both sides like a giant vise. The Hungarian center under Sigismund held out valiantly. But when the Serbians under Prince Stephen came to Bayezid's side, the Hungarians were doomed.

The remnants of the western army fled in panic and confusion, leaving all they had looted behind. Some who managed to escape across the Danube were caught and put to death by the very peasants they had treated so cruelly.

Not only was this a humiliating disaster for European chivalry, it sealed the doom of Constantinople and established the Ottoman rule over the Balkans, which lasted for hundreds of years.

Bayezid thanked Allah for his victory. He felt troubled, though. His face was twitching; his commanders stood apprehensive. Reluctantly, he gave the order to kill every prisoner. This must be done, he explained, in retaliation for the massacre of the Turkish irregulars by the French knights a few years earlier. He also gave orders to spare the rich nobles and hold them for ransom.

"Great Sultan, Prince Mircea of Wallachia and Moldavia," announced his advisor.

Bayezid motioned to his servants, who brought some coffee. They had met in battle only two years before and while Bayezid was victorious, he held Mircea in high esteem.

"With you against me . . ." The Sultan spread his arms as if to say, "Who knows?"

"It was not my wish to fight the Great Sultan." Mircea lay down prostrate before Bayezid's feet until the Sultan touched his shoulder.

"You can share in my glory." Bayezid sat down.

Mircea sat on a much smaller pillow to the right of him. The interpreter, a Romanian gazi, sat discreetly in back of him.

"Great Sultan," Mircea began, "spare the Orthodox priests . . ."

Curiosity appeared on Bayezid's delicate face. "Yes," he finally said. "As you wish, but I think we have captured mostly Catholic priests, perhaps no more than a dozen of the Orthodox faith."

"Give them to me."

Bayezid nodded in agreement. "Tell me why do you want them?" He looked at Mircea, looked searchingly, then smiled. "No, better not tell me. I do not wish to know. Do with them whatever you desire."

120

"Great Sultan . . ." Mircea touched the cup with his lips but did not drink the thick coffee.

"Another wish?" Bayezid was amused and surprised. The Wallachian Prince was unusually brave. No one on this earth would have dared to ask the Sultan to grant him two favors in one day.

"A request . . . there was a woman abducted by the Crusaders . . ."

"A woman!" Bayezid was really amused. "My friend"—he smiled—"I can give you one thousand women."

"This one is different. She is a Wallachian princess; her name is Zerkal; she is among the prisoners. Could you give her to me? I would be forever grateful."

"It shall be done!" Bayezid clapped his hands and gave instructions to the gazi who entered.

The audience was almost over; Bayezid stood up.

"I, too, require your help," he said seriously.

"How can I, a mere Prince, help the magnificent Sultan?"

"I may need your best cavalrymen. There is one Mongol I must defeat, an arrogant man they call Timur the Lame, the Conqueror." Bayezid sneered. "He has already restored the empire of Genghis Khan . . . subdued all of Central Asia, the Golden Horde in Russia, conquered India, Persia, Mesopotamia, Syria. I must defeat him! Allah himself came to me in a vision and foretold me my victory over this Timur the Lame . . ." Bayezid was now rambling on to himself. He paced across his tent and dismissed Prince Mircea with a wave of his hand.

On the Nicopolis plain, the Christian prisoners were being put to death in droves.

Why did the priest describe the meeting of the sultan with Mircea and why the mention of the woman Zerkal? Am I wasting my time again, Startz wondered. Zerkal, such a strange name. Wallachian? No, I never heard a name like that before, but then again, in the fourteenth century names tended to be more exotic. He did think of a mirror. A woman, a princess, whose name is mirror? He smiled and opened another tale.

This one was told by Karl the Second, Duke of Hannover, a soldier of fortune, currently in service of the Great John Hunyadi. The German stated the dates precisely: the city of Buda, June 3, 1445, at four in the afternoon.

121

The Great John Hunyadi, "White Knight of Wallachia," conqueror of two Turkish armies, and the Savior of Christendom, was sitting in the main hall of his magnificent palace while the voice of a lowly Orthodox priest droned on.

A few Hungarian nobles and French and German knights, including myself, stood at the other end of the hall looking with some astonishment at our great leader. How in the world had an Orthodox priest gotten an audience with Hunyadi? Perhaps he was granting a favor to a fellow countryman. Yes, that must be the answer!

Hunyadi listened attentively, looked over the diagrams which the priest spread before him, and finally called his aide, a tall Romanian knight with a long scar across his face. He whispered to the aide at great length, stood up, received the blessing bestowed on him by the Orthodox priest, and walked out of the room. His famous silver armor gleamed in the afternoon sun.

The priest also left, and Hunyadi's aide approached me, the senior German knight, the Duke of Hannover.

Later that evening, a carriage with the priest and Hunyadi's aide, accompanied by a detachment of German knights under my command, left the capitol in the direction of the ancient town of Cluj in northern Transylvania.

Just before dusk, the carriage and the detachment arrived at the gates of a large estate. Two of the knights disembarked and smashed the heavy chain holding the gate together.

"If what you say is true, Father"—the Romanian knight with a scar broke the long silence—"we must hurry." I speak seven languages, including that of Romania, quite fluently, and I understood every word.

As their carriage rolled toward the mansion, several servants appeared on the road, armed with lances and swords. They tried to stop us, but they were no match for the heavily armed German knights who scattered them within minutes. The carriage rolled past the mansion to a small burial plot with an elaborate marble mausoleum. The priest and the Romanian knight wasted no time in jumping out of their carriage and hurrying toward it.

"Take the carriage and the horses out of sight," the priest said. Calmly, he opened his burlap bag and consulted his drawings. "Here," he said, pressing the stones of the wall. Nothing moved. The priest paused. Beads of perspiration appeared on his fore-

122

head. Behind him, I, the Romanian, and my German knights waited patiently, our hands on our swords.

The priest pushed again. He was a powerful man: it seemed that by his sheer strength, he was moving the entire wall. Finally, the panel of heavy stones slid back to expose a very narrow flight of steps leading into blackness. The knights lit their torches. Two of them advanced first, then I, the priest, and the Romanian.

We came to another wall and the priest had to consult his plans again. Then the wall slid open and we were in a round basement.

In the middle of the cramped chamber stood a large limestone coffin. Bats, wolves, and snakes were carved on its sides. While my knights remained discreetly near the entrance, the priest and I and the Romanian determined that the coffin was empty.

It was not an ordinary coffin. Inside, it was lined with metal and filled with brown liquid; patches of green mold swam on the surface, emanating a most foul odor. We turned away, nauseated.

"They will be coming back shortly; we better stand to one side," said the priest.

Silence hung heavy in the dungeon.

"Here, look." The priest touched my hand. From his burlap sack, he extracted a sharp, shiny instrument that looked like a curved knife, with a handle shaped like a cross. My German knights held firmly to their swords and torches.

In the dungeon, there was suddenly a brief movement of wind. No doors or secret passages opened or closed, yet the wind grew stronger and colder. Two clouds of fine white mist appeared out of nowhere and floated toward the coffin. These two clouds began changing slowly into human form: the larger into the figure of a man, the smaller into a woman. My German knights gasped and one of them dropped his sword. It fell with a thunderous noise on the stone floor and the whole dungeon shook.

"Ayyyyyyye!" screamed the man, almost completely materialized, his eyes bloody and hateful, his long, wolflike face howling in agony and fury. The shrill outcry left my knights stunned and immobilized.

The priest, however, was not stunned. He jumped up to the vurdalak (for that is what it was called in Romanian; a simple vampire in our state of Hannover-Braunschweig) and slashed his throat with one swoop of his knifelike instrument. The priest tried to cut off the creature's head, but he succeeded only partially.

The vurdalak, his head barely attached to the rest of his body, flung the priest against the wall and advanced toward him. The priest recovered enough to throw a vial of holy water at the monster's face, which blinded him and seemed to burn through his skull. I advanced and tried to finish him off with my sword, but the vurdalak lifted me into the air and threw me against the coffin. The blood was gushing from his wound, dark red, almost black. He turned toward his companion, who was now transformed into a beautiful lady dressed in black Turkish silk.

"Zerkal," coughed the mortally wounded creature, "flee, my daughter . . ." The woman quickly began retreating into a cloud of mist.

The priest, weakened by the vurdalak's blow, stepped forward with his weapon as did a few of my knights, but she dissolved before our very eyes.

The vurdalak was still screeching and waving his arms when the Romanian knight took careful aim with his double-edged sword and cut off the monster's head. The head rolled, followed by a stream of black blood. I wanted to pick it up, but the priest stopped me.

Very cautiously, the priest wrapped the head in some white embroidered cloth. Then he lifted the burden delicately, careful not to touch any of the blood.

"You must burn this place now," he told the Romanian knight. The knight understood and translated the command to us in German.

"My job here is finished," the priest said sadly. "I must leave alone now, and take this head to a special place, to dispose of it. God be with you!"

"Father—" The Romanian knight stopped him. "What will happen to the woman, the one called Zerkal?"

"I am not certain," the priest answered. "She will have to dwell among the living for a time."

My German knights began setting fire to the dungeon. Outside, the dogs were barking and the cocks crowing and a bright disk of sun was rising above the mountains.

I could not forget that look of the Romanian vampire when he threw me across the room as if I were a mere feather. His look told me of the treasures such as this world has seldom known: gold and precious stones; the treasure which could be mine if I choose to help him. Only how could I help him now? It was too late! The vurdalak also told me by his glance alone that his Prince would reward me beyond anything known to mortal man. I thought of this for some years afterward and decided to pass on my tale to my heirs so that they might one day find this fabulous Romanian treasure.

The letter of young Father Stefan Pavlovic, the new priest of St. Cyril Parish in central Transylvania during the time of the Great Romanian Peasant Uprising. Summer 1907.

My dearest Mother,

I am eternally grateful for the linen and the new boots which you so kindly sent me. My old boots were indeed beyond any repair. As you know, the most reverend Bishop Filaret, who spoke to me a great deal about the tragic death of my father, assigned me to this tiny parish to, as he put it, "test my wings." This testing presumably includes learning to live without money. After three months here, His Holiness has not yet sent me a single franc.

This is a strange place, this village and this part of the country. So different from the Carpathians. This village is situated on the slopes of the great Transylvanian gorge. From my window, I can observe a beautiful panorama of the mountains and castles, a view most spectacular in the evening, when the sun slowly sets over the mountains and the valleys are covered with a light blue mist. There is one point of interest here, the famous Dubrava castle. It currently belongs to a monastery: Order of St. Elia the Prophet. I must confess, I never heard of that order before. Two weeks ago, the Egumen, the spiritual head of the monastery, kindly invited me to conduct the evening service at the castle and to share their simple supper afterward. This was a most pleasant occasion. The monks were quite hospitable: I thought they seemed a scholarly lot. The Egumen explained to me later that the order originated in eastern Moldavia, now a part of the Russian Empire, and that they had bought the castle only a few years ago from a ruthless and evil Hungarian landowner. After tasting some delicious wine which the monks made themselves, the Egumen, whose name was Setozar (later on I could not find a saint by that name in my book of saints), led me on a tour of his monastery. They are evidently a well-to-do order and they have an excellent library. I was invited to use it. As Setozar explained, they need an extensive library because they are historians. Then he said something which I did not understand: that by learning the past, they would be able to predict the future. Well, they had three other things of interest. One was a massive bas-relief of a devil (at least he looked like a devil to me) burning in agony in the main hall of the castle. Because of its nature, its subject matter, the bas-relief remains covered most of the time with thick white muslin. Another place of interest was their wine cellar, which used to be a torture dungeon where the Hungarian landowner tortured and executed his serfs. Finally, there was a carriage of great workmanship. It was without wheels and was not used because, as Setozar told me, at one time it was the devil's toy. I must mention to you that the people here, mostly of Dacian heritage, are a superstitious lot. They are also very proud and, until one gets to know them better, aloof. They still hang wreaths of garlic over every door and every window at the time of the full moon—even in our enlightened age! This is supposed to keep away the local vurdalaks, of whom the most feared is a woman who steals babies from their cribs and who roams at night near a desecrated church and a cemetery not far from Dubrava castle.

There's a legend about her and her master, who is supposed to be the prince of all vampires. Every century, she returns to him reincarnated as a human being, without being aware at first who she really is. When such a time arrives there's a reign of terror through the countryside. Babies disappear without a trace, as well as local shepherds, farmers, in isolated farmhouses, and hunters in the forests. People disappear as far north as Bukovina and the western Ukraine. The police do not interfere, the locals say, because they are bribed by the vampires. The reason so many people are needed, the legend goes, is that the Prince of the Night must replenish his casket with fresh blood. Such fantasy!

Dearest Mother, please send me my father's winter cassock as mine is about to fall apart. Also send me the small yellow suitcase that holds my father's papers. Bishop Filaret specifically ordered me to read them and study them for some reason. And perhaps you could write to the bishop and remind him of my financial plight.

Please don't worry.

May God keep you safe.

Love, your son Stefan.

Last week I had the strangest and most frightening dream, no doubt because of listening to all these silly superstitions. It was so real that for a few days and nights afterward I almost believed it to be a vision. I woke up in the middle of the night, and it was very light outside: the moon here, as in our region, is unusually bright when full. I saw in my window the face of a beautiful woman. She was smiling at me, only there was something strange in her smile. I could not quite understand it at the time, but now I remember: it was her teeth, shining like pearls, and so sharp, like those of a cat. I knew there could not be any real face in my window as I live on the second floor: mine is one of only three houses in the village with a second story.

The woman kept smiling and she begged me to invite her in. I am not sure whether she was actually speaking, however. She promised me joy such as I have not known. I think I crossed myself and she started crying, as if I had hurt her. In my dream, I felt sorry for her and I opened my window . . .

Two pages of meaningless scribbles follow, disjointed words, unclear letters. Then, in a shaky handwriting, the account continues:

She was somehow with me in my room. I realized she was wearing some ancient black silks and was heavily perfumed. I felt rather weak. She took my hand and placed it upon her breast.

What I did later in my dream (dear God, I only hope it was a dream), I cannot write about, for it was all dreadfully sinful and disgusting. She left before morning, I do not know how. She promised to come back the following night to take me to a place, a paradise on earth, where strange flowers and plants grow by the light of the moon.

I felt rather exhausted. After my morning prayers, I decided to visit the castle and talk to Father Setozar, who perhaps could explain the meaning of this dream.

Again, pages of meaningless scribbles and strokes of the pen. Then, in very bad handwriting:

The woman in my dream, my nightmare, returned again in the middle of the night. This time there was a man with her, an unusually handsome young man who wore, of all things, a golden crown on his head. The crown . . . the crown . . . dear God, I remember everything so vividly: the princes of Kiev had worn it for centuries. Wait, instead of our holy Orthodox cross, there was a red, shining ruby in the middle, shaped like a tear or . . . a drop of blood. He kept looking at me with his large, burning eyes and I knew instinctively that I was looking at the face of the most horrible being created by Satan, the one known in our native Carpathia as the Prince of the Night, the dreaded krovopeiza, *the vurdalak himself.*

Of course, I realized that the woman with him was the very Zerkal in the legend, his eternal mistress. I stood too horrified to move. His eyes were burning into my head and my body was becoming weak. I felt my cross and raised it high to ward off the apparition. The woman's face twisted in rage and she turned away. But the vurdalak kept his burning eyes fixed on me and I thought, for a moment or two, that he even smiled. Although he was not talking, he somehow conveyed his thought to me. He was inviting me to accompany both of them to a paradise he called the Moonflower Garden, where illusion and reality are one. I do not recall what I was doing. I suppose I was just standing there in the middle of my room with my cross in my hand. What amount of time had passed, I do not know. I suppose I was saved by my faithful dog, who awakened and raised such a commotion that eventually the vurdalak and his companion vanished and I was free. I felt so weak, I fell down on the floor and did not regain consciousness until morning.

Scribbles again.

I did not go to the castle today . . . must hold services . . . one of my parishioners died during the night . . . a reign of terror? The relatives of the departed fled south, fearing he would return from the dead. Feel ill today and depressed. . . . My dog was killed, someone slashed his throat. A child of five disappeared during the night. All the villagers are boarding up their windows and laying wreaths of garlic and bunches of wild roses around their houses. Nonsense, it will not protect them, nothing will! Nothing! I must flee, must get to Setozar. Perhaps they are right in saying that when the vurdalak appears, great disasters are sure to follow . . . the revolt engulfed all of Romania . . . too late . . . I cannot write . . . a unit of the Romanian army sent to deal with the insurgents is entering the village . . . I must flee . . .

More insane writing.

*The kindly hard-working monks, the good monks are all killed,
massacred to a man . . . God's martyrs, no doubt, placed on the
right of Jesus Christ, our Lord. I cannot endure this much
longer . . .*

This last letter had been on Nikodim's night table on the evening
of Annoushka's death. It was confiscated along with some other
personal papers by Startz and returned when Nikodim was released
with official apology from Brasov prison.

His coffee long gone, Startz was leaning in his armchair, thinking.
There had been no attempt to trace Michea's ancestry except to
suggest that Prince Mircea, a well-known historical figure, could be
the all-powerful Prince of the Night. Ridiculous! If Michea *was* one
of the real Moldavian princes, what particular line did he come
from? Was he the son of Besorab the First, for example? And the
mystery surrounding Setozar was now even murkier than before.
Was he Russian? Was he Moldavian? Where did he come from?
Startz tried to remember who in the Ministry of Interior came from
northern Bukovina, someone who might fill him in on the monastic
order of St. Elia the Prophet. He wasn't even sure that such an
order existed. And another beauty: Zerkal. Another puzzle! Apparently she is only a sometime vampire. Well and good, only what
is she at other times? Plus there was that damned Slavonic manuscript. It's all nonsense, of course, fantasy, superstition. All of it,
except the murders.

Startz winced; he was developing a headache. There was only one
thing he was certain about: the killer would strike again, and very
soon.

He yawned, glanced at his alarm clock: almost three in the
morning. Time was definitely running out.

The time! Startz jumped up, slapped himself on the forehead.
The time, you fool! He paced back and forth across the room. That's
what is wrong with Nikodim's fairy tales and the Slavonic manuscript and even Nikolai's report. The time element, more specifically the lack of it, tied his hands. And it had let him compromise his
integrity and had made him send a criminal, yes, but one who was
innocent of that particular crime, before the firing squad.

Time! Of course! Every legend of any vampire, any vurdalak,
states one indisputable fact: to them, time simply does not exist.
They live in a timeless void. Then, all legends aside, why was

Nikodim so preoccupied with chronology? And the nameless monks writing their letopis were also victims of their own chronological interpretation.

He opened Nikodim's dossier again and leafed through it. Now it began to make sense.

three

Nikodim's morning began as usual: half an hour of calisthenics followed by another half hour of prayers. At precisely seven, he shaved his head, brushed his teeth, dressed, and opened his window. He deeply inhaled the fresh morning breeze, listened to the singing of the birds. God's earth is dancing on mornings such as this.

He noticed several rabbits lurking expectantly under the bushes; they're waiting for some carrots, he remembered. Since Annoushka's death, he had taken up the task of feeding them. He threw out a few carrot sticks; watched the rabbits hop up, grab them, and hurry back to their bushes. He smiled, but this morning he had a heavy, unpleasant sensation gnawing, pressing at his heart. The leaves were already golden, another summer over.

Only a week had passed since his release, and he felt as if he had never left the castle. That Inspector Startz was playing some sort of a game with him, Nikodim decided. At first the policeman seemed to have believed his story; then, suddenly, he'd searched his room and arrested him. He had not charged Nikodim with murder; he'd arrested him on some vague suspicion. Suspicion of what?

The modern jail in Brasov was a far cry from the Bukovina labor camp. Nikodim was even allowed to pray and do his calisthenics. And the food wasn't at all bad. The other inmates—thieves, embezzlers, along with a few political prisoners—treated him with respect, and the guards were young and polite. On the morning of his release, Inspector Startz himself had arrived to give him an official letter of apology. He had also driven Nikodim back to the castle. The castle guards, both Ivan and Janco, were now suspended and the museum was temporarily guarded by six militia men. This, to Nikodim, was a clear sign that Inspector Startz was not any closer to finding the murderer. And that particular murderer would strike again; he had to. On the evening of his release, Nikodim recalled, he'd met face-to-face with Michea, who had been sitting in the library making notations from one of the volumes. They were alone. For the first time, Michea had stood up when he saw Nikodim, managed a smile, and addressed him as "the servant of God."

"Whose servant are *you*?" Nikodim couldn't help asking, although he already knew the answer.

Michea looked him over with his gray, emotionless eyes and, to Nikodim's surprise, broke into an impassioned monologue. "I also serve a god, priest. A different god, one that doesn't promise you paradise, but gives it to his faithful servants right here on earth. Mine is the god of freedom, of the wind and the space, the god of your innermost desires and wishes, the god of cruelty and strength—not your slobbering, puny Jesus. My god, priest, is the god of darkness, the lord of flies: he has thousands of names and thousands of faces: Bes, Velsevul, Satan, Chort. . . . Your God doesn't care about this world or his people. Mine rules it! Oh yes, as well as other kingdoms, the ones you can't even see or feel, kingdoms where an eternity is but one fleeting second . . . you can't conceive of what I am talking about, can you?" Michea had stopped talking and sat back in his chair.

"You are a vurdalak and I must kill you." Nikodim had quietly retorted.

Michea had leaned back and laughed. He laughed, yet his eyes remained serious, watchful, piercing.

"Priest." He'd sighed. "One of your forefathers was indeed successful." Michea's eyes had sparkled with deep anger. "But only once! He studied well, did exactly as old Setozar instructed him to do . . . I know, I could not find the head. But *you* kill *me*? As you should be the first to realize, that is impossible. I cannot be killed by any mortal being . . . and you are mortal, aren't you?" Michea had smiled again, a grand, superior smile.

"I must do it and I will do it, with the help of my Lord Jesus Christ," Nikodim had said stubbornly.

132

"Jesus Christ?" Michea had exclaimed. "He could not even defend himself. What kind of god is he? Listen to me, priest, and listen well. Pack your belongings and leave this castle while you can. I can arrange a job for you . . . I still have a few friends in high places. Forget me. Enjoy your brief existence while you may." Michea had scooped up his notations and walked out of the library.

Nikodim had thoughtfully watched him leave, then had sat down and began leafing through a leather-bound tome that Michea had carelessly left on the table.

After a quick breakfast, Nikodim stopped at Dr. Tagarū's office. He had a relatively free day: the first busload of tourists was not due until noon. There was only a staff meeting to introduce the new assistant curator.

Nikodim felt at ease sitting in the familiar office, across from his old friend instead of facing the smiling, devious policeman and not knowing what was going to happen from one minute to the next.

"It is good to see you back, Father. A cigarette?" Dr. Tagarū knew that Nikodim would never smoke on his own. But he did love smoking, and, under some circumstances, a proffered temptation might be accepted. This was one of those occasions.

"Good to be back." Nikodim inhaled deeply. "Only I now am far from certain that I can fulfill my obligations . . . here."

"What are you talking about? Not that nonsense again, with Michea? That's a grandmother's tale! Not a shred of scientific evidence!" Dr. Tagarū was visibly upset. He took off his glasses and began wiping them. "They should have taught you at the seminary that the laws of nature are very strict and that there are no exceptions, our Creator himself saw to that!"

"I had a brief conversation with Michea," Nikodim continued gloomily. "He freely admitted to me that he was a servant of another god, quite different from ours."

"Nikodim, Nikodim, I have known you for about eight years now . . . and I have known Michea off and on since he was a boy, and his mother . . . he always had a very active imagination. Of *course*, he thinks he's different from the rest of us . . . and he is. He is a Nobel laureate, after all! And who are we? He may even be playing a joke at your expense."

"No, no, not a joke . . . I know it, he knows it."

"You wanted to read the missing pages?" Dr. Tagarū asked him softly. "Well, you cannot. They are still missing. That captain, the big man who began the investigation, he must have them . . . you want to read our forgeries?"

"I don't understand it."

"What is there to understand? The original five pages were never returned to the museum; the ones which, I assume, describe a certain heretical rite."

"Oh, my God." Nikodim sighed. "That is bad, bad for me, bad for all of us."

"You know, you should be very thankful to God, instead of being so gloomy. It is nothing short of a miracle that they let you out so quickly. Look, you have your job back, that in itself is a miracle. And yours is not the worst salary in Romania . . . I value your assistance, both as a historian and as a friend."

"Thank you, Doctor. I am grateful, don't misunderstand. Yet everyone must do what he thinks is right. I am not an exception."

Nikodim looked at his wristwatch. He had to leave at about eleven to check the lights and replenish the souvenirs at the shop. Today's tourists were a group of Russian technicians, part of a trade delegation. Judging by past experiences, the Russians were more interested in the souvenir shop than in the museum.

"You still have plenty of time. Have another cigarette." Dr. Tagarū looked at him sternly. "Listen to me well, Nikodim. I am not a psychiatrist, I am a medical doctor and a historian." He kept looking at Nikodim. "I, too, was a deeply religious man when I was young. But more than religion, more than medicine, I was always fascinated by our history . . . too bad you are a Slav, you wouldn't understand. There is no history so complicated and tragic and so full of riddles as ours. Avars and Bulgars and Pechenegs and Goths and Slavs and Vandals and Huns and Tartars, of course. And the Turks! They all came across our plains. And we Dacians somehow outlived them all. For nearly four centuries there was no mention of us. As if we had disappeared from the face of the earth, yet we survived . . ."

"I see no point, I know Romanian history quite well myself . . ."

"Of course you do! But here I was in 1931, a young lad just out of the university, enthusiastic, and bored. I wanted to know so much more. One of my professors, the famed Nicholae Iorga, told me about a certain Moldavian monastic order that was compiling historical data . . ."

"The Order of St. Elia?" Nikodim exclaimed. Great interest sparkled under his bushy eyebrows.

"Yes, the prophet . . . and I took the train to Jassy. The monks were hospitable; they allowed me to stay and study with them for nearly a year. Their chief historian, who is also their leader—they have quite a different system within their order—is an old wise man by the name of Setozar—"

"Setozar was killed in this very castle in 1907," Nikodim interrupted.

"Evidently not. He was alive and energetic when I last saw him in 1932."

"Then he escaped somehow. And you actually spoke with him?"

"Just as I am speaking with you now. Setozar, though he was an interesting man, shared your delusion, your idée fixe, your fanatical belief or . . . I shall be blunt, your madness."

"It is hardly madness to destroy an evil presence."

"Everyone sees evil differently." Dr. Tagarū shrugged. "Our Communists speak of the opiate of the people . . . Look, throughout centuries, good and evil have changed so much, it's difficult to tell at times which is which."

"I was referring to it primarily in a spiritual sense."

"Is that so different? You just go ahead, go ahead and kill Michea. It will be a simple act of murder, nothing else. You would be the assassin of a very famous person, not of a mythical creature, as you believe. And you will be shot for it as an ordinary criminal. If you're lucky, they might put you into a lunatic asylum, as an ordinary madman. And what about your professed faith in Jesus Christ: 'Thou shalt not kill'?"

"I am not a madman and I am not a murderer." Nikodim wanted another cigarette, but evidently Dr. Tagarū was hoping to end this conversation. "Michea is not a person . . . you said you knew him as a boy? Well, you knew a boy who was nearly eight centuries old. If I kill him—and actually, he reminded me himself that no mortal being can kill him—I will only be killing something that died eight centuries ago."

Dr. Tagarū was serious now. "As a historian, I, too, learned respect for our Romanian superstitions. Therefore, I shall disregard what you just said. Just remember: a vurdalak did not kill our Annoushka; a man did that. Yes, so much has been written and said

135

about our poor vurdalaks, and about all the hideous crimes attributed to them. Tell me, Nikodim, you believe so strongly in the ultimate blood sucker. Tell me, have you ever seen one?"

"May I have another cigarette, Doctor?" Nikodim's huge hand trembled a little as he struck the match. His eyebrows came together and beads of perspiration came out on his forehead.

"Yes, once." He actually blinked a few times. "You can choose not to believe me, of course."

"You're not talking about Michea?"

"No." Nikodim paused.

"Well, go on."

"Are you sure you want to hear it? It is not pleasant."

"Yes, of course, go on. I have never met anyone who actually saw a vurdalak— Oh, what about the legend that once you've seen one, you'll die shortly afterward?"

"The legend is true. I've been living all these years on borrowed time." Nikodim put out his cigarette. Dr. Tagarū waited. "I think the reason I am still alive . . . you see, with me, they don't just want to kill me, they want their revenge. My ancestors killed one of their kind."

"They killed a vurdalak? This is fabulous!" Dr. Tagarū smiled, but his eyes remained serious and worried.

"It happened in the winter of 1917; in the Banat of Temesvár, a small village near the Yugoslavian border. There had been several instances of vampirism; the villagers were terrified. The suspect— one of the local children actually saw him—was a Greek moneylender who lived in an isolated villa a few kilometers away from the village. I'll never forget their story, the snow-covered road they had to walk that day . . . to a small, desecrated cemetery just to one side of the villa and there, in a well-protected crypt, the round dungeon . . . in the middle, a casket filled with blood: the body lay in it, immersed in the blood, only his eyes and his nose were exposed . . ." Nikodim began shaking. He couldn't continue.

Dr. Tagarū picked up his phone. "Olga, bring me some coffee and two cups!" he ordered. He kept watching the powerful man shake uncontrollably. After Olga brought the coffee and Nikodim had taken a few swallows, he recovered somewhat.

"I am sorry, Doctor . . . that creature was described. It looked more like a wolf; the face was covered with coarse black hair. He

136

appeared to be smiling; his giant fangs gleamed just under the surface . . . My relatives were very tired and cold, and it was getting late. Father Seraphim opened his satchels, took out a flask of holy water and a specially blessed knife. He was very nervous. He dropped the knife and the creature began to stir . . ." Nikodim looked again at his watch. Dr. Tagarū sat silently. Nikodim could not judge his reaction.

"Yes, yes, I know what happened afterward . . . I, too, heard a similar story." Dr. Tagarū poured himself another cup of coffee.

"That vampire, before he died, he put a curse on me, on all our family too . . . for centuries to come. Sooner or later, I will die a most hideous death. I'll scream in agony ten thousand times; I'll even renounce my God; I will be reduced to a whimpering coward."

"And you still want to kill Michea?"

"You know, Doctor, Michea himself warned me to leave." Nikodim smiled for the first time. "He said he would even help me to find a new job. He must be nervous."

"Why don't you heed his advice? Why don't you leave?" There was genuine concern in Dr. Tagarū's voice. "I've heard some stories about Michea; he may not be a vurdalak, but he is a very dangerous man. How can you forget what happened to Annoushka?"

"I have been giving it a great deal of thought." Nikodim smiled again. "Jail is a very good place for thinking. Yes, I believe I know what Michea represents . . ."

It was still unclear to Dr. Tagarū whether Nikodim actually saw that vurdalak himself, but he did want to end this unpleasant conversation. To his great relief, the telephone rang at this point and Dr. Tagarū was informed that the bus with the Russian tourists had just left Ploesti.

"Don't worry about me, Doctor." Nikodim stood up, felt for his father's Orthodox cross under his shirt. It was time to begin his working day.

The Russian group arrived late in the afternoon, thoroughly frightened and indignant. Nearly a dozen of them, including two women, hurriedly disembarked from their bus and all but ran into the castle. It turned out that they were unfortunate enough to have gotten the same young driver who had driven Sally and Nikolai back to the village. Evidently, he had narrowly missed colliding with two oil trucks and had driven so recklessly that the first thing the Russians demanded from Dr. Tagarū was that they be given another driver for the return journey.

"I have four children back home," a Russian engineer explained, "and I am not ready to die in any case."

"Comrade," another one said excitedly, "look, two huge trucks were coming directly at us and some army convoy was in back of us, and this cretin continues driving at them, and we were all screaming at the top of our lungs and Lydia here fainted. It's a miracle we are alive!"

"You are completely safe, Comrades," Dr. Tagarū assured them. "I am going to call the ministry about their driver. In the meantime, I hope you'll have an enjoyable visit in the famous Dubrava castle. Your guide, Nikodim Pavlovic, speaks even better Russian than I do."

"I don't feel so well," sighed a Russian lady.

Dr. Tagarū invited her to come have some coffee in his office.

"We have a good selection of souvenirs," began Nikodim, noticing that the Russians were already admiring the blouses and sandals. "However, you'll have sufficient time to select your purchases after the tour. This way, please, Comrades." He led them into the main hall of the castle, reciting the historical data as they went along.

"The Dubrava castle, one of the oldest castles in Europe, was first built in the tenth century, destroyed by the Tartars in the thirteenth century, rebuilt and destroyed again in the same century by the Turks. Stephen the Great lived here as well as John Hunyadi, Vlad the Impaler, and other illustrious princes and kings. Michea the Brave proclaimed the first Romanian state in 1600, only to be killed a year later. King Carol and King Michael both lived here at one time or another. Now it's a wonderful museum belonging to peasants and workers and containing national treasures." He paused.

"That is an imposing-looking devil," observed one of the Russians.

"From the sketches of the great Leonardo da Vinci . . ." Nikodim droned on, leading the group into the library. The Russians were impressed by the number of Slavonic manuscripts.

"You are a Slav yourself?" one of them asked. "Is there a minority problem?"

Nikodim didn't quite know how to reply. "Romanians are not a pure race," he ventured cautiously. "They have Roman and Dacian ancestries as well as some Slavic and Tartar blood . . ."

"We Russians have some Tartar in us, too." The man smiled, satisfied.

Nikodim stopped the tourists at two display cases on the way to the shop. He felt someone watching him intensely. He glanced up. To his amazement, he saw Michea standing with his mother on the balcony, looking at the tourists.

A vurdalak who walks in daylight? Nikodim corrected himself: Michea is not just an ordinary vurdalak. He can probably do anything he wishes.

Michea smiled and nodded. Nikodim turned away and ushered the Russians downstairs.

After the tour, another problem arose with the Russian group. The Ministry of Tourism refused to send a different bus driver and the Russians refused to board the bus. They demanded to see higher officials and stubbornly waited in the museum's lobby.

"Go apologize," Dr. Tagarū implored the unconcerned young bus driver who was sitting in his bus, his feet on the wheel, leafing through an old edition of *Penthouse*.

"I'll have you fired!" Dr. Tagarū was losing all patience.

"I have already been fired," the driver answered. "They fired me last week. But today their driver got sick so they offered me double wages to drive this crazy bunch. They don't want to go back with me? I'll go back by myself."

Dr. Tagarū had an idea. He spotted the militia sergeant and went after him. The sergeant came out and whispered something in the driver's ear. Whatever it was, it worked. The driver put away his magazine and went to make peace with the Russians. The rest of the afternoon was uneventful and the evening came fast.

After supper, Nikodim sat, deep in his thoughts, looking outside at the clear, starry sky. The moon wasn't up yet. It was quiet. Perhaps I should leave? Nikodim was fighting his doubts. It's no use, he'll live until Judgment Day. Nikodim crossed himself. He remembered his grandfather, a Bogomil who believed that this world was created by Satan and that only through death could one enter a better world, the world of kindness and happiness. He also thought about Dr. Tagarū's pronouncement earlier in the morning, that there are no exceptions to the laws of nature. Perhaps just the opposite was true; perhaps nature, along with all its laws, is one giant exception, and normal life, even happiness, does not exist. Not in this world, nor in any other. He remembered Michea talking about other kingdoms, other pleasures. Perhaps we are all put on this planet for some obscure reason: foolish beings, so ready and eager to destroy one another. Who am I to say that Michea and his kind don't have a place in the scheme of things? Am I dreaming? In fact, he had dozed off for a few minutes. For a few minutes? It must have been a few hours. The moon was now very high over the mountains, a bright disc, almost full. One more night . . .

Nikodim realized that he was holding his father's cross in his hand. He also realized that something was outside his window. He felt a chill; he felt the other being's hunger and hatred. The window was slightly open. He stood up and closed it, then put on his sweater and sat on his bed. He heard some rustling in the bushes outside his window. Perhaps some cow is lost? No, he would have heard the bell. Perhaps Michea himself had decided to pay him a visit? No, Michea would wait and see whether he'd run. Something else. Nikodim now heard hoarse breathing right under his window. Shivers went up and down his spine.

"Invite me in." Nikodim heard a very sensual woman's voice, half whispering, half singing. "Please, invite me in . . . I know you are lonely. I know I can make you happy; open your window . . ."

Nikodim ran out of his room and slammed the door so hard that the militia man, one of the museum guards making the rounds, almost dropped his rifle in surprise.

"Something happened, Comrade?" he asked Nikodim.

"No, no. I suppose I had a bad dream." Nikodim took a deep breath.

"Do you want a cigarette? You look so pale."

"I am all right now." Nikodim went back inside. He knew exactly what he had to do. He took his bottle of holy water and opened his window wide. He fully intended to pour it on whoever or whatever it was. But the night was still, the moon was high, countless stars sparkled in the dark sky outside his window. Only the crickets cried now and then in the tall grass.

Nikodim was unable to sleep for the rest of the night. Over and over again, he examined his sketches and drawings of Michea's possible resting place.

For some time now, Nikodim had been aware of a secret garden that was somehow connected to the Dubrava castle. In the earlier writings, it was referred to as a "moonflower garden," a place of beauty and evil where unusual flowers grew and bloomed by the

140

light of the moon. As far as his research indicated, there was no such place anywhere close to the castle. There was a hidden torture dungeon, which Inspector Startz had discovered using Nikodim's own charts. There was a secret passage leading from the library to Michea's apartment, also discovered without much difficulty. Yet there had to be another secret passage, another dungeon—this one had to be round, with the earth-covered floor and the inevitable marble casket in the middle.

The passage would be extremely difficult to discover and discovering it would be dangerous. There would be traps, ingenious traps, pits that opened up, lined with swords and spikes. Arrows and darts with poisoned tips that would shoot from hidden enclosures in the wall. Graveyard snakes, known for their deadly poison, would drop from the ceiling. There would be spiders, pendulums as sharp as razors, just about everything and anything designed to stop and kill an unwelcome intruder.

Why does a vampire need a secret passage? Nikodim often wondered. After all, a vampire can walk through a solid wall or any door if he or she so desires. The answer, according to Setozar's manuscripts, was that once a year the vampire has to bring his victims to his resting place, as the proverbial lambs to a slaughter, during Black Sabbath rites. There was another reason as well: the vampire had to have a passage for any unforeseen emergency. So, if some disaster of nature strikes and the vampire is in deep slumber, his servant or servants—the human ones—can save him in time.

That secret entrance, as inevitable as the casket itself, was the only possible way for a human being to destroy the creature.

How well Nikodim knew it: both he and Father Seraphim had almost been killed by two axes activated by a tiny thread that Seraphim's long walking stick had broken. The axes had swung in front of them with terrific force, evidently moved by some motor hidden under the steps. Had it not been for the long cane, which sprung the trap too soon, both Nikodim and Father Seraphim would have been chopped to bits. The Greek moneylender would still be terrorizing the countryside.

Nikodim studied his drawings again. It was very lucky for him, he thought, that all his personal belongings, including his detailed map of the area, had been returned upon his release. Only the blessed knife, which he would need to cut off the vurdalak's head, was still missing. For now, Nikodim had to rely on his straight razor. The resting place, he felt, was more likely to be outside the castle, and that is why he took more and more interest in the ancient tale of the moonflower garden, a fascinating tale which, at first, he had not connected with Michea.

Michea should not have made his reference to "other kingdoms" back in the library. Other kingdoms? Well, according to a pagan Dacian noble, Neiu (first or second century B.C.), near the site of the present castle "stood a beautiful house with white columns surrounded by lush gardens with ponds and fountains . . ." A Roman villa perhaps? The further reference to wondrous flowers and birds "such as we have not seen" had really put Nikodim on the track. This indeed could be Michea's resting place.

The question was, where could it be?

Nikodim spread out his map, scrutinizing all the familiar notations, all the places where he had walked and searched for clues. The tunnels near the Valley of Blood were the first choice. In his spare time, Nikodim had examined most of the tunnels and the caves. Nothing. The desecrated church and the cemetery in the forest were the next logical places. Indeed, there were signs, and eventually Nikodim had found two headless skeletons, but afterward he had had to abandon that site, too. The ruins of the peasant citadels near the campsite of the German archeologists held only the mass graves of slaughtered peasants.

Toward morning, Nikodim came to the conclusion that the resting place had to be somewhere to the east of the castle, between its walls and the Valley of Blood below. That was a rocky and treacherous slope, and the only area that he had not yet searched very thoroughly. Satisfied, Nikodim began his morning calisthenics.

four

Michea waits, a young handsome prince. The tear-shaped ruby in his crown glistens menacingly in the bright moonlight. This is the night of revenge, the full moon of September. His hand rests on his dagger; his gaze, on the huge iron gates. These gates will open to admit a mortal: the first and last mortal to enter his domain.

Michea thinks of his trip to Bucharest, the faces in the dimly lit theater, the applause. He thinks of fat Babulescu, his pathetic little slave. The writer had had the goal of offering his prince every drop of his blood. But his blood was too watery; Michea had sneered. Not like the warm red blood of the dying Russian warriors so many centuries ago.

He sees a lonely Tartar horseman, a black dot on the giant plain. The Tartar whips his horse into a frenzy; he has a message sewn into his fur cap that must be delivered to the great and mighty Khan. Three Russian riders follow the messenger; their arrows sing in the hot, dusty air and the messenger falls off his horse.

Later that night, Michea sees himself accelerating his Mercedes. Only a few seconds, and the man who now poses the greatest threat will be dead, a few seconds . . .

Michea smiles. History is full of these instants. Yet during those few seconds, as the big man was walking unconcernedly toward his door, an ordinary garbage truck was backing into the alley from one of the side streets. That truck effectively shielded the man and saved his life. Michea pressed down on his brakes and stopped just in time. The Mercedes was a superb machine. Michea watched the big man open the door and walk inside the building, unconcerned. He doesn't even know! Michea put his Mercedes in reverse . . . Another Tartar messenger gallops fast across the endless steppe and the same fate awaits him near the river. The sun is setting into the Black Sea; the great Khan will not get his message. And the history of Europe will be changed for centuries to come.

Michea closes his eyes and listens. Thunderous steps, coming closer and closer, disturb the idyllic serenity. The flowers shrink, the birds stop singing, and the swans swim hurriedly away. This has never happened before.

Michea crosses the bridge which spans the pond and waits. His eyes are now bright with anticipation, his pale hand clutches his dagger. He looks at his small servant dressed in a dark robe. "Open the gates," he orders. He thinks, the priest has come too late, several centuries too late. He smiles again.

The gates spring open, and the priest appears. He steps in very cautiously, holding a vial of holy water in one hand and a razor in the other. He walks slowly toward Michea.

"Stop, priest!" shouts Michea. He knows the priest will not stop. "Remember your own Slavic proverb: an uninvited guest is worse than a Tartar."

The priest advances.

Michea nods his head and a heavy metal net falls over the priest, knocking the powerful man down. At the same time, the servant runs up to him and slips a chain around his waist, locking it so that the priest can't move his hands. Somehow he manages to shrug off the net and get up, but he is now helpless. He cannot throw the holy water, he can barely move his fingers. He is frightened. He turns around to run, but the great iron gates are locked. There is no way out. The servant runs after the priest, slips another chain around his legs, and locks it. The priest can move his legs just enough to walk very slowly. He knows he's trapped. His square face reflects horror. He flexes his muscles uselessly, trying to break the slender metal chain.

"You wish to see my resting place?" Michea asked politely. "And you shall see it, such bravery deserves to be rewarded . . . or is it curiosity? Follow me, priest."

He walks across the bridge and Nikodim follows like a dog on a chain. He stops to look in wonder at the unusually bright, almost blinding moon, at the flowers, which have opened up again, at the swans and the beautiful white mansion surrounded by gardens. This is not possible, he thinks, all this is some kind of an illusion.

"All this is as real as the chains that bind you," Michea answers his thoughts. "Look well."

And Nikodim looks again: at the fountains, the statues, and at the moon hanging so low over the mansion.

"Where are we?" Nikodim wants to ask, and the answer comes to him clearly, although Michea does not even open his lips. We are nearing *my resting place*.

On the steps of the mansion, a woman's figure suddenly appears. Michea stops and angrily waves her away. The woman vanishes into the garden.

"Come, priest, you wish to see my coffin. Well, here it is."

A large round room, tall Roman columns near the walls, a round opening in the ceiling through which bright rays of the moon shine and spotlight a large square casket. The casket is made of solid gold with figures of bats, wolves, and snakes etched in a never-ending pattern. The eyes are rubies, emeralds, and diamonds—gleaming, watching.

Nikodim is astounded.

"Fashioned by the finest Chinese goldsmiths, the very same masters who decorated Temujin's own tomb . . . It traveled across the face of the earth. Are you not impressed?"

Nikodim remains silent.

"Take a deep breath, priest," invites Michea.

Nikodim smells a fresh, pleasant, sensuous fragrance.

"Not a nauseating odor, no rotting flesh. Advance and see the blood . . . oh yes, it is filled with blood, as well you know! But look at it; it's of the clearest red: no filth or mold or slime on its surface, the freshest blood of innocent babies."

Nikodim turns away.

"Now that you've satisfied your curiosity, it's my turn. I'd like to ask you just one question . . . where is Setozar's ritual, the missing five pages?"

"I don't know . . . can't you find it, you the mighty king of the . . ."

He suddenly remembers that he *does* know. Dr. Tagarū had told him that the policeman had them. He remains silent.

"Look at me, priest!" Michea orders. His eyes are getting red, burning through the priest, prying into his mind. "Look at me!"

I must not. Nikodim averts his head.

Now the same thoughts of the vurdalak killed many years ago return to his mind: the hour is near, priest, you will die a hideous death! Before you die, you'll scream in agony ten thousand times, you will denounce your God, you will be reduced to nothing. The familiar, frightening curse!

"Answer me, priest." Michea's voice is now soft and soothing. "Look at me." He pulls his dagger out, and this time Nikodim looks.

"Tell me who is in possession of the ritual and I will shorten your suffering." He places the dagger back in its sheath, motioning for his servant. The servant pulls Nikodim's chain very hard, forcing him to his knees.

"I know *you* don't have the ritual. If you did"—Michea smiles— "you would not come here with your holy water and your silly razor. Watch this . . ." Michea's servant hands him the vial of water and razor taken from Nikodim. Michea pours the holy water on his hand.

"Nothing," he declares. However, he quickly wipes his hand with a plush towel, which is also supplied by his servant. "As for this toy—" Michea snaps the old-fashioned, sturdy straight razor with his fingers, and throws it on the ground contemptuously.

"And this, this, too, means nothing." He tears off Nikodim's father's cross, spits on it, and throws it on the ground.

"Answer me, priest, and you shall die in peace."

Nikodim looks straight into the burning eyes. Michea seems uncomfortable.

"I cannot tell you. You know I cannot tell you!"

Michea sighs, a look of boredom appears on his face. His eyes are gray. There is a movement beside him and Nikodim sees the beautiful American lady, the one who had sat near the policeman at the banquet.

"Zerkal," Michea speaks quietly to the woman. "You must leave us; this is not for you."

But the woman remains, looking at Nikodim with curiosity and hatred.

"Take a very good look, priest." Michea's voice is distant, coming from the tops of the columns. "You have achieved the impossible; you have seen my resting place; no mortal shall *ever* see it again."

Nikodim looks at the gleaming, golden edifice with the snakes, the wolves, and the bats dancing in a wondrous pattern, alive and sparkling among the brightest moonbeams. He hears a soft melody played by some unseen strings; he inhales the intoxicating aroma, so sweet and so pleasurable.

That casket, standing in all its splendor, is the last thing he sees. Michea, standing behind him, bends over the priest, and, in one swooping motion, gouges his eyes out.

Early in the long-forgotten century, across the dusty plain, the third and last messenger was racing desperately toward the silver snake of the river, toward the safety of the Golden Horde. He made it to the river and forced his stallion into the water. The current was swift. The Tartar slid off his horse and swam behind it, holding its tail. On the other side of the river, he shook the water off his sheepskins and grinned in triumph: the Great Khan would be pleased.

The Tartar was still grinning when the Russian arrows cut him down.

Mamaii Khan did not get the vital message that accurately showed the disposition and the strength of the Russian forces. It was sent by a Moldavian prince, a trusted Russian ally turned traitor. He was discovered and had to flee the Russian camp. His messages were intercepted by a bearded Russian commander whose name will not be known to history, and his small unit of archers.

That night Prince Dimitri of the Don stood victorious amidst thousands of dead and dying soldiers. He held his cross and his sword over his head and watched the retreating Tartars. Two Russian horsemen, covered with dust and thoroughly exhausted, stood at a respectable distance away from Dimitri and his officers. He turned in their direction.

"I do not see the head of the Moldavian devil," he said with disappointment.

"He is the very devil, my Lord," answered one of the riders. "We followed him day and night through the swamps and the forests to the Lithuanian border."

"It does not matter," Prince Dimitri said wearily. "Our land is saved. They will never again drink the blood of our people."

He struck his sword into the moist earth.

BOOK THREE

one

Again, Sally was totally exhausted when she got up. She was afraid to look at herself in the mirror. Her dreams were getting progressively worse. Maybe it's just this couch, she thought. I must talk to Nikolai; I must get out of this morbid castle. Another thought contradicted the first: here's where I belong . . . forget New York, forget Nikolai. This is where I must remain.

Evidently, it was very early. The mist hung thick beyond the library's window. Sally stretched. The couch was comfortable, but her whole body ached. Nikolai? No, he mustn't see me like this. I'd better walk down to the village, to our room. She opened the heavy wooden door and looked into the hall. No one was moving. A guard in a military uniform was asleep in a chair, leaning on his rifle. She tiptoed toward the entrance. Not one sound, though, for a second, she thought she heard a horse neighing in the yard.

Outside, across the parking lot, was the now-familiar forest path.

Not too far, not very far, and all of it downhill, she kept telling herself. She realized she had forgotten her Nikon on the table in the library. Hopefully no one will steal it. Steal it? This was Romania, not New York.

As she walked, she began to listen once again to the sounds of the wakening forest. How friendly and familiar were these sounds of the morning. How very much unlike the menacing sounds of yesterday evening. Yesterday? It felt more like a month ago. She was getting stronger with every step. She felt that she could be perfectly at home in the forest at this time—when the morning had not quite arrived and the night had not completely dissolved.

There were rabbits awake and running, a deer eating berries, dozens of birds. The treetops still held some patches of fog, but the sky was getting bluer by the minute.

Sally walked fast. She almost ran past the ancient cemetery with the curious patch of barren earth in the middle, down the path toward the blacktop road leading to the village.

It was warmer now. The sun was rising and its rays skidded across the top branches. Another beautiful day. Doesn't it ever rain here, she wondered. She paused to pick a few wild roses from a thorny roadside bush . . . Mustn't prick myself! This thought was as strong as if somebody next to her had suddenly barked a command. She stopped and then laughed to herself. What if I do prick myself? She carefully tore off a few branches with small pink roses and continued on her way.

Just as she came in sight of the asphalt road, a truck wheezed by very slowly in the direction of the village.

She stopped. What rotten luck! There was still about a mile and a half to go and she was again tired, out of breath. Maybe another truck will pass along, she consoled herself, and continued walking. Five minutes, ten. There were no trucks or cars, but she heard behind her the monotonous bell and the hoofbeats. Her heart stopped. She stood motionless.

The carriage appeared as graceful as the first time—six gray horses, that same sad-looking coachman, the bell, and the face in the window.

A sudden feeling of terror gripped her entire body. I must run back into the forest. I must turn and run. She remained where she was, however, and the carriage slowed down, stopping next to her.

"Please enter, Sally," a familiar voice called out to her. Once again, the face in the window was that of an incredibly gorgeous young man, the man of her recent dreams. Or were they nightmares? The huge gray eyes were smiling, friendly. "Enter freely." He repeated the invitation. The door was open.

Sally could not help herself now. She held on to her roses and stepped into the carriage.

"Do you mind if I pull down the shade?" Michea asked casually, very casually. "The sun is already up . . . sometimes it burns my eyes."

All her fears were gone. She sat relaxed on the very soft seat, holding her roses. He leaned toward her, still smiling. "So, you're going back to the Two Moons Café to your friend, the policeman?" He asked this politely, but there was a trace of anger on his angelic face when he said "policeman."

"Yes, yes, I am." Sally looked at him defensively. "And perhaps we'll leave the village today. He has a cottage on the Black Sea."

"Yes, perhaps," said Michea noncommittally, and became silent.

She wanted to ask him so much. How real were the dreams in which he'd held her in his arms? How could he have changed so remarkably from the middle-aged man in one evening? So many questions, so many mysteries. But she did not dare.

At the Two Moons Café, the carriage stopped.

Michea opened the door.

"Good day," he said. "I pray we shall meet again."

The door closed, the carriage was on its way, and Sally stood alone in the village square.

The water from the fountain near the Hotel Red Danube fell noiselessly into the marble pond.

I should freshen up my roses. She went toward the fountain and stopped again, looking helplessly at her bouquet. The petals were ash gray; the stems had dried out. She gasped and dropped them on the black asphalt where they disintegrated into a handful of dust.

The feeling of terror entered her body once again. She ran into the inn, up the narrow stairs to their room. Everything was the way she had left it. The embroidered quilt lay crumpled at the foot of the bed; the window was open. Sally's hands trembled; the feeling of terror was overbearing. The sun was over the rooftops now and its rays touched the small window. It became unbearably bright and hot. Her only thought was now to flee toward some cool dark place. Yes, to flee back to the abandoned cemetery. To hide there under the bushes and wait for the evening.

two

Around noon, after a most enjoyable drive, Startz parked his Volkswagen near the village fountain. When he and Nikolai walked into the Two Moons Café, the congenial manager met them with something approaching open hostility. He studiously avoided looking at them and kept his face buried in an old magazine.

Only when Startz rang the bell a few times did he turn toward them and growl, "What do you want here, Comrades?"

"To begin with, two rooms," Startz replied.

"We have no rooms. Try the Hotel Red Danube."

"No rooms?" Startz saw only two automobiles parked in the village square. He immediately became suspicious.

"None. Go away." The manager turned back to his magazine.

"Do you know who we are?" Startz asked quietly. For the time being, his voice was only mildly threatening.

The manager stroked his mustache, sighed, and looked at them again, apparently resigned.

"Please, Comrades," he begged, "why don't you leave? Leave us in peace." And, as an afterthought, "You know, you are no longer welcome in this village."

"Why not?" Nikolai was puzzled. He thought his tips were always generous.

"Wait, Nikola." Startz's voice was now icy and threatening, the "obey me or else" voice for which he was famous. "Listen, Comrade, and listen carefully. We did not come here to win popular

154

acclaim. We don't care if we are welcome or not. We are here on state's business. We want two rooms, immediately. And we want to order breakfast." Instead of waiting for a reply, he swung the registration book around. It was empty, just as he had thought. After signing, he walked around the counter, picked out two keys, and threw one to Nikolai, who was watching him with amusement.

"We'd better sit by the window, Nikola. I don't want some idiot letting the air out of my tires."

The young waitress, who was also unusually gruff, managed to spill the coffee twice.

"What's gotten into them?" Nikolai wondered.

"They are proud and independent people, and both of us disturbed their way of life—you with your American woman, me with my snooping." Startz began eating and did not elaborate further. The food was delicious as usual. After their meal, they decided to question the boy who had told Startz that he had seen Sally get into Michea's carriage on the day of her disappearance. His was the last house on the village road, next to a boarded-up Orthodox church. No one wanted to open the door and invite them in. Instead, the boy's mother opened the window and coldly informed them that her son was spending his summer vacation with relatives in Constanza. Then she slammed the window shut and was gone.

The truck driver who had seen a naked woman wandering in the forest used to live in an old barracks near the village. According to his roommate, another truck driver, he had moved away several days before.

"Where is he working now?" Startz asked.

The roommate did not know.

"We might as well drive to the castle." Startz seemed disappointed, though not surprised.

"I thought the man was lying," said Nikolai.

"No doubt." Startz shrugged. "We'll get back to both of them later."

After a pleasant stroll up the castle road, they arrived at the parking lot. A big orange tourist bus was parked near the entrance to the castle and there were quite a few other cars: Volkswagens and Fiats, Michea's gray Mercedes, and an old beat-up half-ton truck that belonged to the museum.

The museum itself was crowded with visitors; a tour was in progress. They found Dr. Tagarū talking to his new assistant, a tall young man with a blond goatee. The older man explained that he was terribly busy, but he agreed to see them in his office. When he arrived, he seemed very cordial, the first person who had been happy to see them. He ordered some coffee, asked them about their trip, and then whispered mysteriously, "Did you bring the manuscript?"

Nikolai took the five pages out of his folder and spread them on the desk. Dr. Tagarū wiped his glasses and began to read. He shook his head a couple of times, muttering "remarkable" at the end of each page. He finished, cleared his throat, took off his glasses, leaned back in his armchair, and closed his eyes.

Nikolai and Startz waited patiently.

Olga came in with coffee and a plate of pastries. Nikolai and Startz helped themselves; Dr. Tagarū still sat silently in his chair.

"Well, Doctor?" Nikolai finally asked.

"Yes, Comrades." He opened his eyes and watched them finish their coffee. "These five pages are *not* the original pages of the letopis currently entrusted to this museum. The content is quite different and, actually, the letters themselves are . . . Hmmm, you see how they wrote the letter *A*?"

"Please get to the point," Startz begged. He was still convinced that these pages had nothing whatever to do with the murders, or with Michea.

"My point, Comrades, is that you've come upon an interesting and valuable discovery. . . . But it has nothing to do with the thirteenth-century manuscript, the enormous historical document which everyone is suddenly interested in seeing, and which I am now keeping locked up in my safe."

"Dr. Tagarū, are you positive?" Nikolai demanded. "Are you absolutely sure?"

"I am absolutely certain." Dr. Tagarū assumed his professional tone. "You see, Comrades, feel these pages yourselves, notice the unusual thickness and the format, as well as the contents . . . quite possibly these pages are from an earlier version of the letopis." He drank his cold coffee.

"Could these pages be . . . a forgery?" Startz was fidgeting in his seat. He felt that enough valuable time had been wasted.

"Not at all. These pages are as authentic as anything I've seen, and," Dr. Tagarū added with great dignity, "I am an authority."

"Can you translate it for us by tomorrow morning?" Startz was really getting impatient.

"Impossible, besides . . ." he hedged.

"What?"

"I must examine these pages under laboratory conditions, take X rays, find out the chemical composition of the paper and the ink, look for secret marks or messages. It may take two weeks or more. I must also caution you, Comrade Captain, not to carry them around in your folder, but to surrender them as soon as possible to Professor Nereu, the director of our national archives."

"So you refuse to help us?" This was it, as far as Startz was concerned. He stood up, smiling.

"With much regret." Dr. Tagarū, too, stood up. "Are you familiar with the general content of the manuscript?"

"In general, yes." Nikolai had an idea. "May we enlist help elsewhere? Citizen Pavlovic, can he translate it for us?"

Dr. Tagarū hedged again.

"Do you have any objections?" Nikolai pressed him. "All we need is a simple translation, nothing more."

"I have no objection . . . and Nikodim—Citizen Pavlovic—is an eminently qualified colleague. But . . ."

"Then it is settled, we'll go talk to him. Thank you, Doctor." Startz and Nikolai stood up.

"Only"—Dr. Tagarū smiled weakly—"I don't know where he is."

"You don't know where he is?" Startz exclaimed. "He is supposed to be working."

"He . . . disappeared. I mean, we couldn't find him this morning."

"This is incredible!" Startz had planned to talk with the priest in any event. He, too, was now gone.

"I am sorry, Comrades."

Both Startz and Nikolai were already walking to the priest's room.

"I came for some answers," Nikolai mused, "and all I am getting is more questions."

"My mistake, Nikola, I should have had him watched. I thought he was so happy to have his old job back. He really tricked me."

Dr. Tagarū was hurrying after them with passkeys. "His room is locked; all his belongings are inside." He opened the door for them. "It's as if he vanished into thin air."

"You may leave us now, Doctor, we would like to be alone." Startz went to the window, noticed that it was closed from the inside, opened it, looked below: a good three-meter drop. "It's possible, of course." He shrugged.

"Damn it, Startz!" Nikolai smashed his fist on the chest of drawers. "It's vitally important that we have the manuscript translated as soon as possible. I don't know why it's so important . . . but there's something in it, something more than either the pagan or the Christian rituals it describes. Something concrete."

"Carrots!" Startz replied, unmoved. "Look at that . . . and look at all his charts. Hey, here's one drawing that's new . . . a garden, no less." He examined it closely. "Look, Nikola, he calls it the 'moonflower garden,' a garden that both exists and doesn't . . ."

"Where?"

"Between this wall and the Valley of Blood."

"Nothing there except some sharp rocks," Nikolai replied.

"I know," Startz said slowly. "And the priest must have known, too. He certainly knew every inch of this castle. It's because of his charts we discovered the torture dungeon. You want to see it, Nikola?"

"No, thank you. Look, I'm not even supposed to be here. If Bugash discovers, he might literally hang me."

"A *moonflower garden?*" Startz looked out the window again. "Nikola, give me the carrots." He threw a couple down, watched the rabbits run up and grab them, and smiled. "The afternoon is still young, Nikola. I feel like taking a drive to the Valley of Blood. Why don't you join me?"

Fifteen minutes later, they were standing in a field of tall grass and poppies, looking at the bushes of wild roses and vines clinging to the ancient walls and tunnels on the hillside. The castle seemed larger from the valley side, leaning forward, with its tower and walls outlined against the sky. A commercial jet flew slowly over the castle, leaving a streak of white. Chattering sparrows flew from one rosebush to another.

"A poppy grows for everyone who died here, in this valley." Nikolai was moody. "I almost died here, too, Startz, during the war . . . I hid right by those rocks, where we're going." He noticed new grass and vines near the wall, over the diggings where he had first discovered the bodies.

"What do you suppose they were really looking for?" he asked.

"Gold." Startz replied matter-of-factly.

"Gold?"

"Yes, gold, Nikola. After you left, I began wondering what two top German archeologists would be doing, really, in a Transylvanian valley. Well, they were searching for our Romanian 'Eldorado.' "

"But our gold mines are at least fifty kilometers to the north."

"Of course." Startz kept on walking, stopping now and then to consult the priest's drawing.

"What happened after the German authorities received their bodies?" Nikolai caught up with him and forced him to stop.

"Nothing really. Angry notes were exchanged, then the matter was dropped."

"They didn't really come back to life, did they?" Nikolai smiled.

"Apparently not. As far as I know, they were both cremated. Also, they died not so much from the loss of blood as from internal injuries."

"That's not the report I heard."

"You read only the preliminary report. I ordered two additional autopsies."

"And Annoushka?"

"Very similar. As if she were caught in a vise."

"Not the loss of blood?"

"That, too, would have killed her, but not so quickly."

They walked silently up the slope.

"You know, Startz." Nikolai smiled again. "I was a fool to go back with you. On such a beautiful day, I could be sleeping on the beach near my cottage. This place smells of death. I am still alive."

"You don't want to be a policeman anymore? . . . I understand." Startz continued climbing.

"I think not, not after what happened." Nikolai thought they would never find Sally and that thought hurt him deeply.

"Well"—Startz stopped and looked at the drawing again—"looks like we've come to the point where he indicated his secret garden."

"Tell me, Startz, how did you find out that they were looking for gold? It's strictly forbidden to even look for it without a special permit."

"I know, illegal as hell! They were looking for some ancient treasure, a tomb of some kind. An interesting little pair. Their scientific permits were just a cover . . ."

"Tell me," Nikolai persisted.

"Old man Rusai, of all people, the caretaker at the castle. I pressed him and pressed him and he eventually cracked. He told me that he took food to them a few nights before they died. They were drinking, embracing, and kissing each other, and singing in German. They even invited Rusai to have a few drinks and tipped him generously, for once. The older German, who spoke Romanian, bragged to Rusai that they were both going to be among the richest men on earth. He kept mentioning gold, and he showed Rusai a thick gold ring with a ruby in the middle. The next morning, however, the Germans gave him some money and asked him to forget the foolishness of the night before. And he promptly forgot it."

"I just bet he did!"

"Not only that. I called the State Archeological Commission and they confirmed the existence of a legend." Startz stopped. "Did you hear something, Nikola?"

"No." Nikolai looked around. Everything was quiet; some birds, perhaps, or a rabbit stirred.

"Well." Startz frowned. "Let's search the area. Here, Nikola, you take this part, and we'll meet up there, by the wall— Wait a minute! Listen!"

This time they both heard a weak, high-pitched whine followed by a moaning noise. The sounds were emanating from a rocky area directly above them. They both climbed toward it, and stopped.

In a tiny clearing, between two large rocks, was the body of a man, still alive.

In their many years as policemen, both Nikolai and Startz had witnessed incidents of cruelty and torture. But *nothing* in their experience prepared them for what they now saw. The worst of it was that the body, horribly tortured and mutilated as it was, still breathed; although its tongue was cut out, it kept making weak, imploring sounds.

Nikolai was the first to recover. He slowly took out his pistol, took careful aim at the priest's bloody head, and shot twice. He then turned around, shaking so hard that the pistol almost fell out of his hand. Then he ran down the slope to where Startz had parked his Volkswagen.

When Startz caught up with him, Nikolai had recovered a bit. He sullenly held his pistol and did not utter one word until Startz stopped the car by the entrance to the castle. Nikolai jumped out

160

and, pushing aside some startled tourists, ran into the main hall of the castle. He looked up at the balcony, and as had happened more than thirty years before, he felt rage exploding within him, a rage he could no longer control. He saw Michea and his mother standing at the head of the balcony just as they had on that fateful day in 1944. Michea was smiling again. *Smiling!*

Nikolai raised his pistol and fired at him twice. The shots, loud as cannons, reverberated through the ancient castle. A horde of tourists screamed and stampeded outside. The militia guard opened his mouth wide but did not move.

Nikolai knew that he had missed. He saw Michea running into his apartment and slamming the heavy door. Nikolai himself was running up the stairs, taking three and four steps at a time. He tried to break the door down with his shoulder, but the solid oak resisted. He shot at the lock and it opened. Startz was screaming at him from the hall, but Nikolai was beyond caring.

As soon as he was in Michea's apartment, something small darted toward him: Michea's old servant armed with a curved knife. Nikolai swung at him with his pistol and knocked the old man out. In the living room, he felt Michea's mother's claws as he slapped her hard, easily knocking her to the ground. She continued clinging to him like a leech, trying to slow him down and bite him on the leg. Nikolai picked up a heavy Chinese vase and broke it over her head. But still she clung to him. He bent down, grabbed her by the throat, tore her away from his leg, and threw her across the room. Then he crashed through another door and burst into Michea's bedroom.

"Out, bastard!" Nikolai screamed as he began to search frantically, recklessly. He found Michea hidden behind the drapes near the huge bed—a terrified, middle-aged man, heavy black circles under his eyes, face bloated, lips pressed tight.

Nikolai raised his pistol slowly. He wasn't going to miss this time. Michea put up his hands as if to shield himself from the bullets. He was not begging for mercy, but he was trembling.

Nikolai did not shoot. He advanced toward Michea and hit at his hands with the pistol, determined to see the eyes of his adversary.

"On your knees," he ordered. He didn't know why he said it, but Michea wasn't arguing.

Too easy to let him get off clean. Nikolai hit Michea again with the

161

butt of his pistol. Blood spurted out. Michea immediately pressed the cut area with his hand. Nikolai struck him once more. Now was the time to shoot him.

Nikolai put his pistol to Michea's forehead and began pressing the trigger. Blackness enveloped him.

The blackness gradually dissolved into a soft, gray-blue mist. In that transparent space without beginning or end, Nikolai saw images, sometimes lovely, sometimes hideous. He was a boy of twelve, his last day at his home. Janco, big as a mountain, was comforting his mother. We will take good care of your boy . . . Nikolai held a rifle for the first time . . . the endless marches through the forest. Sally appeared and drifted slowly toward him, dressed in a long, black dress, more beautiful than ever. *I have never left you*, she seemed to say, *I will come for you soon. I will never leave you!* Her smile was soothing, her voice, as she began to sing, was his own mother's voice . . . a young man dressed in black appeared behind her. Nikolai couldn't see his face . . . the man was warning Sally to keep away.

The mist became brighter. Now he heard clear, familiar voices. One speaker, whom Nikolai recognized at Startz, was concerned with what had happened to Michea . . . why not with what happened to me? Nikolai felt sadness. . . . Am I dead, too? Where am I?

"The bullet grazed his forehead," the other voice replied. "No, he would not let me dress it. His mother bandaged him."

Now Startz was concerned. "Nikolai?"

"No danger, however, take him to a hospital . . . concussion."

Startz was silent. The other voice, whom Nikolai recognized as Dr. Tagarū, kept chattering nervously. "He is screaming, 'banditry,' 'assassination'! And he's right! I don't see why I agreed to help you. This may well be the end of my career."

"Don't worry, everything was done on my authority; it's my career that's at stake, not yours. The telephone switchboard remains closed?"

"Just as you ordered."

"Good."

Nikolai tried opening his eyes but couldn't.

"I think he'll regain consciousness very soon now." Dr. Tagarū spoke sorrowfully. "Poor man, poor man."

162

"I can't blame him for what he tried to do." Nikolai felt Startz sitting down beside him.

"You can't blame him?" Tagarū was incredulous.

"Not after we found . . . you might as well know. Your colleague Pavlovic is dead. Tortured and mutilated by a person or persons as yet unknown. But not just tortured. I've never seen anything like it. He was flayed alive, his ears and nose had been cut off, his fingers . . . Nikola put him out of his misery . . . and you know the rest."

"What will happen to him?"

This was something Nikolai also wanted to know very much. He tried to open his eyes and succeeded . . . Where am I? Leather-bound books, paneled walls, in the library, on the couch. Nikolai tried to sit up, fell backwards. His head ached.

"Lie still, Nikola. If my plan works, nothing will happen to you." Startz stood up.

"I . . . didn't kill him?" Nikolai mumbled. He had to be sure.

"No."

"Damn . . ." Nikolai felt the bandages on his head. The room was beginning to swim around him. "What are we going to do?"

"Not us," Startz corrected him. "You are out of this play. I am now going to have a serious conversation with Michea and, early tomorrow morning, I am driving you all the way to your beautiful cottage by the sea, where you'll tend to your roses. That is, unless you wish to spend the next ten years in prison."

"Swallow these." Dr. Tagarū gave Nikolai two red capsules and a small glass of juice.

The room began dancing even faster, the mist closed in again.

"How long will he be out, Doctor?"

"I'd say until tomorrow morning."

"Can that secret panel be opened?"

"No. It has been padlocked and only I have the keys."

"I am grateful for your help, Doctor. Now you may wish me luck, I am going up to see our genius. I'll stop by later tonight."

The militia man guarding Michea's apartment felt very uneasy. "I do hope you know what you are doing, Comrade Inspector," he told Startz. "I am only a corporal following orders . . . that man is a very famous person . . . he was screaming that we'll all be in jail. He wants to talk to some minister."

"Is he still screaming?"

"Not anymore. How long do I have to stay here?"

"As long as I tell you to stay!" With that, Startz entered the apartment.

Michea was in a foul mood, which was understandable: his head and ears were heavily bandaged. He sat on his luxuriously plush couch, being comforted by his mother. His servant stood anxiously before him, a plum-sized purple bump on his forehead. Startz took the first chair he could find and sat, facing Michea.

"Leave us, please," he said, motioning to the woman and the servant. They both left, but only with Michea's nodded assent.

"I'll see your friend shot," he hissed. "Pure banditry, an assassination attempt! How long do you think you can keep me incommunicado?"

"As long as it takes," Startz replied quietly. "I believe you owe me a small measure of gratitude. I saved your life, after all."

"Thank you very, very much." Michea touched his bandage. "Now we are even; what do you want?"

Startz moved his chair even closer. He studied Michea carefully. He leaned forward and painstakingly enunciated every word: "I want you to forget this entire incident."

"Another madman!" Michea exclaimed. "Forget it? Oh, no, I'll remember it, I'll remember it so loudly that from now on you'll be inspecting nothing more exalted than rotten potatoes in a labor camp. *Forget it?* I have an agreement with the politburo. I *know* that this attempt on my life was not sanctioned by the government. And wait until the foreign press finds out! Forget it? Please leave my apartment, we have nothing more to discuss."

"Don't you understand?" Startz spoke slowly and evenly, looking Michea straight in his watery eyes. "No one will find out anything, *in any event*. Unless you play my game, I have no choice but to kill you, your mother, and your servant. And *I* will not botch the job!"

"You are an amazing man, Inspector." Michea's voice was now low, rational, almost conciliatory. He looked at Startz as if seeing the inspector for the first time. "You're joking, of course. You cannot get away with anything of this sort."

"I am very serious and I most certainly will get away with it. I have been a policeman for almost thirty-five years, a good policeman, I am told. If you don't believe that I can kill you, or someone else, for that matter, and get away with it, then you are sadly underrating my intelligence and I am overrating yours."

Michea was now thoughtful. He touched his bandages again. "Why not simply kill me now?"

"Because I have a sense of justice and fair play."

Michea laughed, rather nervously. "You, a secret policeman?"

Startz ignored him.

"Well then, Inspector, all I have to do is to give you my word?"

"Not quite. You'll also have to sign an affidavit, which I'll prepare later this evening."

. Michea thought some more. "I'll do it, but on one condition." His gray eyes were now sparkling with anger, burrowing into Startz's. "And if my condition is not met, well"— he paused dramatically— "then you might as well try to kill me."

"Please go on!"

"That your friend Nikolai"—Michea spat out Nikolai's name with distaste—"will never, ever disturb me again. That he will never return to this area."

"I am driving him home tomorrow. He will not see you again." Somehow Startz felt that Michea would demand more, some document or some further assurance. To his relief, Michea winced, touched his bandage again, and said, "Agreed. Now, Inspector, please leave. My wounds are beginning to hurt."

Startz relieved the militia man and walked slowly down the stairs. There were still many loose ends to be tied up. He felt tired.

three

———————

Toward midnight, all the excitement died down. Startz, exhausted after supervising the ambulance team that had been sent to retrieve the priest's body, slept soundly on one of the cots in the guard's room. Nikolai was sprawled out on the library couch. The new guard was sitting at attention in the main hall of the castle on a specially provided hard chair so that he could see almost everything in the museum. Everyone else was asleep. There were no lights in Michea's apartment. The countryside, too, was peaceful and silent. The moon was hanging like a bright silver coin just above the mountains and billions of stars shone like diamonds in the clear mountain air.

The only room with light and movement was Dr. Tagarū's office. At supper, Startz had managed to persuade the good doctor to translate Nikolai's manuscript in view of what had happened and on the assumption that Nikolai, like any other experienced policeman, had developed that rare and valuable sixth sense. If he felt it was important, it just might be important. And in the morning, they both would take a long drive.

Dr. Tagarū was greatly distressed by the death of his friend and colleague, the second such loss in two months. He was also confused about the vurdalak theories. He set out to translate the manuscript, fiercely determined to succeed, and hoping that the ancient pages would shed some light on the mysterious and tragic events.

When he had refused to translate the manuscript earlier, he had been decidedly modest about his laboratory facilities. In fact,

166

during his four years as chief curator, he had managed to assemble a tiny laboratory, complete with X ray and infrared equipment. Though anything really complicated had to go to Bucharest, the laboratory was adequate for the basic tests. The translation itself went smoothly. The text, mid-thirteenth century, detailed two similar rituals for killing and exorcising vampires: evidently the monks of the Order of St. Elia took the creatures very seriously indeed. While both rituals described how the vampire could be tracked down and rendered powerless, both the pagan and the Christian version mentioned the existence of a prince or a king among these creatures: one who could not be destroyed by a human being. Whenever that particular evil creature appears, disasters of great magnitude follow: devastating wars, massacres, plagues, and floods. Pagans believed that only Perun's mighty arrows (bolts of lightning) could kill him. The crafty Volos, another major Slavic god, was thought to be an ally of the vampires. And the generous and kind god Dazhbog, had his own way of dealing with them: to flee the land infested by a vampire. The Christians felt that only God's direct intervention, through either the Archangel Michael or the Prophet Elia, could send the creature back to hell, where he belonged. The vampire king can appear anywhere on earth, since speed and time itself are of no consequence to him. Unlike the rest of the vampires, he can appear in broad daylight. However, three nights out of each thirty, he must rest in the tomb that is hidden in his garden.

Garden? Dr. Tagarū jumped up from his chair. Could that be the moonflower garden that appeared on Nikodim's charts? When Dr. Tagarū had read the manuscript earlier in the day, he had missed the significance. The garden where illusion and reality blend into one. *The secret garden*—that's where Startz and Nikolai had found his friend. Dr. Tagarū eagerly translated the rest. "The tomb, a casket of solid gold which is filled with the blood of infants who have not yet reached the age of one year . . ."

And that was all they knew about King Vampire. There were some general references and charts explaining how the moon, especially the full moon, affected the vampire's movements. And that was all. Dr. Tagarū sat silently for a few minutes, then gathered the pages together again. Now, he felt certain, would come the most interesting part. He turned off the lights, locked his office, and went to his small laboratory at the end of the corridor.

On the way, he noted with satisfaction that the new guard was not asleep. Everything was peaceful. He stopped by the library and listened to Nikolai's snoring. Good, good, he thought, Nikolai needs his sleep after that heavy blow on the head.

Dr. Tagarū entered his narrow laboratory, turned on the overhead light, and carefully locked the door.

The first step was to X-ray the pages. He turned the overhead light off, lighted a table lamp, took out his magnifying glass, and slid the first pages into the machine. He knew immediately that he had stumbled upon a great discovery. The first page contained a map. It was a map of a large medieval city and, to his amazement, Dr. Tagarū read that the city was Kiev. Sweat poured down his face. Excitedly, he took off his glasses and cleaned the lenses and his magnifying glass. Then he looked again. He almost went to fetch Startz and Nikolai, but decided that they could wait to see the discovery in the morning. Feverish with anticipation, he sat down and slid the second page into the slot.

The next three sheets contained a *bylina*, or Russian folk poem, describing the Tartar invasion of 1240, when the "Glorious mother of all cities, Golden Kiev, where Vladimir the Red Sun brought Jesus Christ to our Russian people" fell to the invaders. The author of this lament was a Russian *voevoda* prince, Dimitri, who had led the gallant defenders. He was wounded in the battle and brought before the Great Khan, who was so impressed by the Russian's bravery that he spared his life. There was a vivid description of treachery within the Russian camp: a few hundred Pechenegs led by a Moldavian prince opened the city's south gates at the crucial moment and allowed "the sea of Tartars to drown our spirit." The traitor prince attended Dimitri's audience with the Great Khan, wearing a crown with the "blood stone in the middle." Eventually, Dimitri learned that the prince, whose name was Michei, was *krovopeiza*—he who drinks blood. That was how the tale ended. Dr. Tagarū had yet to see the fifth page of the manuscript.

He hesitated before sliding it in. Something seemed to dart past the closed window. If I don't finish it now, he thought, I'll soon be seeing ghosts. It must be very late. He looked at his watch, which had a habit of stopping. It was stopped at half-past one. When he finally slid the fifth page into the slot and looked, *he literally froze to his chair.*

The whole page was covered by a pen-and-ink drawing, a portrait of Michea—young and arrogant, his large eyes almost leaping from the page, wearing a crown with a tear-shaped red jewel set in it.

Dr. Tagarū did not know how long he stared at the portrait. He got up and examined it closely, but there was no mistake; the resemblance was uncanny. It was Michea. Wearily, he sat down and reached to extinguish the overhead light.

"Wait, Doctor, not yet." He heard a familiar deep voice and the sound of it sent Dr. Tagarū into a spasm; strong electric currents seemed to run up and down his spine. The voice itself was friendly, even somewhat amused. "Let me gaze a few moments more at my portrait!"

Dr. Tagarū was petrified and embarrassed at the same time. He felt warm liquid running down both sides of his trousers. He bit his lip very hard, hoping there was no one in the room. It's a hallucination, nothing more, he told himself. Sheer overwork.

"Excellent, considering it was done from memory." The voice continued, calm and friendly. "Yes, Dimitri was a better artist than he was a military leader. He fled later into the forests and became a monk . . . as well as my enemy. It does not matter, he died a very long time ago. You may turn the light on."

Dr. Tagarū cautiously flicked the switch. Now, he thought, all this will disappear. How can anyone be inside? I locked the door carefully, and I have the only key. I must turn around. Everything will be fine. I must! And he did turn around.

Michea stood behind him, dressed in black, wearing the ruby crown; he was once again the young and vigorous king depicted in the portrait. Dr. Tagarū closed his eyes and stretched out his hand to feel the apparition. Michea was solid, his cape felt like velvet.

Michea smiled. "Do not be alarmed, Dr. Tagarū, I did not come here to suck your blood."

The doctor, however, was still alarmed.

"I simply wish to take what is rightfully mine . . . my portrait. Only one page. You may keep the rest."

Dr. Tagarū began to tremble.

"Do you not find me handsome?" Michea almost laughed. "I said, I shall not harm you . . . I may need you in the future."

Dr. Tagarū closed his eyes again.

"Open them," Michea ordered. "I am not a figment of your

imagination." He now looked bored; his amusement had vanished. After removing the page, he switched off the machine, then looked sternly at Dr. Tagarū.

"You will remember nothing of my visit, my portrait." His eyes grew huge and red. He stood motionless until Dr. Tagarū's head and body were limp. Then he arranged the doctor's body so that his head was resting on the table.

Dr. Tagarū was now sound asleep.

Michea turned off the overhead light and left the room.

four

Everyone was asleep in the ancient Dubrava castle, even the new and alert guard. The morning was coming, as it inevitably does, the mist rising in the valleys. Nikolai kept tossing and turning. He finally fell off his couch and continued sleeping on the floor.

He still felt the warm embrace of the woman, her caresses so wonderful and sometimes so painful. Just as months, centuries ago, in their small room at the Two Moons Café . . . He felt every sensation even more now. On the floor, he felt she was becoming distant. He held her hands, begged her not to leave him.

"I cannot leave you," she seemed to whisper. "I don't want to leave you . . . I must leave you, my love." Her hands were strong, much stronger than his. Ancient heavy rings were on her fingers; she covered the lower part of her face with a black scarf in the manner of an Arabian woman. Only her eyes were visible. They held him, controlled him—his body and his thoughts. He felt helpless.

"Wait," he wanted to shout. "When will I see you again?"

"When I come for you," her eyes answered and immediately flashed a warning. "I will come to you, do not look for me *anywhere*."

With that, she was gone. Only morning mist hung on the castle walls. A big man on the floor of the library tossed and turned and moaned in his sleep.

Two dark figures were standing on the steps of the mansion, a man and a woman. They were communicating without speaking.

The man impressed on the woman that she must leave, that it would be fatal for her to remain any longer. She must journey back to her own country, to another continent thousands of miles away. She must adapt to her new existence and never again visit her former lover, as she had earlier in the night.

She no longer needed lovers.

The woman protested. She did not want to leave. Her place was beside the man, in this mansion, in this beautiful garden. She also hoped to visit her lover again, to spend another night with him, and another.

"Never!" The man was firm and, she thought, even jealous.

"You must leave, the sooner, the better."

He promised that he would see her soon, in her own country, in her city. The necessary preparations had been made. But for the time being, he must remain here. She must not be concerned; he would survive the holocaust. He would see her soon, he repeated. And they would remain together for all eternity.

The woman was still not satisfied. She felt hungry, cold, and lonely. She kept staring in the mist, trying to see the castle, the room where her lover slept, his face. She wanted to touch his warm body.

"You must never think of that man," her companion angrily ordered. Then he smiled and embraced her. Now she felt warm! She was being cared for and protected. She felt pleasure beyond human comprehension.

Then the figures were gone. And soon the mansion itself vanished in the morning fog.

five

Startz heard the alarm clock ring and ring and ring. One more minute, he told himself, just one more.

"Comrade Inspector, wake up!" One of the militia men was gently shaking his shoulder. Startz sat up and yawned. They must leave as early as possible. He sent the militia man to wake up Nikolai, then Dr. Tagarū and, finally, Olga, the cook. He dressed within two minutes.

At the breakfast table, his companions were a frightful sight. Nikolai was unshaven, pale and listless; Dr. Tagarū's face was red and swollen, and huge circles were under his eyes. He ate silently and, Startz thought, was falling asleep over his eggs.

Startz tried cheering them up. "Comrades, look outside. Another wonderful, wonderful morning . . . listen to the birds. . . . Wake up, Nikola." He noticed that Nikolai was really close to sleep in his seat.

"What did you give me yesterday?" Nikolai asked the doctor.

"Hydrochloride . . . sleeping pills."

"I feel like I slept a whole week." Nikolai drank his coffee, his juice, and started eating his sausages.

"I have the translation ready for you in my office." Dr. Tagarū remembered his great discovery. "And wait until you see the X rays! A discovery of first magnitude. Soviet historians would be especially interested. I must notify Professor Nereu."

After breakfast, Startz and Nikolai accompanied the doctor to his narrow laboratory. They did not seem very impressed with his discovery.

"Don't you realize what it means?" Dr. Tagarū asked.

"Well," Startz replied, "I don't see any connection with what we are trying to do. Do you see any connection, Nikola?"

"No," Nikolai had to admit. "You showed us only four pages, Doctor. Where is the fifth?"

"I . . . I don't know." Dr. Tagarū searched all around him. "I must have it in my office. However, it contained nothing, as you can see, the tale ends right here." Dr. Tagarū was really worried. As soon as he had awakened, he had searched the laboratory and his office. The fifth page had disappeared somehow, and he was in trouble.

Much to his relief and surprise, neither Nikolai nor Startz made an issue of it.

"Please see to it, Doctor, that the manuscript is delivered to the proper authorities," murmured Startz. He thought he'd follow up on the matter of the missing Slavonic manuscript upon returning to the castle.

"Of course, of course."

"I suppose that is all; we'll be leaving shortly. I shall be back within two days . . . wake up, Nikola," Startz yelled. "What's the matter with you? Is your head all right?"

"It's still there."

"You'd better take him to a hospital," suggested Dr. Tagarū.

"No, no . . . I am waking up." Nikolai had the strangest feeling that somehow he had seen Sally during the night. Not only that, but that they had made passionate love, the most sensual kind of love. There was something else, too. Something about death and resurrection. He shook his head. "I *am* waking up."

Less than half an hour later, both Nikolai and Startz were sitting at the Two Moons Café. Nikolai had decided he was hungry again, and Startz wanted more coffee. The manager was in town, the waitress was friendlier, and the food was delicious.

Early that evening, Startz slowly pulled into a narrow driveway and stopped by a small white cottage almost hidden by several tall rosebushes. Beyond the cottage, he could see sand dunes and hear the gentle murmur of the waves.

"Wake up, Nikola, we have arrived."

Nikolai stretched and smiled. "You know what I am going to do, Startz? I am going for a swim. Why don't you join me?"

Startz was ready to protest that he didn't have swimming trunks. Nikolai was already undressing.

"Come on," he invited. "We are going naked. The nearest cottage is two kilometers away."

Startz kept looking at him. He felt a queasy sensation in his stomach. Obviously, Nikolai had not bothered to look at himself in the mirror this morning; otherwise he would have surely noticed two small red punctures at the base of his neck.

six

Startz did not return to the Du-
brava castle in three days, as he had planned. After leaving Nikolai
in the cottage, he returned to Bucharest to discover that a major
purge had taken place in the Ministry of the Interior. Both Minister
Radū and Colonel Bugash, along with most of their underlings and
messenger boys, had been retired, some "with honors," some not.
Temporarily, the Central Committee had assumed direct control of
the ministry; the chairman of the committee was an able, young,
hard-working bureaucrat. He also happened to be one of Startz's
longtime admirers. The brief confusion that accompanied the
change of power allowed Startz to bury certain questionable aspects
of the Dubrava affair, especially those aspects which he did not
understand, including Nikolai's absurd behavior. As calm returned
to the ministry (the purge was accomplished without violence and
many deserved to be fired anyway), Startz was called to the office of
the new minister, the same bureaucrat who headed the supervisory
committee. To his utter amazement, Startz was promoted to full
colonel and given the directorship of the foreign section, a very
lucrative and challenging position. Startz was also given a new
apartment in the city's fashionable downtown section, an official car,
and a new office overlooking the city. There was so much work at
first that it took Startz three weeks before he could drive to Nikolai's
cottage.

As the two of them walked along the magnificent white beach,
Nikolai was in a somber, uncommunicative mood. He had lost a
considerable amount of weight; large circles had appeared under his
eyes, and his face was haggard and unshaven.

Startz told him of all the developments at the ministry. The new minister spoke highly of Nikolai, both as a policeman and as a friend. Nikolai should see a psychiatrist. He had an administrative leave, but if the minister should see him now, he'd immediately send him to a hospital for observation at least.

"Tell me, Nikola," Startz finally asked, "would you rather be around people? Perhaps in your apartment? You know, here you live like a monk . . ."

"No, not at all," Nikolai suddenly interrupted him. His eyes lit up, his face became animated. "She comes here, Startz, really, almost every night . . . perhaps not in person." He was doubtful for a few moments. "But she's here, I tell you. Please believe me! At least, she is with me in spirit."

Oh, my God, Startz thought. His friend had definitely snapped. Outwardly, the good policeman did not betray any emotions. "How can you be so sure, Nikola?" he asked gently.

"I am sure." Nikolai was stubborn. "Every night . . . almost every night . . . she comes here to look at the sea. You can't understand." He was now impatient. "Let us go kill a bottle or two. I caught some fish, we can fry them for supper."

"Of course." I'll ask him when he's drunk, Startz thought. It was just possible that Nikolai was on one of his famous benders. If that's the case, it's all right. Startz hoped he *was* on one of his drinking sprees. That was something real to deal with, instead of a nightmare.

Nikolai was more agitated when they reached the cottage. His spirits were picking up; he poured himself and Startz a full glass of fine Romanian cognac, downed his, and began scaling the fish he had caught earlier in the day.

He also began talking rapidly, disregarding what Startz told him. He offered his own interpretation as to why the purge had taken place. His opinion was, to Startz, depressingly paranoid. Nikolai thought that Michea had arranged for both Radū and Bugash to be removed because they had both read his report. The fact that Startz had been promoted meant nothing. The new minister, while possibly not one of Michea's worshippers (Nikolai did use the word "worshippers" exactly), would be manipulated by Michea's allies.

Startz sighed, drank his cognac, ate some fish (which was excellent), and drank some more.

"Why do you suppose she comes to you only at night? And what do you do, I mean, does she climb in bed with you? Do you make love?"

"I wish she did!" Nikolai was finally getting drunk. They had a third bottle on the table and he was drinking very fast. "She doesn't." He threw his empty glass at the wall. "You know, Startz, it is as if she teases me, tortures me, laughs at me. I can't understand it. I am going insane."

That may well be the first rational thing you have said tonight, Startz thought. "That is possibly a recurring dream."

"A dream? It is a nightmare. I wake up, she is not there, I am in a cold sweat, my blanket is wet from my sweat. Maybe you are right, I should drive back to Bucharest and face the new minister before he fires me." He smiled. "I saw in the newspaper that our friend has written a new play, something about the Tartar invasion . . ."

"Nikola," Startz said, slapping him on the shoulder, "believe me, I did not even have the time to fart once, these past few weeks. I was so busy I never even looked at a newspaper."

"I did," Nikolai said slowly. "I have nothing else to do here. I read Babulescu again, and here is Basarab's latest volume of poetry." He threw the thin book at Startz. "It was published last month. Not bad really, but frightening."

They sat silently for a few moments.

"Are you going back to the castle?" Nikolai asked.

"Yes, I am going, when I have time. Are you?"

"I am going when I get the sign."

"The what?"

"The sign, an indication . . . you know, a signal."

"What kind of signal?"

"I'll know when it happens."

It was getting rather late now; the red moon hung over the Black Sea and the beach. It was very quiet outside.

"Don't worry, Startz," Nikolai smiled again, the second time during the entire evening. "You take my bed, I have a sleeping bag."

"Do you think she'll come tonight?"

"I don't think so."

"Why not?"

"She comes only when I am alone. I can't explain, but with both of us here . . . no, she won't come."

"So, you still believe in vurdalaks?" Startz drank again, cautiously; he did not want to be the first one to pass out.

"Vurdalaks? I don't know, honestly. But I do know that there are mysterious, unexplainable things in this world, and Michea is one of them . . . beings. Whatever the hell he is, he is not human!"

"Don't worry, I will take care of him in my own way. I cannot do it now, but I promise you, Nikola, I will"—Startz smiled as he used the word that had been so prevalent a few years back—"eliminate him."

Nikolai threw back his head and laughed. He stopped abruptly when he noticed the hurt expression on Startz's face.

"We'd better get some sleep," he suggested, spreading the sleeping bag on the floor.

"Nikola"—Startz was serious—"I gave you a promise."

"Let's go to sleep." Nikolai climbed into his sleeping bag and remained silent.

"Nikola," Startz insisted, "have you ever known me to break a promise?"

"This is different; you can't harm him. I feel, somehow that only *I* can be a real threat to him. And I think the woman knows it, too. Come on, Startz, let us get some sleep."

Startz was dead tired. There was so much more he wanted to extract from Nikolai, but the big man was already snoring. What a strange statement, he thought: a woman and a signal? I must study his report, Startz decided. Perhaps there is something I have overlooked. And I must have another competent translator for that curious manuscript. Dr. Tagarū is not entirely trustworthy. An independent scientist not connected with the museum might uncover something. Meanwhile, this Dubrava affair was far from finished. But he was effectively prevented from concluding his investigation. He had neither the time nor the mandate to continue it.

Michea would still be riding in his carriage. Perhaps Nikolai's paranoia did have some basis in fact. Perhaps Michea had managed to manipulate the whole thing to his advantage. Doesn't matter, Startz thought grimly. My promise will be fulfilled. But how?

Doctor Tagarū's fortunes began to improve as soon as he "discovered" and translated the manuscript. Not only were his colleagues in Bucharest astounded, but they hailed his find as a major contribution to the history of eastern Europe.

The Ukrainian Academy voted to give him the Order of the Red Banner for Labor; the Romanian Academy reinstated Dr. Tagarū as a full member. There were serious discussions as to whether to restore him to his university post and, in the meantime, he was given a slight raise in salary.

One thing that puzzled him and that he could not possibly explain was the last missing page. He attributed the vampire business to the perverse Russian kind of mysticism. Why worry? Yet he was worried; he couldn't sleep. He thought of Annoushka, longed for the time when he could leave this dreadful castle and go back to the university, back to civilization.

He did not see Michea very much after the new curator arrived. There was so much to do and it seemed to him that Michea was avoiding the museum. The poet now used another stairway that led directly into the yard whenever he wanted to use his carriage.

Two militia men remained at the castle as a precaution. Brasov militia officials now conducted the investigation. They had asked Dr. Tagarū if he had any additional information about the mysterious deaths. And that was all.

Dr. Tagarū hoped that the little Startz would not come back to stir up the hornet's nest again. This morning his career seemed assured. He finally had received a letter from the University of Bucharest that he had been reinstated as a full professor. After a period of thirty days, during which he would familiarize his successor with the duties of the museum, he was to return to Bucharest where the apartment assigned him near the university would be ready. Thirty more days, only one month! Dr. Tagarū was overjoyed. He put an empty piece of paper on the wall over his desk and wrote a large 2 on it. It had taken one day for the letter to reach him. Twenty-eight days to go. He stepped out of his office and found himself face-to-face with Michea. An unpleasant surprise.

"Good day," he said, trying to bypass him.

"Good day, Comrade Professor." Michea chuckled. "I came to ask a slight favor."

Professor? How did he know? He has many contacts; somebody at the ministry must have told him.

"Certainly, if I can be of help." Dr. Tagarū smiled his best official smile. Can't jeopardize these twenty-eight days.

"It's very simple, Doctor." Michea's face looked fatter than ever; there were gray sacs of flesh under his eyes. He had put on quite a bit of weight. "A dear friend will be arriving from Bucharest in about two weeks—you have met him, our famous Babulescu. He will collaborate with me on a play I have been working on for some time now. And well, he is somewhat of an eccentric, he loves to work alone. I would be forever grateful if, for a few days after his arrival,

180

you would close the museum's library to tourists. Then he could do his writing and research undisturbed."

This request did not please Dr. Tagarū at all. The library was, after all, a part of the museum, mentioned in all the catalogues and tourist brochures. To close it would be a breach of protocol.

"You might say to the tourists that the library is closed for inventory or repainting." Michea read his doubt. "It would be no problem, the season is almost finished."

Dr. Tagarū thought it over. On the one hand, he would be breaking the regulation; on the other, the library's ceiling needed a new coat of paint anyway. And Michea was a powerful man. Who knew how many powerful friends he had. He was a bastard too, and possibly something worse. Dr. Tagarū was still unsure of the vampire theory and, at this point, didn't much care.

"Certainly, I'll see to it that Comrade Babulescu is undisturbed."

"I will be grateful." Michea smiled. "Dr. Tagarū, should you need a favor someday, do not hesitate to ask." He walked up to his apartment.

Dr. Tagarū, greatly relieved, hurried to see his new assistant curator.

seven

Nikolai's long-awaited signal arrived unexpectedly on a blue September morning. The air was still, the Black Sea was calm. Nikolai was reading in his cabin when he heard a distant roar, and almost immediately the walls of his cottage began to shake. He ran out on the beach and almost fell down; the earthquake was so strong that the glass shattered in the cottage's windows and cracks appeared in the roadway. The ground shook for a few minutes, then everything became still once again. This, he knew, was his summons to the Dubrava castle.

First, he wanted to find out what was happening, but the state-operated radio stations were off the air. The earthquake must have been devastating farther west. Nikolai threw on his leather jacket, stuck his pistol in the pocket, and ran to his Land Rover. A few minutes later, he was racing down the deserted and increasingly dangerous highway toward Constanţa.

There he saw the first signs of the earthquake and confusion, as well as the first roadblocks. His identification helped to get him through to Hîrşova, where the new bridge over the Danube had been severely damaged and all the traffic had been turned back. He had to drive north at least fifty kilometers to Măcin, where he took a ferry to Brăila. That bridge was open only for military vehicles, but Nikolai persuaded the captain in charge to let him through. All the main highways were now closed to civilian traffic. The army officers at the roadblocks were unmoved by Nikolai's identification and his threats. He was forced to continue on the dusty country roads, crisscrossed by cracks in the earth.

At Busau, row upon row of new apartment buildings were lev-
eled, streets were impassable. Stunned, angry people were standing silently, surveying the ruins of their homes. Red Cross units
stacked the dead bodies.

Nikolai had picked up Route 10 and driven another fifty kilometers when an army patrol stopped him and requisitioned his Land
Rover. An army truck driver carrying the wounded to Brasov gave
him a lift to a crossroads near Cheia. From there, Nikolai traveled
on foot to what was once the beautiful village near Dubrava castle.
The village was largely destroyed. The Two Moons Café was reduced to rubble; the Hotel Red Danube had collapsed along with
most of the other houses. The wounded were being evacuated in
army buses, and there were piles of corpses on the ground at the
village square. But the central fountain, miraculously, still spouted
clear mountain water.

No one recognized Nikolai, nor did he want to be recognized. He
walked toward the forest and found an old bicycle leaning against
one of the few remaining houses.

The castle was burning. The main tower had collapsed, and the
walls were crisscrossed with huge cracks. He decided not to go
there. Not now anyway.

Acting on blind intuition, he rode the bike off the road into the
forest, but he did not see the thin uprooted tree directly in his path.
The bike struck the yellow dirt, and Nikolai flew over the tree trunk
and landed in a ditch. He got up, climbed over the branches, and
examined the bike. It was now useless.

Startz was standing in his bathroom, a cup of hot coffee in his hand.
He was dressed, shaved, and ready to go to his office at the Ministry
of the Interior. He was contemplating whether to trim his gray
mustache himself or to let the barber do it during the afternoon
recess, when he heard a very loud, expanding roar, as if twenty
Russian tank divisions were rolling into Bucharest. In fact, the
thought momentarily crossed his mind. The roar reached a crescendo and his building began to shake. Startz had just enough
foresight to drop his cup, run into his bedroom, and dive under the
bed.

The walls and ceiling of his modern apartment house on the
fashionable Megeru Avenue fell apart, exposing the unusually blue,
clear sky and gray concrete beams. Fortunately, Startz did not live
in the main twelve-story apartment complex, but in the small three-

story addition, built mostly to house offices and stores. His apartment was on the second floor and by the time the earthquake was over, he found himself buried, nestled safely betwen a tractor and what appeared to be a conveyor belt, in a store displaying Japanese farm machinery. Every part of his body ached, but as far as he could determine, nothing was broken. After two hours, he finally dug himself out of the debris and climbed into the street.

What devastation! A whole row of new high-rise buildings had collapsed like houses of cards; the university was gone; the new computer center was a pile of rubble; fires were raging throughout the downtown area. The great city, a jewel of eastern Europe, was reduced to a bombed-out skeleton.

Shaken as he was, Startz walked across the rubble toward the ministry. The last earthquake, in 1940 as he remembered, was nothing compared to this. Even the ultra-modern Hotel Continental had visible cracks in its white walls. So much for the quality of the new apartment complexes. Startz was bitter; everyone knew how badly they were built. Nikolai had told him several years ago that structurally they were all unsound. Now they had all been reduced to piles of rubble, with trapped people screaming underneath.

At the ministry he was immediately summoned into a high-level, super-secret meeting about how to deal with citizen discontent and the possibility of an open rebellion arising out of the disaster. The situation in the rest of the country was critical. Ceausescu had declared a state of emergency and the Romanian army had already begun search and clearing operations within the capitol. The earthquake, which registered 7.5 on the Richter scale, was centered in the Transylvanian Alps northwest of Bucharest, and had caused widespread damage in cities as distant as Rome, Moscow, Athens, and Ankara. The giant factories in Galați and Craiova were hit the hardest. All the factories in the Budapest area were either destroyed or closed down. At Ploesti, the oil refinery center, which had been devastated by an American air raid during World War II, was now out of operation, and the city itself had suffered great damage, with more than three thousand apartment units destroyed. The river port of Zimnicea was almost completely destroyed; the cities of Gheorghiu-Dej and Brasov were heavily damaged. The list seemed endless.

When Startz arrived, roughly thirty gloomy officials were sitting in a basement auditorium at the Ministry of the Interior, looking at a giant map of the country, and listening to the military emergency network which had been set up secretly in case of a Soviet invasion and which was now, ironically, the only available means of communication. The minister, usually a handsome and youngish-looking man, now hobbled on crutches and displayed a purple scar on his forehead. He stepped to the podium and came directly to the point.

"Comrades, I just left the president. Our revolution has suffered a severe setback, possibly a setback of several years. From what we now know, the damage is estimated at fifteen to twenty billion *lei*, not to mention the lives lost and the injuries sustained by our citizens. Politically, the repercussions may develop into an ominous trend. The shoddy quality of construction . . ." He paused. "I will personally shoot the builders of my apartment house! My wife and my daughter"—his voice quavered—"are among the confirmed dead.

"We discount any possibility of insurrection or organized opposition, but . . . we must try to turn the average citizen's attention to reconstruction, not recrimination. We must, working along with the Ministry of Information, light the spark of traditional Romanian patriotism in the face of adversity, to push on with the reconstruction, while"—he raised his voice—"at the same time, weeding out and isolating the malcontents, the critics, and the other social outcasts. This is the time to be gentle, but also the time to be firm. I hope, Comrades, you understand what our country and our party expects of us. Your specific orders will be given out by my secretary." He hobbled off the podium.

The messages again began pouring in on the teletype and two junior officers were busy, once again sticking various colored pins into the giant map of the country.

Startz stood up. At least, he thought, we have a competent minister instead of the hysterical Madame Radū. And evidently there was not going to be a widespread purge, at least for the time being.

"Wait, Startz." The minister approached him, followed by his aides. "This may be of interest to you." He tried to smile even though his front teeth had been knocked out. "Last night there was quite a gathering of famous people at our Dubrava castle, a testimonial dinner of sorts." This was said with great irony. "And we had an agent on duty too. I felt there was a breach of security at the castle anyway. Hmm . . . all highly respected people . . . some were foreigners; one was a high official of our great neighbor to the east."

The minister took Startz by the arm and lowered his voice to a whisper. "That agent of ours last radioed an incredible report. There was a religious service of some kind in progress. I stress the word 'religious' because this agent thought it was a black mass. They were wearing long black robes. And listen to this: they were waiting for their master, the devil himself, I assume, to appear in a cloud of mist and provide them with some nourishment. Normally, I'd suspend my, our, agent for drinking on duty and for slandering such luminaries. Or perhaps give him three months at hard labor to clear his head. Only, when another agent came to relieve him at his post, he found that our man was dead . . . horribly mutilated, his throat torn open. And that was the last I, we, heard from our second agent. Apparently the service, gathering—whatever it was—continued up until the time of the earthquake. Now all the guests, with the exception of our novelist Babulescu, are presumed dead, buried under the walls."

"Babulescu?" Startz asked. "Did he say anything?"

"He's in shock, in a hospital."

"The castle walls collapsed?"

The minister looked closely. "Do you believe in miracles, Startz, or, well, coincidences that are too outrageous to contemplate?"

"No, Comrade Minister, I do not."

"And neither do I," said the minister. "Yet, according to our seismologists, the epicenter of the earthquake originated directly under Dubrava castle."

Startz waited, trying not to betray his emotions.

"Well, it did!" The minister evidently was in pain and wanted to end the conversation. "The ruins are presently occupied by a detachment of soldiers. Four corpses were found in the castle. Michea's was not among them. His whereabouts are currently unknown. I am more concerned, however, with your friend and mine, Nikolai, who was stopped twice, driving like a madman in the direction of the castle. He is a good policeman and I do not intend to lose him. Do not spend very much time on this, but inasmuch as your orders are for the Brasov area, find him for me. And also see if you can find our elusive Basarab. I am more and more interested in that character."

Very late at night, Startz's helicopter landed at a military base outside the city of Brasov. Two jeeps were waiting.

Early in the morning, Startz stood drinking a cup of coffee and watched the sun come up over the ruins of the Dubrava castle. The soldiers were loading books and manuscripts into wooden boxes. Dr. Tagarū and his new assistant curator were busily examining and stamping the boxes. Dr. Tagarū's hands were bandaged, as was his head.

"We had absolutely no warning," he explained to Startz. "A miracle saved us. When disaster struck, several members of my staff and myself were in the yard trying to catch Michea's horses. They had freed themselves somehow during the night and were trying wildly to get out. Perhaps they knew."

Startz thought, *the animal instinct?*

"The rest had no chance whatsoever, except that novelist, Babulescu. He escaped somehow."

"And Michea?"

"Michea!" Dr. Tagarū jumped up as if someone had hit him.

"Yes, Michea Basarab, Comrade Adelescu. What of him?"

"Excuse me, Comrade, I am very busy." Dr. Tagarū went back to stamping his boxes and manuscripts.

Startz chose to ignore the doctor's peculiar reaction. He could always question Tagarū later.

The commander of the rescue unit, a serious-looking, middle-aged captain, related in great detail how they had searched the castle, found and identified the bodies, and cared for the wounded.

"You did not find Citizen Babulescu there?" Startz interrupted.

"No. That I find quite amazing because I personally searched the entire library shortly after our arrival. No one was in it then."

"Library. Could you elaborate?"

"Yes, he said he was in the library doing some research and was saved when several bookshelves fell, shielding him when the ceiling collapsed. And he said there was another man in the castle."

"Oh? Where is Comrade Babulescu now?"

"As far as I know, he is on his way to Bucharest. He was worried about his apartment."

"He said there was another man in the castle? Did you check it out?"

"Yes, Comrade, and we posted guards around the walls immediately afterward."

"But not before?"

"No." The captain's face reddened.

"Did Babulescu describe the man?"

The captain thought. "Comrade Babulescu was quite shaken and

187

bruised; perhaps he had a concussion. He said the man was very large, a hunter who offered him some vodka . . . also something about a guard. I thought he was referring to our guard."

Startz looked again at the remains of the castle.

"Could there be other bodies out there?"

"Of course, it's possible." The captain shrugged. "But I don't think so. We have questioned all survivors at length; everyone is accounted for . . . except . . ."

"Michea Basarab?"

"Exactly!" The captain was relieved. "You know where he is?"

"I wish I did."

"No one at the museum had seen him for several days prior to the earthquake. His automobile is gone. Possibly he was—"

"Never mind, Captain. We'll find him if and when we need him. What I need right now is two soldiers with weapons and a driver."

The captain gave the orders.

eight

Nikolai abandoned his bicycle and cautiously walked up the narrow forest path. Exactly two kilometers, he remembered. The small cabin was so well hidden that his own partisan unit, returning from a mission, had once missed it completely.

Almost thirty-seven years ago. He remembered Janco then, lifting him up and tossing him in the air at their victory party. This afternoon, he hoped Janco would again be sitting behind the crude wooden table, a bottle in one hand, his submachine gun in the other. He wanted to see the small red banner waving proudly above the door and his old comrades sitting in the tall grass outside, smoking, resting, and waiting for instructions. The forest wasn't the same anymore. The silence was total, a certain smell of death hanging in the air. Here and there were signs of the earthquake: hundred-year-old pines had been uprooted and thrown around as if they were matchsticks. Not a single animal in sight, not even a bird. Nikolai walked on. Fresh ditches, heavy underbrush, uprooted trees, fallen branches. It was getting dark.

I'll never find the cottage. He touched his pistol to reassure himself. Then he realized that he was hopelessly lost. He sat down, lit a cigarette. The first stars appeared; the sky was clear. He climbed one of the trees to have a look around. I must be three or four kilometers from the castle, he thought. The mountains were in the right place; the castle was not visible. The cottage *had* to be somewhere around here. He climbed down and began walking in an

189

ever-widening circle so as not to miss it again. Another half hour of searching and he saw a light. There was the cottage, and someone was in it.

The cottage was larger than he remembered it. A thin stream of blue smoke was coming from the chimney. As he approached, a smell of spicy stew reminded him that he hadn't eaten all day. He knocked on the door, on which he had carved his name so long ago.

"Do not move!" he heard Janco growl from the inside. "Turn around and walk back, whoever or whatever you are. I am counting three; if you are still there, you are dead."

"Janco!" Nikolai screamed and kicked the door open.

His friend was sitting at the same old wooden table, a Russian submachine gun in one hand, a bottle of vodka in the other. Some things never change. He was drunk, but his eyes were alert and suspicious. He looked Nikolai over, but he kept hs hand on the trigger.

"Cross yourself, Nikola," he said.

"What?" Nikolai stopped cold in the doorway.

"Cross yourself three times." Janco was serious, dead serious.

"Whatever for?"

"Just do it!" Janco shouted and raised his gun.

"Have you gone crazy?" Nikolai sighed and crossed himself three times.

Janco put down the gun. Now he was the same Janco, a giant madman, a huge grinning bear. He got up and embraced Nikolai, lifting him in the air just as easily as he had when Nikolai was a boy.

"You came back, Nikola. I knew you were coming back. I am very proud of you. You did not lose your courage."

At Janco's insistence, Nikolai drank some of the vodka.

"Why did I have to cross myself? Are you becoming religious in your old age?"

"I don't know what I believe anymore . . . I am just being careful. These days, you don't know who is out in the forest."

Nikolai sat down on some old ammunition boxes and drank some more. Vodka relaxed him; his confidence returned.

"Tell me, Janco," he said quietly, "tell me all you know about . . . the vurdalak."

"That is why you came back? Don't deny it. I know you came to kill. You walked so softly, even I didn't hear you until you knocked on my door. Good thing, too. If you hadn't knocked, you'd be dead already. So, you came to kill our Prince of the Night?"

"What?"

"That is one of the other names for a vurdalak. Michea, your bosom friend, you came to kill him?"

"Yes," Nikolai answered very quietly. Now he felt tired. He took another pull on the bottle and, without asking Janco, picked out a piece of meat from the pot on the stove. He ate the meat quickly, burning his lips, then drank some more.

"Will you help me again?" he begged. "Just this last time?"

"I will help you simply because you will not be able to succeed without my help and, also—" Janco was now sad. He took the bottle away from Nikolai, drank fast and long. "I too, have a score to settle with the fiend. Sit down here, Nikola." He invited him to a small fur-covered cot. "Sit down and listen. We have plenty of time on our hands. You must rest."

He stirred the stew, put some of it on a tin plate, and handed it to Nikolai. Noticing that the bottle was nearly empty, he flung open a burlap curtain behind the stove to reveal a small brass and copper still above which, on two large shelves, stood approximately fifty more bottles, some of them broken and empty. He took out one of the full ones.

"That earthquake!" He shook his head in sorrow. "It missed me by about three kilometers. A little closer and all my little babies would be gone." He handed the bottle to Nikolai, who was busily eating the stew. Then, to Nikolai's surprise, he opened one of the old ammunition boxes in the corner and took out a large wreath of garlic.

"Myself, I don't believe in it." He shrugged. "But people around here think the smell repulses the night visitors . . . hmmmm." He peeled one of the cloves and took a healthy bite. "You want some, Nikola?"

"No, thank you."

Janco took another bite of garlic, washed it down with some vodka, and hung the wreath outside on a nail above the door.

"You know we must kill her, too . . . your beautiful American woman . . . if, indeed, she is American or, for that matter, a woman."

Nikolai did not answer.

Janco was watching him closely for any reaction. Nikolai kept eating.

"She probably tasted your blood, Nikola," he said very quietly.

Nikolai did not move.

Janco watched him for a few more moments, smiled, and slapped him on his back.

"Relax and don't be too concerned. It is not a coincidence that you came to me this evening. Perhaps we are not as helpless as we would have been before the earthquake."

"Go on." Nikolai put away the plate.

"Normally, I'd say we have no chance against them whatsoever. Remember what happened to the poor priest?"

"You know about that?"

"Sure, this is a small country."

A wolf howled outside.

"One of his friends?"

Janco listened. "A wolf is only an animal. What we are going to hunt, just before the sun rises, is . . ." He searched for the right word.

The howling stopped abruptly.

Strange, Nikolai thought. He suddenly had the feeling that he was being watched. Janco evidently thought so too. He put down the bottle and wiped the sweat off his face.

The wolf howled again, much closer, almost outside the door. They both jumped up.

"It begins," said Janco, reaching under the old boxes. "How are your nerves lately?"

"Not too bad. What are you doing?"

Janco threw the boxes aside. Underneath was a cache of various weapons: old rifles, daggers, swords, lances, and an ancient bow with a few wooden arrows. He grabbed the bow and the arrows.

"You know," the policeman in Nikolai finally spoke out, "you can get ten years just for your still, and ten more for all these illegal weapons."

Janco grinned. "You should see my other hiding places."

He put the bow and the arrows on the table, reached again for his shelves, this time taking down a metal flask. Carefully he put the flask in the middle of the table and began dipping the tips of the arrows into it.

"Poison?" Nikolai forgot about the wolf. He was fascinated.

"No, just plain, ordinary holy water."

"You mean the wolf is not real?"

"Oh, the wolf is real. This is not for the wolf. Him, I am going to shoot with this"—he pointed to his gun—"if he ever howls again."

"Remember that other wolf?"

"Of course, I do." Janco finished with the arrows, tried out the bow, tightened it a bit, and sat by the table.

"I suppose now we have to watch out for snakes?"

"I don't think so," Janco replied calmly. "This time he'll come in person, his royal highness."

"And you are going to shoot him with those arrows?"

"What do you suggest? The bullets won't kill him."

"And why not? I almost killed him back at the castle with this very gun."

"No, you could not have killed him." Janco dismissed the notion with a wave of his hand. "They, the vampires, live in a different time and space . . . it is like shooting at that wolf when he is no longer there."

"Your arrows are even slower."

"Let me tell you how an arrow such as this once saved my life."

Janco listened to outside noises. Everything was now quiet.

"Long before the war, I was a carefree, young hunter roaming the forests and the mountains from here all the way to Trans-Carpathia. Now, superstitions aside, every hunter knows that there is a species of giant bats living in the mountains. They are very shy and nobody ever proved that they are vampire bats . . . very few of them are left today. But, Nikola, these bats frightened many a brave man. I saw six of them once. Their wingspan must have been, oh, perhaps a meter. They flew very fast over the treetops and I shot one of them down. I thought it fell, perhaps a hundred meters ahead of me, in a small clearing. And I decided to find it so I could stuff it and sell it to some rich merchant. Giant bats were rare even then. As I was walking toward it—it was just before daybreak—I heard some rustling in the bushes, some large animal. I reloaded my shotgun and kept walking. Whatever was in the bushes followed me. I tell you, I suddenly became very frightened. I thought, to hell with that bat. I started running."

Janco stopped and listened again. Nothing.

"I ran faster and faster. In my panic, I dropped my shotgun. I was out of breath. I stopped in the middle of the clearing and then I saw him. An enormous bat, circling over and swooping toward me. I ran again and this time I fell into what must have been a mass grave. Bones, skeletons, skulls of people. The bat was just above me . . . and it was coming toward me very fast, faster than anything. I turned away, knowing that I couldn't defend myself. Actually I could have used my hunting knife. As I turned, I hit my chest on an arrow stuck into one of those skeletons. I quickly pulled it out and just as the bat was almost on top of me, I stuck the arrow up to defend myself. The bat must have impaled itself on it . . . it let out an ear-piercing shriek. The arrow was out of my hand, and I lost consciousness from sheer fright. When I woke up, in that same ditch, the sun was shining, the birds were singing, everything was normal. It was some kind of nightmare, I decided. Possibly brought on by some poisonous mushrooms I'd eaten earlier. I found my shotgun and walked back to the village."

Janco stopped just in time. There were some scratching noises outside. Both he and Nikolai stood up, Nikolai holding onto his pistol and Janco to his bow and arrow.

"Stay here." He nodded to Nikolai, cautiously opened the door, and peered into the darkness. "Look there." He grinned.

The wreath of garlic was gone. Janco closed the door and sat down again.

"So much for garlic."

Nikolai remained standing.

"Relax, Nikola, they can't come into this hut. They can only enter if somebody invites them in. And I am certainly not going to invite them in. And you aren't going to invite them in either . . . are you?" He added thoughtfully, "I forgot about the woman."

"What about the woman? She's long gone; she's probably back in New York." Nikolai was irritated.

"Oh, you think so?"

"What makes you think otherwise? Why bring her into this anyway? She is not a vampire. Stop talking about her! Give me the bottle."

Janco kept watching him.

"And stop staring at me! Better tell me all you know, all the superstitions about vurdalaks. I feel the more we know, the sooner we can kill Michea."

"So, you finally believe in vurdalaks?"

"I believe . . . I don't believe, I don't know." Nikolai drank some more. "Just tell me."

"I don't really know any more than most people around here. I think the legend begins from the time of the Tartar invasion. It is said that the Tartars were drinking human blood, that by drinking it, they hoped to avoid getting killed in battle."

Nikolai clearly heard a woman singing the song he and Startz had heard in the nightclub in Bucharest.

"Nice song," Janco interrupted, not at all surprised. "Let me continue. There are many legends; few of them contradict one another. In Moldavia, people say one of their princes was born a vurdalak and that he led the Tartars into Romania. Who knows?"

"What I want to know is how do you *kill* one of them?"

"Certainly not by driving a stake through its heart. I believe you have to cut off the creature's head and burn it far away from its body. Oh, and one must be very careful, because they are said to have black blood. If that blood touches your skin, you become infected and die—you might even come back as a vampire."

"That's more or less what we read in the ancient manuscript." Nikolai noticed that the woman had stopped singing. "Anything else?"

"Now, the trick is, of course, to find them first, when they're asleep or just getting ready to go to sleep. Where exactly did you find the priest?"

Nikolai told him.

"There is another legend around here"—Janco was now very thoughtful—"that somewhere near the Dubrava castle exists a magical garden, a beautiful place with flowers and animals such as no one has ever seen. The flowers bloom by the light of the full moon and in the midst of it stands a mansion, a tomb of some kind, where the Prince of the Night sleeps in a golden casket, immersed in human blood. Oh, and no human being can enter it unless he is invited by the Prince Vampire."

"His private domain."

"I think so. Now, I know there cannot be such a place because I have walked every square meter of the grounds around the castle. But I did find many interesting things: knights' armor, muskets, helmets, lances, scimitars. Once I found an entire battery, four medium-size cannons, that Napoleon's army must have left in the woods. They were so well camouflaged, I discovered them only by stumbling on one of the barrels."

The policeman and responsible citizen in Nikolai spoke up once again. "Why didn't you inform the museum's staff of your discoveries? Dr. Tagarū would have been so pleased."

Janco's reply about the museum staff, Dr. Tagarū, and the government in general was a solid curse. He drank some more vodka.

"In any event," said Janco, "they fired me again, just a few days ago. I'd been snooping around; I found ancient books and banners and silver and gold coins and even precious stones . . . but," he whispered, "never a place such as this garden."

They sat silently for a few moments. It was quiet outside.

"And yet," Janco continued, "I believe such a place *must* exist. Our legends usually have some basis in fact. That is why I think the earthquake might help us . . . help us find the garden and the prince. Maybe also his princess."

Janco lit another candle, helped himself to his stew.

"Have more," he offered.

Nikolai didn't feel like eating. His stomach was tied into a knot. After a surge of high tension and energy earlier in the day, he now felt tired, lethargic, depressed. What was he trying to accomplish in the first place? Madness! I am slowly going mad, he thought. Actually, not so slowly. Deterioration, vurdalaks, centuries. Now we are in a new era. Man went to the moon and back and here I am about to hunt a vurdalak? Ridiculous! Rest, rest is what I need- . . . this insanity will pass. He stretched out on the cot.

"You can rest," Janco warned, "but don't fall asleep!"

"Why not? What are we doing anyway, sitting around and talking? I think all I need is a good sleep. Tomorrow I'll go back and forget this nonsense. Rest . . . perhaps Startz was right, perhaps I need a very good psychiatrist."

"Talk, Nikola, talk all you wish, only don't go to sleep."

"I know everything about vurdalaks." Nikolai rambled on and drank some more vodka. "I read the old Slavonic manuscript. I know all there is to know and I know nothing. She can't be here. She must be in New York. Startz would have found her if she were in Romania. Janco, you only meet a woman like her once in your lifetime . . . Janco, listen to me, tell me if I am insane?"

"We're all insane." Janco picked out the last piece of meat and swallowed it.

"I *am* insane. I keep seeing her every night in my dreams. I can almost smell her perfume and touch her hair. She laughs at me when I reach out, tells me I cannot have her, that she belongs to her master."

"Don't think about her!" Janco was concerned. "She is not even a woman."

"I cannot have her, and that is all that matters to me now. I want to see her again, and touch her."

"Shut up, Nikola. Drink! Only not so fast. We musn't get drunk."

"Why not get drunk? And sleep it off. And forget about Michea. But I cannot forget him . . . must kill him! You said you, too, have a score to settle. What did he do to you?"

"Not to me." Janco looked out his tiny window as the moon came up over the forest. "I have two daughters. One was recently married and had a son, my grandson, a fine boy. He disappeared less than a week ago. Other babies have disappeared from around here as well."

Nikolai sat up. "Why didn't you inform the authorities?"

"Authorities?" Janco laughed bitterly. "They notified the local militia. She was told to keep her own baby's disappearance a secret. Authorities!" He spat.

"Who was it she spoke to? I'll have him shot."

"They're all like this, Nikola, have been this way for centuries. The peasants around here believe—"

Once again the scratching noises began. This time they heard muffled sobbing outside the door.

"We better be alert now. I think our guests have arrived."

Nikolai suddenly felt chilly. He held onto his pistol. Janco placed an arrow in his bow.

"We are supposed to be the hunters." Nikolai felt like going outside and forcing a direct confrontation. "Seems to me they are hunting us."

"Have patience, Nikola. They will try to destroy us first, you especially."

"Why me?"

"Because you must be dangerous to them, to Michea."

"I am not dangerous to him sitting in this hut. And in what way can I be dangerous to him anyway?"

"You were in love with his woman. Maybe she loved you, too. There's that saying: 'Love conquers all.' " Janco smiled, but his eyes remained serious.

197

"Oh, be quiet." Nikolai rubbed his eyes, irritated. "We should just go and get it over with one way or another. I can't take much more of this waiting."

"We have to sit here until just before daybreak, then it will be our turn to go hunting." Janco again flung open his magic curtain and grabbed a fresh bottle.

"You know"—Nikolai finally smiled at the irony of their situation—"if we ever catch Michea, we can drown him in your vodka. That will kill him for certain."

"Be quiet." Janco put a finger to his lips. He carefully put the new bottle on the table. Then, like a cat, he walked back to his cache of weapons and picked out a curved dagger and a Turkish scimitar. He kept the scimitar, gave the dagger to Nikolai. "Forget your pistol for the time being," he whispered.

Nikolai examined the dagger, which was decorated with Arabic writing. Jewels glinted in the ivory handle. He tested the blade gently with his finger.

"Hey!" he cried out. The edge was razor-sharp. He sucked in the blood, doused the wound with vodka. The cut was deeper than he'd thought.

Suddenly he sensed an unexpected stillness. The crying had stopped, and he actually heard tiny thuds as the drops of his blood hit the old floorboards.

Something was about to happen. Nikolai raised his dagger. Janco held onto his bow and arrow, his eyes very alert: an old hunter anticipating the animal's deadly strike.

A gust of very cold wind suddenly struck their shelter. The walls of the hut began to shake. Part of the roof flew off. This was no earthquake.

The small window blew open; splinters of glass flew across the room; the candles sputtered; Janco's bottles shook and fell to the floor.

At that very instant, the heavy wooden door of the cottage fell off its hinges and landed near Nikolai's feet with a thunderous crash. The wind howled wildly, and a form appeared, outlined in the eerie moonlight. Michea stood at the threshold of the hut. Long, dark hair fell on both sides of his pale young face, black velvet enshrouded his slender body. The jewel in his crown, like his huge red eyes, burned with an unearthly fire. His features were contorted with rage.

He stared directly at Nikolai. No words were spoken, but Nikolai understood his terrifying message. He trembled uncontrollably; the dagger fell from his hand.

Janco stretched his bow to the limit and took careful aim.

Michea saw the movement. He raised his left hand, and Janco froze, paralyzed, unable to release the arrow.

Michea communicated the rest of his message. The wind died down.

Finally, Janco managed to release the arrow. It flew into the open space. The doorway was empty now; the arrow whistled sadly across the clearing and hit a tree.

Janco was the first to recover. He shook his head, lifted up the door, and leaned it against the wall. Then he lit the candles, examined the broken hinges, and shook his head again.

Nikolai sat quietly, staring into the night.

"Wake up, Nikola!" Janco said, almost pleading.

Nikolai closed his eyes. Janco pressed the bottle to his friend's mouth, made him swallow. Nikolai coughed, opened his eyes.

"He is trying to scare us, Nikola." He grinned. "He is only trying to scare us!"

"He *did* scare me," Nikolai said, though the vodka revived him somewhat. "He scared me so much . . . to the marrow of my bones. Before this, I did not know the meaning of fear. Let me have some more."

Janco went to his curtain. More than half of his bottles were now broken. He picked up a full one, gulped about a third of it, and gave it to Nikolai. Nikolai drank another third, put the bottle down, and put out his hand.

"Farewell, Janco, my friend, I must go home."

"You are crazy! That's exactly what he wants. How far do you think you'll get out there?"

"He promised that I won't be harmed if I go back now."

"*He* promised? And you believe him?"

"I must go," Nikolai repeated dumbly and started for the door. He did not see Janco's large fist coming at his head. Stars and moons exploded and then he felt nothing.

Janco picked him up gently, like a child, carried him to a cot, and covered him with a sheepskin.

Nikolai's finger was still bleeding. Janco bandaged it with a piece of cloth, picked up the dagger, and sat by the table.

It was very quiet outside. From where Janco sat, he could see the full moon hanging over the trees. The night was still young, and, he thought, the worst was yet to come. Too bad Nikolai had gotten so frightened . . . but that could mean only one thing: the vurdalak himself was frightened. Why would he give such a warning? He must be frightened of Nikola, Janco decided. I was right. Somehow Nikola is very dangerous to them.

Suddenly Janco felt confident. He drank some more. The morning was as yet far behind the Carpathian Mountains, but the old hunter's instinct told him that the prey was now on the defensive. He thought for a moment about his grandson. Even if this is the last act of my life, I'll kill them for him. For him, and all the other children.

A woman began singing outside the cottage. She was singing a lullaby and she had his mother's own voice. Janco crossed himself and the singing stopped. He grinned and drank some more. On the cot, Nikolai was still unconscious.

nine

Several hours later, Janco's confidence began to fade. I should not have drunk quite so much, he thought, as he put the fourth empty bottle aside. The 150-proof alcohol was beginning to affect even him. Janco felt drowsy, sleepy. Nothing was happening outside; there was not a sound, just dead, heavy silence. He caught himself napping a few times. To shorten the waiting time, he paced in the hut every fifteen minutes and once even ventured outside. When we come back from our hunt, he thought, I am going to repair the damned door. Nikolai was still asleep, snoring loudly and, from time to time, talking nonsense in his sleep.

Another hour. I can last another hour. Almost four now. Another hour and we are going to hunt. Such a long day and night. That magical garden must be where Nikodim's body was found. And nowhere else! In his mind, he once more went over the jagged terrain: all the rocks and all the small gullies and ditches, all the possible hidden entrances.

The earthquake had almost split the castle in half. The main tower had collapsed immediately; huge cracks had appeared in the massive walls; fires had broken out inside. Once again, the famous Dubrava castle was a smoldering ruin.

Janco had arrived at the castle just after the earthquake had stopped, in time to watch the evacuation of the museum staff. He'd observed the comings and goings from the forest beyond the parking lot. Those survivors who could walk had been loaded into an army truck. The stretcher cases had been wrapped up so that Janco could not tell whether they were dead or seriously wounded. All of them were the "upstairs people." Michea's mother, his servant, and another body. Michea? Janco had thought so at the time. The stretchers had been loaded into an army ambulance, which had then sped away across the ditches and cracks in the road. Six or seven soldiers had remained to guard the castle.

When the soldiers had finally gathered for lunch, Janco had entered the ruin through a large crack in the wall. The main hall was in shambles: the bas-relief of the devil was split evenly in the middle; the hideous head had been knocked off completely. It was on the floor, broken into several pieces. There had been no access to Michea's apartment from the hallway because both stairways had collapsed. Janco had skirted the rubble and strolled into the library. Rusai, the old caretaker, had once assured him that there was a secret passage connecting the library and Michea's apartment. The library, too, was destroyed. The bookcases were overturned; the ceiling had collapsed. As Janco was looking for the passage, he heard moaning and saw a man's leg protruding from under one of the bookcases. Then he saw another leg. Without much difficulty, he had pulled out a chubby little man, bald and bewildered, but unhurt. The man had stared past his rescuer, apparently in shock.

What if he starts screaming? Janco had realized that they would probably both be shot as looters by those trigger-happy young soldiers.

The man had kept staring past Janco, even when Janco had slapped him gently on his puffed cheek. Apparently, when the bookshelves had fallen down they had knocked the man to the ground and he had been trapped beneath them, which explained how he had survived. Had he been standing in the room, the falling ceiling would surely have killed him.

Babulescu! Janco had recognized the famous writer who often came to visit Michea and to stay at the castle. When Janco was younger, he had even read Babulescu's books. Everyone did.

"I have to be going, Comrade," Janco had said gently. "Can you walk? Feel your feet." Janco had begun to worry about the soldiers outside.

"Wait, please wait," the writer had whispered.

"Comrade, you just walk to the entrance and tell the soldiers who you are. I have to go in another direction."

"Wait," he'd whispered again. "Do you know who I am?"

"Yes, yes, you are Babulescu, the writer."

"But do you know"— he seemed confused—"what has happened in this castle?"

"Of course, Comrade, the earthquake."

"No, no! You do not understand . . . not an ordinary earthquake," he protested, waving his hands. "God himself intervened! Don't you see, we are helpless."

"What the hell are you babbling about?"

"We are powerless, helpless!" He had looked at Janco imploringly.

"You are not helpless, damn you! You can make it outside." I have to disappear fast, he had thought. The passage leading to Michea's apartment was exposed to full view. The bookcases concealing it were down. Janco disappeared into the darkness.

"Don't go there," Babulescu had whined. "Our master will not forgive you. Our master cannot be destroyed! Our master . . . " Frantically, he had unbuttoned his shirt and grabbed a round golden medallion, the size of a small coin, from his neck. He had pulled it off, breaking the chain, and had held it high toward Janco as if it were a talisman. In the middle of the medallion was a tear-shaped ruby which glistened once or twice in the semidarkness.

Janco's passage had been completely blocked with massive stones. He had run back down. Babulescu was no longer in the library. That bastard would come back with the soldiers any second now. As Janco had escaped through his chink in the wall, he'd heard soldiers shouting and running into the castle. But he had been running too; he had run most of the way back to his cottage.

Now, in the cottage, one hour before sunrise, he remembered the writer's words.

According to legend, the vampires surround themselves with people of influence and importance, powerful allies who eventually become their servants. If Babulescu was one of them, his words on that fateful morning might be an important clue. "We are *helpless, powerless.*" Who did he mean by "we"? Michea? His mother?

Janco often wondered just what role Michea's mother was playing. Obviously, a vurdalak does not need a mother. While the legends mention his woman companion, she is called Zerkal, the mirror. There is nothing about a *mother*. And a very old mother at that. Hardly another vampire. The old caretaker thought she was a witch. Now that may be more like it. A protector of his highness . . . Well, whatever she was, she had been carried out on the stretchers, so she couldn't be much of a protector now.

Helpless . . . powerless, too? God's intervention? I hope they are helpless! . . . Helpless? He shook his head. Michea had not looked helpless when he appeared. For a few seconds, Janco had thought he would leap into the room and tear both their throats out. But then, he had not been invited. Janco grinned. At least that part of the legend held true, thank God!

What puzzled and disturbed Janco was the fact that now, almost before dawn, no attempts had been made to lure him away. The silence continued, dead and ominous. He did not like it.

"Wake up, Nikola!" He shook his friend and Nikolai jumped up.

"We must get ready. Soon it will be our turn to go hunting."

Nicolai rubbed his eyes, touched the big lump on his temple.

How long have I been out?"

"About four hours. I had to do it, " Janco apologized. "You were about to go outside."

Nikolai felt his parched lips. "Do you have any water?"

"Of course, I have water. Hey, wait—" His teakettle was empty, overturned on the floor. The brook with clear mountain water was only a few dozen steps behind the cottage. But something was wrong!

"Janco, I am very thirsty," Nikolai insisted. "I must have some water."

"Drink this." Janco pushed a bottle of vodka toward him, but Nikolai refused.

"Just give me some water."

Holy water! That's it, Janco remembered. Nikola wouldn't know the difference. He poured a cup out of the flask. Nikolai drank it all at once. Janco poured him the rest, and Nikolai guzzled it down.

"Now I feel better." He sighed. "Well, let us get ready."

It was that gray time when the night is over, but the morning has not yet opened its eyes. The dew was heavy and clear, the rabbits and the birds were beginning to wake up, and the mountains were enveloped in a tender blanket of mist. Two figures walked cautiously across the small clearing and into the silent forest.

Two kilometers along the road, in the Valley of Blood, they sat down in a patch of tall grass to rest before their climb. It was getting light now. The castle was curiously tilted to one side, ready to fall.

Here and there, large, deep cracks in the ground ran menacingly across the meadow.

"I don't like it, Nikola." Janco was concerned. "They are not making any moves."

"Maybe they are hiding?"

"When I was at the castle today . . ." Janco related the meeting with Babulescu.

"He might have meant that Michea himself is helpless, powerless?"

"Oh, sure, helpless. Almost knocking our hut down?"

"Lead the way." Janco stood, his bow at the ready.

Another fifteen minutes of climbing. Some overturned rocks and earth.

"Nothing here." Nikolai felt his bump again. "I told you there was nothing. Perhaps we should split up."

"No, no, Nikola. We are going together. Come on!" They circled around some more. Nothing.

Just then, Janco noticed a glint of light in the bushes next to a very large boulder.

"Stop!" he whispered. "Take a look."

Nikolai looked. For a split second, he also saw the brightness. For some reason, Nikolai felt much better, refreshed from his sleep in the hut. The nightmare was almost over. For the first time since he had left the castle, Sally had not appeared laughing at him in his dreams. Janco was already walking toward the big boulder. Nikolai followed. Stupid, he thought, my holding onto this dagger. He held it firmly nonetheless.

There was nothing in the bushes, at least, nothing was shining anymore. Must have been some kind of reflection, thought Nikolai. Both of them wanted to see something, anything, and here was this flash—just a reflection. Perhaps some drops of dew, maybe an indirect ray of sun, although the sun wasn't due to come up for at least another half hour.

"Watch out!" Janco yelled. They both stopped, then tried to run. Too late.

Right under them, the very earth was turning around: the bushes, the rocks, everything was moving upside down and in a circular motion. Suddenly they were floating in a space vacuum. The sky was under their feet; the mist was so thick that they could barely see each other. And everything moved even faster, around and around. The sensation they both experienced was like taking a hot shower and an ice-cold shower simultaneously. They were flying through some giant wind tunnel without beginning or end. Faster and faster! When their lungs felt ready to burst, the phenomenon ended as suddenly as it had begun.

Once again, their feet were firmly on the ground. But it was a different kind of ground. And the terrain around them was also totally different, different and strange. They both rubbed their eyes to make sure they were not imagining things.

They were in a narrow passage between two huge mountains of solid black granite. There was no grass, no vegetation. The passage was littered with sharp, jagged stones that shone like shards of colored glass. At the end of the passage, massive iron gates stood ajar, just wide enough for one person to squeeze through. Near the gates sat a ragged old woman holding a candle.

"This is not happening," Nikolai said aloud, mainly to reassure himself. He still had the dagger; Janco, his bow and one arrow. The rest of his arrows were gone.

"Let us see if the old hag can talk," Janco replied.

"Where are we?" they asked.

The ancient woman moved her lips, but no sound came out.

Nikolai noticed tears streaming down her wrinkled, toothless face.

ten

The old woman cried silently, and Nikolai had the feeling that her tears were meant for the two of them. He wanted to tell her something, to console her. She looked terribly old; her grimy rags hung loosely around her emaciated body.

The tops of the two black mountains around them were shrouded in thick purple mist. There was no way for them to scale the slick granite. The passage on which they stood led back only fifty meters or so and then it was blocked by another granite mountain. A trap!

The iron gates next to the old woman were a marvel to behold. Nikolai and Janco had never seen anything like them. They were about five meters tall, topped with vicious-looking spikes. Had the gates been closed, Nikolai thought, even a shell from a medium-size cannon could not have penetrated the massive iron. Janco bent down and noticed old engravings near the bottom: animals such as no one had seen, and dragons. And, within a circular pattern, sometimes solidly rusted over, the inevitable: the snake, the bat, and the wolf—symbols of the vampire. They had come to the right place after all. The old woman's candle flickered and died. Now the only light emanated in eerie multicolored rays from somewhere inside the gates. There were no locks on the gates. They were open just enough for a big man such as Nikolai to squeeze through sideways.

Nikolai said, "I think we're invited."

"That's what I am afraid of." Janco still clung to his bow and arrow. "I don't like being invited."

"We can't go back anyway," Nikolai reasoned, and pushed himself through the narrow opening. Janco followed.

As soon as they stepped inside, the old hag sprang to her feet with alarming speed, screeching in triumph. She did have a voice, and what a voice! In one motion, she slammed the gates shut as easily as if they were made of straw. She screeched and laughed on the other side for a few more minutes. When she stopped, Janco whispered, "Let's try and push them open." They both tried, but nothing happened. The gates seemed sealed forever, and outside the old woman now lay dead. The trap was tightening.

Janco cursed long and hard. He reached in his knapsack and pulled out the last bottle of vodka. Without offering any to Nikolai, he drank from it while carefully watching the scenery unfold in front of them.

If, indeed, any human being can conceive of what paradise might be, this was surely the place. There were more lights in front of them, wonderful colored rays coming directly at them from all sides. They were standing on something soft and pleasant. Their tired feet felt very comfortable, even warm. There were distant sounds of music, like the strings of a mandolin. They were on a path lined with flowers, translucent blossoms which emanated the most sensual aroma. A pond with dark blue water was nearby, its banks covered with blooms resembling giant pink waterlilies. Exotic birds flew overhead, singing. A pheasant walked importantly across the path. On the pond's surface, three white swans swam proudly toward a wooden bridge which connected both shores.

Nikolai was gazing about when Janco raised his bow. They heard a roar overhead and a massive metal net fell down on the path, knocking the bow out of Janco's hand and crushing it on the soft ground. Immediately, a tiny man, wrapped from head to toe in a robe of brown cloth, appeared at the edge of the net with several leather thongs in his hands. He looked at the empty net in amazement, frantically searching for his quarry. His net had missed!

Janco grabbed the little man and lifted him up. The little man cursed and dropped his leather thongs, scratching and biting at Janco's huge arms. With one hand, Janco held him tight by the scruff of his neck.

"Let's see what you look like." He took the hood off the man's face with his other hand and brought him into the light. Nikolai and Janco turned away.

The face was actually a shrunken skull with a few black hairs and fragments of flesh stuck to the blackened pate here and there, slits of what had been Oriental eyes leered out from under the gnarled brows. He apparently had once been a Mongol.

Revolted, Janco dropped the hideous creature to the ground. The ghoul jumped up and scurried into the bushes. Janco threw his hunting knife after him. The creature stopped, reeling from the terrific impact of the large knife, fell backward with a moan, and lay still. Janco walked over and pulled the knife out. The creature was dead.

"Look, Nikola, no blood, just some slime." He wiped off his knife and stuck it back in its sheath. "Nice place this is!" His hands trembled slightly as he drank the rest of his vodka and threw the bottle into the magnificent pond, startling the swans.

"You know what's really amazing?" He turned to Nikolai. "We must be in a giant cavern. I thought as much when we entered, but now I'm almost certain. These lights must be reflections from stalactites and crystals. This is an underground lake. But why are there no signs of an earthquake?"

Nikolai, too, felt they were in some enormous cavern. The weird lights, quite probably a reflection, created an illusion of the bottomless sky above, and the aroma of flowers—but . . . how could anyone explain the flowers and the animals and the birds?

Janco consulted his compass; it was not working.

"We must be almost under the castle. You'd think that this cave would be the first thing to collapse."

They both felt strangely relaxed, exhilarated, their first triumph compounded by an unreal feeling of invincibility. They sat down near the bridge and looked across the water at the other side. Near the opposite bank, a mansion resembling a Greek or Roman temple appeared to be flying on a cloud of thick mist. The magnificent building was surrounded by gardens, statues, and fountains spouting clear, sparkling water.

A small, very appealing animal resembling a koala bear walked across the path, stopped by Janco, and put his head on the hunter's knee expecting to be petted. When Janco stroked his head, the animal made soft purring noises and then wandered off under a bush with fiery red and green flowers.

"We'd better be on our way." Janco shook Nikolai's shoulder.

Nikolai now felt he could stay on this sensuous mosslike ground forever. The mandolins, the aroma, and the beauty of the place were making his head swim. He reluctantly lifted himself up and they walked across the bridge.

Why am I carrying this stupid dagger in such a wonderful place? Without hesitation, Nikolai stopped in the middle of the bridge and dropped his dagger into the dark blue water. One of the swans swam over to the ripple and lowered his head twice as if to thank Nikolai for his friendly gesture.

"You idiot!" Janco shook him again. "What the hell is the matter with you?"

"We don't need it, we don't need any weapons." Nikolai was smiling, a faraway gleam in his eyes. He stared at the mansion, which was bathed in a soft reddish glow. Sally would be there waiting for him, he was sure of that, and nothing else mattered. She would welcome him, dressed in her mysterious black silks, wearing strange jewelry and scented with her strange, intoxicating perfume. Time would stop; he would be with her for all eternity. Nothing else mattered.

"You *idiot!*" Janco interrupted his reverie, and Nikolai suddenly wished that the gruff hunter would go away and leave him alone. How could there be any danger? A tiny, fantastic bird with shimmering, multicolored feathers landed on Nikolai's shoulders and sang to him of things only he could understand, of secret desires and things he yearned for, of supernatural pleasures. He could have it all now, in a few more steps.

"Leave me, Janco," he begged, as they crossed the pond. The bird flew away.

On the other side, the ground was even softer. They were walking on a down mattress, on a soft cloud. Many more flowers appeared, and birds. The statues were white, highly realistic. Mongol warriors, frozen in the midst of their charge, converged on the mansion from all directions, their faces contorted with rage, their weapons held at the ready. Yet even this harrowing sight failed to break the feeling of happiness, of wondrous anticipation that gripped Nikolai so strongly when they sat down to rest on the path. How meaningless his life had been until now. His marriage, his army days, the war, his career—all of it amounted to less than nothing. Until now, he had been blind, a mere human being, a sheep. Now he was stepping over some miraculous threshold into greatness, into a state of love and timeless joy.

Janco stopped to touch and examine the statues.

Forget him, an inner voice told Nikolai, *he is a trespasser and he will be severely punished. You and I, we, belong here, in our moonflower garden. I can stay here forever. I will stay here forever with you.*

Nikolai walked quickly past the first few statues, toward the mansion, aglow and warm, a shimmering palace of pleasures and delights. And eternity was here, right here, in this magical garden, within these plants and flowers, between the glorious blossoms and the bottomless sky. He finally saw the familiar black silhouette, the vision he had longed for every night in his beach cottage. Behind one of the statues—a glimpse! He ran, but she wasn't there. The black figure was near the entrance to the mansion now, her arms outstretched toward him.

"Hurry, my beloved," she sang to him. "The sun is approaching; the master may return at any moment, hurry."

Nikolai ran toward her. Once again she disappeared. This time he was sure she was inside, waiting. He thought of nothing except her silks, her eyes, the strangeness of her kiss.

He heard Janco shouting, hurrying after him. . . . He saw a statue topple from its pedestal, shaking the ground. He ran, jumping over the steps. Within seconds, he was inside the mansion.

Janco knew that they had been deceived when the first statue fell down. He abandoned any attempt to stop Nikolai; instead he knelt to take a closer look at the fallen statue. Something unusual about the grotesque figure alarmed him.

The statue was a remarkable piece of work: a Tartar warrior armed with a lance, poised to throw his weapon at something or someone in the mansion. Janco remembered how he himself had been prevented from releasing his arrow, how Michea's raised hand had frozen him like one of these statues. Perhaps, he thought, these stone warriors had once been real soldiers sent to destroy the mansion and its occupants.

Feverishly, Janco began to examine the other statues. Each one was damaged in spots, as if it had fallen down before and then been reassembled. Large cracks disfigured the white limestone. The weapons were real: wooden lances with copper points, stout bows strung with gut, arrows with soft feathers at one end, cold iron at the other.

He pushed one of the cracked stone warriors and the statue began to topple. It fell to the ground with a loud, hollow thud and broke into several pieces. Then, almost in unison, the other statues began to fall and break apart, their weight shaking the ground of the cavern.

This totally revived Janco. He was again an alert, crafty hunter. And not a moment too soon.

The lights began to change dramatically. The cavern was now dark, bright red beams outlining the mansion. An icy wind blew from all directions; Janco was forced to shield his face and turn aside to escape the gusts.

He felt pain, something very sharp cutting into his left shoulder, cutting to the bone. He spun around and saw Michea standing behind him, a curved, shiny dagger raised in his hand. Janco jumped back again, pulled out his own hunting knife. His left hand was hanging useless, the pain in his shoulder increasing. Michea struck again, with lightning speed, but this time he missed the hunter completely: the dagger swung through the empty air a hair's distance from Janco's throat.

Janco kept retreating. I can't keep it up any longer, he realized. Michea is too fast and I am losing too much blood. He stumbled backward and fell over one of the fallen statues. Again, Michea's dagger struck nothing but air.

My knife! God, Janco prayed, one good throw. Just let him stay in one place for a few moments. One throw is all I need.

Michea did pause, looming over his prey, his dagger raised, his long hair flowing in the wind. In the red light, his face looked thoughtful, even gentle, like the face of an angel on a Byzantine icon illuminated by a *lompada*.

"You found me, hunter." He spoke in a barely recognizable ancient Moldavian dialect. "You found me and now you must pay the price. Only your blood will settle this debt. Oh, yes, I must have it! It is the only substance I need."

Keep talking, Janco thought, I am almost ready.

Michea had a curious expression on his face, a mixture of boredom and sadness. He hesitated with his dagger.

"We have something in common." He actually smiled, revealing sharp, catlike fangs. "We both hunt. You hunt defenseless animals, taking their lives and their skins . . . I hunt human beings." His face twisted with revulsion. "The whimpering, stupid, sniveling, treacherous beings who are lower than the lowest pig."

"Why, then, do you take human form?" Janco asked. Whatever Michea might do, he was ready now. But time was running out.

"I take many forms." Michea's gaze was now transfixed on Janco's bleeding hand and his shoulder. "I am the mist, the wind, the vurdalak. But hear me, hunter, before you die. I don't hunt or kill or torture for my pleasure. I need blood, and I am tortured beyond any suffering known to man. My pain is eternal," he added grimly. "You are much more fortunate; you live and you die, while I must continue."

Not if I can help it. Janco aimed his knife at Michea's throat, threw it, and then passed out.

Outside the cave and the castle, after a fierce night battle, fifty of Tamerlane's hand-picked soldiers were searching the grounds. They looked under every bush, turned over every stone near the Valley of Blood. The sun was high; the Mongols were tired. Finally, their commander, a very tall, lean Tartar stood up and shook the scalps and the bones of his vanquished enemies which were sewn to his leather caftan, and raised his curved sword, still red from last night's bloodbath. He whistled loudly. The small horses reared up and had to be restrained, but the warriors stood absolutely still. Wide grins appeared on their savage faces. They had found the entrance to the sanctuary; their task would soon be accomplished. They could now return in triumph to Samarkand, and the glorious court of Timur the Lame.

One hundred of them had left central Asia with orders to bring back Michea's head. There was no force in the world capable of stopping them. The Tartars of the Golden Horde were mere boys compared to these fighters. Outnumbered twenty to one by Michea's Moldavians, they fought a series of daring ambushes, forcing Michea to abandon his troops and flee. Relentlessly, they pursued the Moldavian prince across the endless steppes and snow-covered mountains, across burned-out cities and forest villages, until they had tracked him down to his sanctuary.

Michea drank the blood slowly, savoring every drop. Then, as the pulse grew fainter, he made an incision under the hunter's heart and drank directly from the wound. The blood of the dead was poison, the blood of the living was his nourishment.

Hunted, he thought. I myself was hunted: many humans have hunted me through the ages, but I always drank their blood as they died. All except the priest. Michea remembered with great satisfaction how the priest had finally broken down under torture and squealed like the pig he was. *That* priest, Nikodim, the last of his troublesome family. Now only Setozar remained, of all his enemies. Michea saw again that scene deep in the Russian forest. He was so engrossed, he almost missed the moment of the hunter's death. Michea stood up, wiped the blood from his face, looked down at the large man, dignified even in death. Courage was the only human quality he had learned to respect. At first, he attributed it to sheer stupidity: the stupidity of Tamerlane's soldiers, the stupidity of Batu Khan, Murad the First, Bayezid the Thunderbolt, Ivan the Terrible, Mohammed the Second, John Hunyadi, and countless other rulers. Fools! They all wanted immortality. But, he had come to feel, there was more to courage than simple foolishness.

He remembered Tamerlane's warriors climbing over his gates, impaling themselves on the spikes so that their comrades could climb safely over their bodies. That had been a frightening hour for Michea, the only time he had ever felt fear. The only time he had felt threatened. Until now.

He remembered them screaming and running across his beautiful garden. The devil himself could not have stopped them! He had felt the Tartar's sword as it severed his head from his shoulders, and the total blackness and emptiness that had enveloped temporarily the prince of all vampires.

He touched his neck where the hunter's knife had cut him a few minutes ago. The wound had already healed.

The hunter's aim was good; his courage had lasted to the very end. Michea turned to look at the red rays shining on his mansion. The sun was already over the Dubrava castle; it was time to immerse himself in his casket, to rest, to dream, to travel in space.

Why do I take the human form so frequently? That question from the dying hunter bothered him. To survive, he thought, to continue. There had been hundreds of vampires on this earth as recently as the nineteenth century; tens of thousands of people worshiped me as god, among them great and mighty rulers who sought the same kind of immortality. Only a few hundred humans worship me today. Immortality? Michea sneered. Now there were no more than a dozen vampires on this entire earth. And they are rapidly losing their powers, becoming careless and stupid. And most of the present-day rulers only believe in things they can see and understand. The bat, the wolf, and the snake, they no longer matter. The wolves are nearly extinct; there are so few of them left in the Carpathian Mountains.

These humans, though, multiply and multiply. Surely they'll destroy one another . . . but not before destroying every other creature.

Zerkal! He remembered. My dear, unfaithful companion. She cannot remain here. She must go back across the ocean to the people she knew as a human, the people who did not believe in anything except gold. Their blood is young and strong. She must leave before the coming sunset. The time is drawing near. And I must kill her lover. Nikolai can still destroy us both, though he does not realize it. Another stupid, arrogant man. Michea smiled in anticipation of torturing his rival; he imagined the breaking point, when Nikolai would whimper and cry out in mortal agony. If only I could spend an entire night with him as I did with the priest. If only the circle of time was not drawing so perilously close.

I must summon the gypsies immediately, he decided, to make suitable travel arrangements for Zerkal.

He became aware that other humans were now searching the grounds above, trying to find the entrance to his sanctuary. It did not matter; the sanctuary did not exist anymore, the iron gates were torn asunder.

I, too, must leave, he thought sadly, to find another sanctuary, to create another moonflower garden, a paradise for all my senses. He looked past Janco to where his beautiful pond had been. The water was gone, exposing hundreds of tiny human skeletons lining the bottom.

Human form? Again, he looked at Janco. Perhaps my human form is no longer useful, not in this time of transition. He bent down, placed his dagger near Janco's head, and struck the ground twice with his fists. A large gray wolf ran swiftly into the ruins of his mansion.

eleven

Nikolai was touching her one moment; the next moment, she was gone. Just as on the beach beyond his cottage, he felt hot and cold at the same time. He looked past the golden sarcophagus, past the crumbling columns. Not a sound. White mist entered the chamber, bringing paralyzing fear. His euphoria was gone. "I must find her, I must, I must," he kept repeating, as if his own salvation depended on it. He tried moving toward the sarcophagus but couldn't lift his feet. He realized that he was no longer even standing on the mosaic-laden floor. He was hanging, suspended, in some unknown void. Time itself had stopped. He was no longer inside Michea's mansion. On second thought, he felt he was wrong. Time did not stand still in this damp, frightening void surrounding him. It was somehow turning backward. He was moving. He was not suspended motionless in the void anymore. He was being shot through it like an arrow, hurled backward with incredible speed and force.

Then he felt himself slowing down; some objects began coming into view. He was still an object flying from point A to point B, but his feet were beginning to touch the ground. He was moving slowly, very slowly, until he felt planted firmly on marble, on what he realized was the floor of the main hall of Dubrava castle. He was standing several steps removed from the remains of the bas-relief of the devil, the famous tourist attraction cast from the sketches of Leonardo da Vinci.

The hall was dimly illuminated by two black candles on top of a podium covered with scarlet velvet, just underneath the bas-relief. There were about a dozen other figures in the hall, all wearing long black robes. Most were chanting or praying. A strange ritual of some kind was in progress.

Angrily, Nikolai noted that the museum guard, his rifle leaning carelessly against the wall, was fast asleep near the entrance. He thought of walking over and waking him up and having all the trespassers arrested. But he quickly found out that he could not move, not one muscle! He was a captive observer. Why did Michea bring me here? he wondered. What is he trying to tell me?

Nikolai's curiosity was now functioning fully. Although the figures were wearing dark robes, their faces were not covered. Nikolai recognized among the dancing, chanting figures moving in a semicircle around the podium two prominent Romanians: one a deputy minister for cultural affairs; the other, the novelist Babulescu. And others seemed familar, too. Strangely enough, Nikolai did not feel uncomfortable or even frightened. Just the opposite—he felt a new kind of energy surging through his body, a pleasant, reassuring sensation. He looked more closely: a policeman is always a policeman! Nikolai took pride in the fact that once he had seen a face, he never forgot it. This was indeed an interesting collection! Besides the Romanians, there was an English lady wealthy enough to buy half of Europe, a top-ranking American diplomat, a Japanese industrialist, and what was this? Nikolai's hair began to stand up. A lieutenant general from his own Ministry of the Interior, a man of unblemished reputation! Another man, dancing and chanting in some unknown language, was the chief theoretician of the Communist party of the Soviet Union, a man whose power was exceeded only by Brezhnev himself. What had happened to his entourage, his bodyguards, Nikolai wondered. There had to be some logic, even in an illusion. And what a fantastic illusion this was! He felt he was physically present at some ancient pagan ceremony.

I . . . why am I here? Because Michea wants me to be a witness. This has something to do with Sally. And I must save her. I must survive!

The chanting and the silly dancing, which consisted of hopping and whirling like dervishes in a trance, grew more frantic, more intense. But not one figure bumped into Nikolai. This, he thought, was interesting too.

As the chanting reached a crescendo, two clouds of fine white mist appeared in front of the podium and dissolved into two figures: a man and a woman wearing ancient black attire from the Romanian past. The man was also wearing a small gold crown. He was unmistakably young Michea.

The couple stood, their backs to the bas-relief, facing the semicircle of followers. The woman's face was very pale. The lower part was covered by a silk veil. Only her eyes were visible. Black and empty, two pieces of coal, but Nikolai recognized them. He gasped, but no one heard him. Michea held a small bundle in his arms. To his horror, Nikolai realized what it was. Howls of delight went up from a dozen throats. A dozen very hungry animals were ready to devour their favorite meal. With a rather bored movement and contempt in his eyes, Michea threw the bundle into the midst of his followers, then turned to face the bas-relief of the devil. The bundle landed among the black robes. There was an innocent cry, then a shriek. Tiny limbs were being torn apart. The blood sprayed the bas-relief. The howls and grunts continued for a few more seconds.

Nikolai felt ill. He could not breathe. At that moment, he very much wanted only to die.

As it became quiet again, Michea turned back to his followers. He reached for his jeweled dagger, pulled it out of its sheath. He held it high with his right hand. With his left, he held the slender hand of the woman.

His followers dropped to their knees, their faces covered with their bloody hands, their foreheads touching the ground.

Michea spoke in a Moldavian dialect: "I am nearing the end of my loneliness," he said quietly. "No longer shall I endure the agony which only my master can understand. Zerkal is now prepared to share my journey." He turned to the woman, made a quick incision on his, then on her arm, tiny incisions; only a drop or two of darl blood was visible on their white skin.

"So that's what it was! He wants me to be a witness to his wedding ceremony." A supreme insult. Anger was filling Nikolai's entire body, but he could do nothing.

Michea looked at his followers. Something was bothering him. "On your knees!" he shrieked. A strong gust of icy wind blew across the hall.

Nikolai felt his legs knocked from under him. He was kneeling on the floor. He touched the marble with his hands.

Michea's shriek, however, had not been directed at him. One

218

figure, tall and powerful, remained standing near the stairway. The wind and the force of Michea's order had failed to move him.

Very slowly, the tall figure approached Michea, who was standing with an expression of both astonishment and fear on his young face.

"Who are you?" Michea asked. He asked it as if he already knew the answer. "How dare you disturb my ritual?" Michea's face was transforming rapidly from that of a handsome, almost angelic-looking young prince into a hideous animal resembling a large wolf. Long yellow fangs appeared at the corners of his mouth; gray hair grew on his hollow cheeks; his eyes changed; sharp, hairy claws held the dagger. His dagger was pointed straight at the heart of the intruder.

The stranger removed his robe, letting it fall to the floor of the castle with an ear-splitting crash. The walls and the floor shook; the dark figures on the floor cringed and whimpered.

Silence again.

The tall, lean figure advanced toward Michea and Zerkal, advanced slowly, confidently. He was dressed as a hunter, in a brown bear-fur coat and deerskin boots. He had long white hair and a beard. Nikolai noticed a deep red scar across his face. He held a large double-edged sword in his hands. On his head was a small crown. It was similar to the crown Michea wore, except this one had a cross in the middle, a simple cross of gold, which shone in the semidarkness of the castle.

Zerkal gasped, turned to the bas-relief, and covered her eyes.

Michea did not move back. He watched the intruder and waited, ready to spring. Then, when the stranger was near, Michea swiftly struck a mortal blow with his dagger.

It was the fastest movement Nikolai had ever seen. There could be no defense against it. Yet the intruder almost laughingly moved backward and raised his huge sword, easily deflecting Michea's dagger, sending it flying out of the vurdalak's claws and across the hall.

Michea moved backward next to Zerkal, next to the bas-relief. He looked up at the devil as if begging him silently to intervene.

"You cannot kill me, vurdalak." The stranger laughed. His laughter reverberated throughout the walls of Dubrava castle, sending another wave of anguished cries and moans from Michea's followers, who were afraid to look up from the floor or even move. "And I cannot kill you." The language he was speaking was mysterious; it certainly was not Romanian, but Nikolai understood him, and apparently Michea did as well.

"Why are you trespassing in my domain?" Michea's eyes reflected sheer terror. Once more, in a desperate effort, he sprang up, seizing the man's throat. He tried to tear it out with his huge fangs and claws. So ferocious was his assault that the man was almost knocked off his feet. His crown with the cross fell on the floor, along with his sword. The struggle continued for a few seconds until the intruder managed to lift Michea up in the air, throwing him against the bas-relief.

Then he calmly picked up his crown and sword, and laughed again.

"I cannot harm you, vurdalak, and you cannot harm me. I am but a messenger of my master. And my master has a fine sense of justice."

Michea understood. He screamed, howled, jumped at the stranger again. "No, Setozar," he cried. "You cannot!" His assault this time was sluggish, weak. Setozar pushed him back against the bas-relief without any effort.

Setozar looked at the helpless vurdalak and raised his sword. He held it raised for a moment, then struck with it, not at Michea, but at Zerkal's black silks.

Even as an incredibly bright bolt of lightning cut the bas-relief of the devil in two, as smoke appeared, as the walls of the castle began to crumble, as the ceiling and balcony collapsed and the floor began to sink . . . even as Michea's followers began to jump up and try desperately to escape from being sucked into dark holes which began to appear in the middle of the floor; even as chaos and panic enveloped the castle, it was Michea's agonizing scream that was the most frightening sound, rising high above the terrible earthquake.

Setozar's sword, which had struck Zerkal, remained imbedded in the marble of the bas-relief. Some of Zerkal's silks hung on the blade, while some fell limply to the floor. There was no blood, no body. Nothing remained of Zerkal. Michea stopped screaming. He picked up a piece of the silk, pressed it to his chest.

Now the stairway of the castle collapsed. Everyone seemed doomed.

"Where is she, Setozar?" Michea asked imploringly, a young king once more, with great sadness on his beautiful face. "Tell me," he whispered. "How can I find her?"

220

"You cannot find her, vurdalak," Setozar replied, also with a trace of sadness. "Part of her went back in time. Another part traveled into the future. You will not find her. Not until the Day of Judgment."

Nikolai realized now that the floor was no longer under his feet. He was disappearing into a large dark crack in the ground. Wind, flames, and dust engulfed him. He was flying into an abyss.

The abyss grew wider. Clearly there were great fires at the bottom. Huge rocks, other bodies—some naked, some still dressed in black robes—were flying past him. So this is death, he thought. And this is the inferno? At precisely that moment, Nikolai managed to open his eyes.

His feet were now firmly planted on the ancient mosaic tiles. There was no more white mist. Ahead of him stood the familiar small figure of Startz, his service revolver raised, pointed toward Michea's sarcophagus.

"Startz!" Nikolai cried out, putting his hand on his friend's shoulder. "Let us go. No need. You *cannot* kill him." His hand suddenly lost all strength; he was passing out.

twelve

"Excuse me, Comrade Colonel, could this be what we are looking for?" The young blond sergeant showed Startz a deep, narrow crack in the ground, just large enough for two men.

Startz sat by the side of the chasm, aimed his flashlight. The crack ended some fifteen meters below. There was a reddish glow at the bottom.

"It may well be. Get the ropes." Startz was forever grateful to the serious-looking captain for insisting that they take complete mountain-climbing equipment, including ropes, picks, kerosene lamps, axes, and even a first-aid pack.

"Radio our position," Startz ordered the driver, "and wait for us here no matter what. If we are not back within an hour, be sure that your captain sends out a search party."

Startz and the two soldiers began the climb down. The descent was relatively easy. The crack, which was actually much wider at the bottom, led into what appeared to be a giant underground cavern, complete with subterranean vegetation. The cavern was illuminated by a reddish glow, a reflection of some indirect light that glinted on the long stalactites and crystals lining the massive ceiling. Signs of the earthquake were all around them. Mountains of stones and black granite blocked their paths. Startz walked cautiously ahead, followed by the soldiers, holding their lamps in one hand, their automatic weapons in the other

But as they progressed, Startz realized their potential peril. "Put your weapons down," he whispered. "One single shot and the whole cavern will collapse."

They went farther in; there was more exotic vegetation: red and green translucent flowers emanating a sweet, strong aroma. A bird flew from one of the bushes, a most beautiful bird, its feathers illuminating the darkness with all colors of the rainbow. A strange animal darted from one bush to another, scaring both soldiers.

"Comrade Colonel," one of them asked, overwhelmed, "what have we found?"

"Whatever we find"—Startz was speaking in his commanding tone of voice—"however improbable it may appear, all of it, everything must remain a state secret. Not one word of this can escape, not even to your captain."

The soldiers did not like this order, but what could they do? They followed Startz reluctantly, looking around with their mouths hanging open in utter disbelief.

Their first inkling that the cavern might have been occupied came when they happened upon two pieces of the fallen gates, one segment partly buried in the earth, the other wholly visible, spikes and all.

Startz held his breath. So these were the legendary iron gates? The soldiers were alarmed.

"Comrade Colonel," stammered the sergeant, "how could these things get in here? They must weigh at least ten tons. And look at those spikes!"

"This must be an accursed place," the other soldier said. "I heard about it when I was a child. Please, Comrade Colonel, let us turn back."

Startz, too, was astounded by the size of the fallen gates. What an archeological discovery! How had they been installed so far below the ground? A marvel of engineering; such skill had gone into the hinges and mechanism. Perhaps when Michea was a real prince, he might have sent hundreds of his entrusted slaves to install them.

Startz was suddenly aware of the soldiers' fear. "What are you?" he asked. "Old women? And you, how did you ever earn your rank?" he asked the sergeant. "Follow me!"

The soldiers followed, more reluctant with every step. They saw the metal net buried under an avalanche of colored stones. Then they came to what had once been a pond. All three gazed silently at what was now a valley of skeletons, most of them the remains of small children.

"This is the work of a vurdalak," said the soldier who had begged to return. He slowly crossed himself, turned around, and walked back. The sergeant wanted to stop him.

"Let him go," said Startz. "Are you with me?"

"I am with you," the sergeant replied. "If you have the courage to walk across, so have I."

On the other side of the bridge they found Janco's body. Behind it, the ruins of the mansion were illuminated in a menacing red glow.

Poor hunter. Startz crossed Janco's hands on his chest. Then he saw Michea's dagger, picked it up, and dropped it in his knapsack. "You hold it." He gave the knapsack to the sergeant. "I am going alone from here."

"Comrade Colonel, I cannot permit you to go." The sergeant was determined.

"Well"—this time Startz gave an order—"you *will* wait for me outside these ruins. Do not go inside! If I am not back within fifteen minutes, return to the surface as fast as you can."

They both heard a distant rumbling sound. Another tremor, however slight, could bury them forever. Startz climbed cautiously over fallen columns and walked toward the mansion. The interior was not too badly damaged. The mosaic floor had been cracked deeply; some parts of the massive walls had collapsed, shattering several of the columns which stood in a circle. At the center of this unholy sanctuary, on a pedestal of solid gold, lay a huge open coffin of beaten gold, engraved with grotesque bas-reliefs of snakes, bats, and wolves, and studded with precious jewels which glittered in the eerie reddish light.

So this was the treasure that had lured the archeologists to their doom.

Startz held his breath, his heart pounding. This was, at long last, the place. He stepped over a crack in the floor, advanced toward the casket.

He studied the incredibly exquisite engravings and bas-reliefs of snakes, bats, and wolves; their eyes were large rubies and emeralds. The writing was unlike any known language. It resembled Egyptian or Assyrian hieroglyphics. For a second, Startz could not help but

224

think that in terms of money alone this treasure, this casket, must be worth billions of *lei,* hundreds of millions of dollars. No wonder the German archeologists were so interested.

He noticed that several of the columns around the casket were leaning, cracked in places, and just about ready to fall.

There was no time to lose. Startz slowly pulled out his revolver, pressed down on the safety catch, and climbed the pedestal to look into the casket.

There was a body in it: a man. His youthful, naked body was reclining comfortably. For a moment, Startz was reminded of a bather at a fashionable spa. The body was immersed in blood, which looked innocent in the deceptive light—like rose wine. The man's breathing was even, his eyes closed; an expression of total bliss radiated from his white face.

Revulsion and horror ran through Startz's mind as he remembered the tiny bones on the dry lake bed. He took careful aim at the sleeping man and prepared to pull the trigger. Something stopped him, paralyzed him. He watched Michea slowly open his eyes and raise himself in the casket.

Michea did not get up completely. He sat gazing at Startz, his face expressionless, his eyes devoid of all feeling. It was as though a giant were looking at an ant.

"Put down that toy," he said in a language Startz barely recognized. "I command you."

thirteen

When Nikolai's hands touched him, Startz managed to tear his eyes from the vurdalak. He felt that the powerful spell he was under was somehow broken, and that they both had a chance to escape the terrible creature in the golden sarcophagus. Startz's mind began functioning again. He realized that Nikolai must have come from another passage, somewhere to the left. That had to be the way back to the garden.

"Nikola, wake up. You must wake up. We have no time!" He dragged Nikolai across the floor toward the entrance. He prayed the blond sergeant would still be waiting. Nikolai's eyes had a glazed, faraway look. He tried getting up but did not have the strength. His mouth was open; he was whispering some nonsense about how he wanted to die anyway, that there was no use dragging him out of here.

Fortunately, he did not have the strength to resist being pulled. When they passed the last column, the sergeant was still there. He ran over to help. Both of them dragged Nikolai over the statues, across the garden toward the pond.

Startz stopped to catch his breath, to look at one of the statues. The head of a giant Tartar warrior lay on the ground, his saber twisted. For a fraction of a second, it seemed to Startz that the savage, horribly scarred face was actually smiling; a flicker of life appeared in the narrow lime-colored eyes.

With Nikolai still protesting weakly, they struggled past Janco's body, across the bridge over the lake of bones, and ran toward the tiny shaft of light that penetrated into the devil's lair. The rumbling was loud and close now. Another tremor was surely on its way.

As if in a dream, Startz found himself lying in a sea of poppies. The sun, the real sun, blazed in a cloudless blue sky! He rolled away from the crack, filled his lungs with the clean air of the earth.

Next to him, the blond sergeant was crying and crossing himself repeatedly.

The tremor was approaching. Startz saw a column of dust and small stones fly up from the hole. Then the ground moved slightly; the crack closed. Everything was still. Startz got up, looked at the place where the crack, the hole, had been. He looked at it for a long time.

Another jeep, with the captain and two medics, one of them wearing a Red Cross armband, pulled up.

"Comrade Colonel"—the captain gently touched Startz's shoulder—"you three were really lucky. We pulled out just as this hole was blowing up. You fainted. Too much gas. These gases could be dangerous."

Next to Startz, Nikolai was grinning from ear to ear.

"Nikola, we made it. And what happened down there—" Startz stopped. A thin spray of dust and gas was still coming from the earth where the hole had been.

"I don't know what happened down there." Nikolai was still smiling. "I remember only—" He scratched his head. "What's the difference? We're no longer in danger." He stood up, looking thoughtfully at the castle.

Unfortunately, Startz knew better. The legend was true. It had been true in the past, and it would be true in the future. Nikolai was in mortal danger. So was he, for that matter. *To see the face of the vurdalak* . . . He remembered the ancient saying. He thought of notifying the Bureau of Mines about the possibility of excavating the casket, the king's treasure. Forget it, they would never find it!

"Please, Comrades." The captain sounded concerned. "I realize what you must have been through down there. Please, take my jeep. Let Dr. Tagarū examine you."

"Thank you, Captain." Startz was now all efficiency. "I am leaving everything in your capable hands. I will certainly mention you favorably in my report. Everything that has transpired here must remain confidential, for the time being."

"I understand." The captain returned Startz's salute.

"Should you need to get in touch with me, I will be at the Ministry of the Interior building in Brasov." Startz gave him the telephone number. The captain wrote it dutifully in his notebook.

"Drive on, Nikola." Startz slapped him on the back, jumping into the jeep. There was another tremor, this one very light. Nikolai started the engine, looked at the castle once again. The cracks in the thick walls were becoming even wider. It wouldn't be long before they collapsed completely. The Dubrava castle would once again be a ruin.

He drove like a maniac across the field. There was so much work to be done in the aftermath of such a disastrous earthquake.

fourteen

Nikolai's cottage, the white dunes. The Black Sea is choppy, mysterious, unfriendly, and cold.

Across the table, Startz was absorbed in reading the latest dossiers on the legation personnel assigned to the United Nations in New York.

Nikolai looked out his small broken window—it had not been repaired after the earthquake. The autumn was in full bloom. The leaves on his rosebushes were all gone and so were the happy German tourists racing down the road in their VWs and motorcycles.

An incredible summer was clearly over. The memories were vague. Like forbidden thoughts and feelings, they lingered. Transparent shadows, like the smoke from the burning leaves.

Nikolai's life had returned to some semblance of normalcy soon after his return from the ruins of Dubrava castle. He'd felt a great surge of energy. He'd thrown himself into his work. He began seeing his friends.

But there was a great empty place in his life. And sometimes in the middle of his working day he would stand up and remember the first night he'd met Sally in New York. The sea of lights and the East River bridges. Before going to sleep, after taking a second, third Seconal, he would think of how much he wanted her, how happy he'd been with her in that Transylvanian village.

The village had been wiped off the face of the earth. The Two Moons Café, and that menacing giant bird, the Dubrava castle, no longer existed. The two punctures on his neck had healed. His memories were getting more indistinct now. But he still wanted her very much.

"I can't forget Sally." Nikolai rubbed his temples. "I can't forget what happened. And I don't want to forget! I go to sleep, and in my dreams I want her. When I wake up . . . I am insane, my friend, am I not? This is a new form of insanity." He made an attempt at smiling. "Being in love with a vurdalak, a blood-drinking beast and a murderess. Our psychiatrists would love to study me. What do you think, Startz? Should I just say to hell with it all and put a bullet through my brain?"

"Don't do it," Startz quietly implored. He wanted to say much more. He wanted to explain that Nikolai was the best friend he had ever had, that if he died there would be a great void in his own life. He could almost share Nikolai's pain and confusion.

"So, Startz, what do I do?"

"Forget everything that happened up there in Transylvania," Startz firmly replied. "The world is not some romantic place with fairy-tale castles, dragons, witches, princesses, and vurdalaks. It's just ordinary, dull people, good and bad. This is a world of facts and facts only. One person murders another and they call us to find the murderer. The murderer tries to hide the facts; he covers his tracks like an animal fleeing deeper into the forest. But the facts are there. And we will find them. Perhaps it will take time, but we will find them."

To this Nikolai sadly replied, "Do you really believe that gibberish?"

His friend smiled and sheepishly shrugged his shoulders. "What else am I to believe, Nikola?"

Startz was right, Nikolai thought, ten thousand times right. We can only believe in something that we know.

Two friends, they looked at each other—their looks saying more than all the conversations they had ever had.

Nikolai was the first to break the silence with a loud, healthy laugh. He slammed a bottle of good Romanian cognac on his table and poured the golden liquid into two tall glasses.

"Drink up, Startz! I am driving you to Bucharest tonight. And I am paying, too."

Then he sang the song the gypsy had sung that fateful night at the Lido Café so long, long ago:

You shouldn't tell my sheep about my death,
tell them that I got married,
to a beautiful Empress,
the world's bride.
At my wedding, a star fell,
the sun and the moon held my crown . . ."

He stopped, downed his cognac, and lifted Startz up like a little child.

"At least I held a real empress, a fourteenth-century Wallachian princess, in my arms, Startz. And not once, but many, many times." He grinned and put his friend down. Now he was the same Nikolai: a big bear with a devil-may-care twinkle in his dark eyes.

"And here we are, Startz, at the end of the twentieth century. What do we know? What do we have?"

He poured himself another glass and drank it. "We still have the gypsies and their violins and the moon." He laughed. "Yes, the moon." He was thoughtful for a moment. The moon did appear over the Black Sea, a strange, menacing disk.

"I am driving!" Nikolai firmly repeated. "Any objection?"

"You are crazy, Nikola," Startz said softly and embraced him. "You are as crazy as you have been all your life."

Later that summer, a tiny gypsy caravan of three brightly painted horse-drawn wagons reached a secluded beach on the Adriatic coast near the city of Dubrovnik.

The sun was setting into the azure blue sea, not one boat on its shiny surface. Silence. A pastoral watercolor.

In the last wagon, four burly gypsies, assisted by a young boy, were straining, trying to lower a large wooden crate to the ground.

The setting sun and the sea now blended into one shiny orange disk.

The gypsies were nervous.

They deposited the crate on the white sand and hurriedly departed.

Silence again. The orange disk spread across the horizon.

Minutes later, a motorized launch arrived. In it were four sailors and an officer. The sailors loaded the wooden crate into their boat. The officer kept looking through his binoculars, watching for any sign of the Yugoslav border patrol.

231

Another minute and the launch sped across the darkening sea toward an old Panamanian tanker, *The Gray Eagle*, which waited discreetly outside the limit.

The launch and its heavy cargo were hoisted up and the tanker sailed immediately—Jersey City, U.S.A., was its official destination.

That night, one of the ship's experienced Lebanese sailors fell overboard and all efforts to find him proved futile.

The following night, another sailor swore he had seen a beautiful lady wearing a long silk dress and some large ancient rings and medallions, standing on the deck. He said she had a very strange smile.

No one believed him.

fifteen

Leonard Reiss parked his blue Rolls Royce in a tiny parking lot behind his elegant office, actually a converted firehouse, on East Sixty-sixth Street. It was almost eleven in the morning and all four of his associates were "in the field." Leonard's secretary, a striking Japanese woman named Miharu, brought him his morning mail, newspapers, and a cup of black coffee. Telephones rang. This morning Leonard was in no mood to talk with anyone on any subject. He slowly drank his coffee, thinking that he really had to find out for himself what the hell was happening in his problem brownstone on East Seventy-seventh Street between Fifth and Madison. Always something. I wonder what it is now? He relaxed somewhat as he let Miharu's firm fingers massage his tired shoulder blades. Maybe I should get rid of that house altogether, nothing but trouble!

Right now, the problem was simply money. The brownstone was divided into three duplexes and all three tenants were behind in their rent. The architect who occupied the semibasement and the first floor was living with his mother in Florida. The interior designer, second and third, was currently in the St. Paul's Hospital psychiatric ward. And Sally Edmondson, who occupied the top two floors, had gone to Europe earlier this summer and hadn't been heard from since.

Reiss and Associates, Ltd., a substantial real estate firm, catered mostly to the beautiful people and those on the way to becoming beautiful, and never once in the firm's twelve-year existence had

Leonard had to resort to such mundane things as eviction notices. However, while the architect and the decorator were only two months behind, Ms. Edmondson was three months behind and, what was even more disturbing, nobody, it seemed, knew where she was. Leonard's tired muscles were beginning to relax and he was developing a better frame of mind. This morning he had the eviction notice ready. So, he'd be out three grand. It was still better than being awakened in the middle of the night with the cheerful news that another one of the tenants in that creepy house had either committed suicide or run amok down Fifth Avenue. I am going to try to unload it, he decided. To hell with it! He told Miharu he'd be back sometime in the afternoon and to call and tell the old super at Seventy-seventh Street to meet him there in fifteen minutes.

"Hi ya, boss." Old Vlas had been with the firm for over ten years. A thin, phlegmatic man in his sixties, of eastern European background, he took care of four brownstones, including the "problem one." He had his keys ready, opened the front door, and let Leonard in.

"You sure nobody's here?" Leonard asked.

"Sure, Boss! Nobody 'cept mice . . . don't worry, boss, I bring my cat."

Leonard bent down, picked up all the letters in the hallway and examined them. One caught his interest. It was from a well-known Wall Street firm and it was addressed to Edmondson. He lifted it up to the light, trying to see what was in it. He hesitated, then he took out his penknife and carefully opened it. Wow! Inside was a check for twenty-five thousand dollars. At least the lady wasn't destitute. Maybe I should wait with my eviction notice, he thought.

"You got her keys, Vlas?"

"Yes, sir."

They both walked confidently up the stairs. There was no light in the hallway past the second floor. Vlas took out his flashlight.

They stepped on some glass—a broken hallway mirror.

"I don't know, boss." Vlas saw that both light bulbs in the table lamp at the end of the hallway had been unscrewed and were lying on the table. "Maybe we call cops?"

"Just open the door!"

Vlas opened both locks and pushed in the door. It opened, but only a crack—it had a heavy chain on the inside. Vlas whistled.

"You said nobody was in." Leonard had the unpleasant sensation that whoever was in, he did not want to meet him or her.

"Ms. Edmondson," Leonard called softly. "I am terribly sorry to bother you . . . it's your landlord, Mr. Reiss."

No answer.

"I go call cops, boss!"

"Wait, wait!" Leonard wasn't going to be left here alone.

"Ms. Edmondson"—he raised his voice—"is anything wrong?"

They both now heard something behind the partly open door. It was a slurping, wheezing, cackling sound—the kind of sound that told them in essence: run, run, while you still can. They both stood, nevertheless, as if glued to the plush carpet.

"Hmm." Leonard ventured cautiously, hiding behind Vlas, who, in the meantime, took out his hammer. "Ms. Edmondson, we'd like to know if you're okay. Just say yes or no."

The wheezing and hissing sounds not only continued but were coming closer and closer to the door. Vlas turned around and ran downstairs with his hammer.

Shit, thought Leonard, shit! He, too, wanted to turn around and run, but that wasn't, well, dignified. So he continued standing, like an idiot.

He saw some movement just beyond the door.

"Ms. Edmondson?" he repeated, backing away a little.

"Yes!!" That was the strangest "yes" he had ever heard, hissing and metallic, not quite human, but it was a "yes" and that's all Leonard wanted to hear.

"It's Mr. Reiss. Please call my office," he managed to say while he turned to go down the stairs. As he hurried off, he heard another chilling "yes."

"What were you afraid of, old man?" he chided Vlas, when he reached the safety of the bright sunshine.

"I dunno, boss. Who make that noise?"

"Noise, noise. Maybe she's sick, ever thought of that?"

She'd better be sick. Poor woman, probably cracked, just like that interior designer downstairs. I hope it's not catching. He suddenly had an idea.

"Hey, Vlas, how would you like to earn an extra twenty bucks?"

"What I have to do?"

"Put this notice on her door." He thought, whatever happened, an eviction notice wouldn't hurt.

And Leonard did not feel like going back to that house, ever again.

"That's all?"

"No, wait a minute . . ." Leonard had another idea. "I'll give you fifty bucks, twenty-five now, the rest tomorow. You put up this notice and then stay downstairs tonight. See if she goes anywhere."

"Okay, Boss," he said without any enthusiasm.

Leonard went back to his office, now empty. He had a tentative appointment for lunch with one of his clients, but he did not feel very hungry, so he sat at his desk and sorted out his mail. Then he almost jumped up out of his chair. Messenger service? The letter was from the same brokerage firm that Edmondson had used for that huge check. Leonard tore it open and there it was—one paragraph plus a neat cashier's check for $3,000, her three months' rent. Shit, I'm still going to unload that house. I don't need this kind of aggravation. The phone rang. Usually Leonard would not pick it up himself, but this time he did, reluctantly.

The voice on the other end identified itself as belonging to the senior partner of that same brokerage house. It was a polished baritone with just a trace of a foreign accent. He explained the situation: Ms. Edmondson was well, uh, indisposed (Leonard thought that was an understatement), and therefore required absolute privacy; also, she desired to move (welcome news to Leonard).

After the call, he locked the check in his safe and went through the rest of his mail—nothing unusual. He was still glancing through the papers when his secretary came back from lunch. Leonard watched her straighten out the pearls on her gray dress. I have two bottles of Château Lafite Rothschild 1937 left in my refrigerator, he thought. Upstairs he had a lavishly furnished apartment, a home away from home, to get away from his problems. This afternoon seemed a great time to use it. After that experience with those weird sounds, he certainly deserved it. As he was going up, his hand around Miharu's slender waist, he remembered that there was no need for poor Vlas to hang around that creepy house. Well, to hell with him! He opened the wine. This was going to be a great afternoon.

Leonard should have called poor Vlas and he should have taken the time to read the day's papers. They were full of interesting items. There was, first, a rather lengthy article in the *Daily News*, with three photographs, entitled "The Mystery at Sea." It described how the Coast Guard was still trying to unravel the mystery of the "ghost" Panamanian tanker, *The Gray Eagle*, which was sitting on the sand near the Barnegat lighthouse on Long Beach Island, New Jersey. It was first thought that the crew had abandoned ship in the mid-Atlantic, although it was unclear exactly what had caused them to do so. A thorough search of the vessel by Coast Guard personnel unearthed one sailor, still alive, who'd evidently locked himself in a tiny compartment near the engine room. He had gone mad during his ordeal, and his questioning was postponed pending a psychiatric examination. The tanker did not carry any oil; that was emphasized. It was towed away to Jersey City and impounded.

The second item was in the *New York Times* Arts and Leisure section. It was an article about the American-Romanian cultural exchange program. There was an exhibit of contemporary Romanian art opening soon at the Serge Korn Galleries. There were plans for the Romanian state orchestra and opera to appear at Lincoln Center and Carnegie Hall. And last, but not least, there was a new play by the world-renowned Romanian poet, Michea Basarab (pronounced *M-i-kh-a-y-a*)—a world premiere in English, at the Old Chelsea Theater. The article then went on to describe the great works of the "Romanian Recluse," as Basarab was sometimes affectionately called.

Finally, in that same section of the *Times*, there was a modest ad to which nobody except perhaps a few lovers of exotic and far-out entertainment would pay any attention. The ad read:

The Soviet American Friendship
Association
presents
The legendary Volga Tartars
direct from their triumphant
European tour—an evening of
musical and visual excitement.
Company of 28, dances, songs.
One week only.

The dates roughly corresponded with the Romanian events.

And while Leonard and his gorgeous Japanese secretary were deep into the pleasures of the flesh, Vlas, the old super, was preparing himself emotionally for spending the night at the brownstone. He was getting drunk. He sat in his tiny room, behind a large boiler, stroking his cat, finishing his first pint of Cossack vodka, and eating his stew—his own recipe, which consisted mostly of garlic, with a potato and a couple of pieces of meat thrown in for good measure. Little did he know that this very stew might prove to be a lifesaver. Vlas finished the first pint and opened up another. A couple more hours and he'd try to walk to the brownstone. At least, he figured, I won't be feeling any pain.

In fact, he didn't feel any pain. He managed to weave his way to the house, made himself a nice bed out of three chairs, and slept soundly through the night. As morning came, Vlas awakened with a terrible hangover and stiff muscles. He left the house, called his boss, and told him that nothing had happened during the night, that nobody had gone out or in, and that he would be stopping by for his twenty-five dollars.

Had Vlas been awake around midnight, he might have seen a lady in a long dark dress gliding down the stairs—not walking but moving as if she were riding on an escalator. The lady had stopped by him and looked him over. Then she had glided straight through the locked door and out toward Central Park.

Had Vlas been awake, he would have seen, too, that the lady was wearing a large gold pendant around her neck, a round medallion with a tear-shaped ruby in the middle: like a drop of blood. Being from the old country, he would have realized then that she was a vurdalak, and that that was why the upstairs hallway mirror was smashed and the lights were out. He'd also have seen that, up close, the lady was no longer beautiful—her face was changed; her eyes had grown large and bloody, reflecting nothing but hunger and hatred. Her mouth was wide open and it wasn't the mouth of a woman. Rather, it was that of some kind of animal—sharp little teeth were protruding between her lips and she had two thin white fangs, such as those of a very large snake. She was hissing, too, exactly like a snake—the same sound he had heard upstairs. And her hands were not the hands of a woman anymore: long sharp claws grew at the ends of her fingers; coarse gray hair grew on her palms. She leaned over poor Vlas, over his neck. She stopped, her nose wrinkled in disgust. Perhaps it was Vlas's stew, or the vodka, or a combination of both.

On a rock across from the Central Park boathouse, a lonely dark figure kept an unusual vigil. The woman was no longer hungry or hateful. She was gazing at the nearly full orange disk and begging for answers. She was in a trance. The visions, reflected sometimes in her eyes, sometimes on the moon's surface, were vague, disturbing.

She saw her beloved moonflower garden devastated by the earthquake, the Romanian mansion a ruin. She saw the terrible man with the sword advancing toward her and felt the rage and the fear of her master. Why am I here? Why am I no longer with him? she asked the moon over and over.

The beautiful flowers were crushed by giant rocks, the swans were dead, the birds were not singing. The woman felt desperate. She wanted so much to communicate with her master, at least to find out whether he still existed.

She saw another woman, so familiar and so distant, and a lover from another time, and a village inn. Everything was getting so blurry, so transparent. The sounds of cars and planes overhead distracted her.

She tried to concentrate once again. She must continue; she had to survive, to be ready for her master.

The morning was not far away, a most dangerous time. She finally saw the faint rays of moonlight shining on the ruins of some ancient castle. She saw once again the tall hunter advancing toward her. The small golden cross in his crown hurt her so much! Red wine spilled on a clean white tablecloth. Now! She was now near the place that she wanted to see: the golden tomb, so familiar and pleasant. She easily read the Babylonian hieroglyphics: "I am Membuchazzarr, the Prince who rules the Night. I am being vanquished, destroyed by the Power greater than Velsevul himself. The multitudes of my slaves are being tortured and slaughtered and the blood of humans needlessly colors the eternal river. Know my curse oh All Powerful One: three thousand years from now, another Prince will appear to take my place."

She stopped reading; the tomb was empty. The gold and the precious stones did not shine as brightly as she had remembered.

It was getting light. Another plane went over the park.

The figure on the rock across from the boathouse had vanished into the morning air.

That evening she had a visitor.

A distinguished-looking man in his fifties nodded his gray head deferentially and waited for her to come down.

"Everything is arranged," he informed her, holding his hands together as if preparing to pray. On his left index finger, he was wearing a gold ring with a miniature ruby in the middle, an exact replica of the larger ruby in her medallion.

"Sandor," he said, his head remaining lowered, "your servant."

He did not expect the very hard slap from her, a slap that sent him flying across the corridor.

"Where have you been?" she hissed. "You know how badly I need the earth; you know I cannot sleep in this four-wall enclosure."

The distinguished-looking gentleman now lay prostrate before her, his face to the floor. He didn't dare to look up.

"In your new home you have a round basement. You have the earth," he whispered.

"Where is my place?" She saw a tiny stream of blood coming from his nose. Her mouth was now wide open. "Where is my new resting place?"

The man told her. He looked up at her in terror. Her face was so near; this was the end. He closed his eyes.

When he regained consciousness, she was no longer there. The man touched the wounds on his neck; he knew he was dying. His only thought was that he mustn't compromise her; he must not be found in this house. He tried getting up. The room and the walls were a large white blur. He reached for the door, opened it with great difficulty. He fell down the stairs leading to the street. He tried to walk again, without any success. He knew he only had a few seconds. He reached the door of his Cadillac, parked near a fire hydrant. He opened it. He knew this was the end. Just before expiring, he managed to take off the ring with the ruby and let it fall on the pavement. He had a happy expression on his face. Zerkal would be safe now. His lord would be pleased.

In a narrow loft building on Mercer Street near Canal in Soho, the new tenant examined her domain. The first two floors, the basement, and, most important, the subbasement: the round brick wall, the earth, and the casket.

Everything was as it should be. The earth was still a little moist, and its sweet aroma reminded the creature of a wondrous garden, its animals, and its beautiful flowers. Her nostrils expanded. She cautiously climbed into the casket. She was now indeed in the timeless euphoric capsule, safe from her enemies and waiting for the reunion with her master. She closed her eyes and then opened them again. Something was *not* right. Strange sounds.

She stood up, touched her medallion, glided up the stairs to investigate.

Those sounds. Loud experimental music was coming from the wide-open third-floor window of the building, facing the airshaft. The music was very disturbing. There were hissing sounds that were all too familiar; the ringing of bells which was also familiar; drums and wailing. All of this disturbed her.

She flew toward her second-floor window. Now she could see a handsome young artist painting a large canvas. He was unaware that anyone could be watching him from that angle and he was working in the nude. His lean muscular body was smeared with paint and glistened with perspiration. From time to time he would run to his stereo panel to adjust the sound.

She watched him silently, intently: a large boa constrictor watching a helplessly trapped deer. She felt her mouth expanding and sweet pains of hunger rushing through her veins.

The artist must have sensed danger. He stopped painting, turned down his stereo, peered into the darkness outside his window. Seeing nothing, he lit a cigarette and thoughtfully examined his canvas.

He heard a slight rustle, felt a breath of cold air on his back. Suddenly he jumped up and turned to face the creature. Her eyes, her fangs, her claws were only inches from his throat. The artist screamed. That scream seemed to stop her for a split second. It was not the scream of a frightened human being. It was a warrior's scream that she had heard somewhere before. And he was a warrior, a veteran and a martial arts expert who still taught part-time at the downtown kung fu academy. He had seen horrors during the war, but none quite like the one that was confronting him now.

He sprang at her with a combination of kicks and blows that were deadly enough to kill several men. It was useless. It was as if he were fighting a statue made of steel. He thought the creature was grinning at him, a hideous hungry mask.

When she pushed him, he stumbled back across the room, overturning his canvas and his easel. He tried to get up, but with a swiftness he had never encountered, the creature flew and sank her claws in his shoulder blades, pinning him to the floor, her mouth moving inevitably closer to his throat. The artist was not a religious man, but he closed his eyes and cried out with all his being, "My God, my Lord, please help me, help me!" He managed to push the dreaded face an inch or two away. Repeating to himself, "God help me, please help me," he reached toward his stereo and turned it on full blast.

The creature shrieked, covering her ears. For a moment, amid a wild cacophony of sounds, the two beings looked at each other. He saw her face change to that of a very attractive lady. Then there was nothing! He was alone. Someone from another apartment was banging on his door to complain about the noise.

He got up. His body was shaking. He turned down his stereo, closed the window. The banging on his door stopped. He looked at his torn canvas and overturned easel. He lit another cigarette.

He tried to tell himself it was all a dream or someone's practical joke. But he knew better. He sat down at his drafting table. His hands still trembling, he drew a pencil sketch of the attractive lady whom he was sure would be coming back to kill him.

At the moment, however, he wasn't thinking of his own safety. He looked at his sketch of the lady with the strange medallion. Suddenly, once more, he felt like praying. He dropped down on his knees and prayed that his sketch would find its way to someone who knew, someone who could help, someone who could put an end to this horror.

epilogue

The great Russian forest, so serene and majestic. A small river, Moskva, runs through it. On its bank, in a sunny clearing, stands a tall, bearded monk who looks thoughtfully at the rushing clear waters. It's a summer afternoon, in the latter part of the twelfth century. The tall man is at peace with himself and his God. His name is Dimitri. He was once a prince, a military leader, the last Russian ruler and defender of the golden city of Kiev. For thirty years now, since the fall and the destruction of his beloved city by the Tartar hordes, he has been a hermit, a holy man, living in the wilderness with only animals and birds as his friends. Until one month ago. Having finished his task, Dimitri walked down along the river for three days and nights to a newly rebuilt frontier settlement called Moscow to see another priest, Gleb. This done, Dimitri returned to the forest.

Dimitri lowers a basketful of berries and mushrooms he had collected earlier in the day. The berries are to be shared with his tame bear, Ivan; the mushrooms will be dried for the winter. He sits down to rest on the soft grass near the river, absorbed in his thoughts.

He sees himself, a much younger man, wearing his armor, standing with his gloomy commanders atop the Golden Gates. Tartars were all around the city, as far as the eye could see. More of them than blades of wheat in the fields near Kiev. Dimitri was waiting for the messenger he had sent to Batu Khan begging him to spare the women and children. The messenger arrived, tied to the back of his horse, a bloody hulk; his legs and arms were cut off, as well as his tongue. The battle began.

Miraculously, the Russians managed to fight off the first few assaults. Thousands of Tartars lay dead or wounded at the base of the walls. Dimitri felt the tide was turning. He was going to release his cavalry in a bold strike at Batu Khan's main encampment. Then treachery reared its ugly head. Dimitri sighed and crossed himself.

It was all over. Hordes of Tartars were pouring inside the city, burning and plundering. Dimitri fought until he could fight no longer. His comrades were all dead. He was bound hand and foot and brought before the Great Khan.

Batu, a tiny man dressed in orange silks, sat on the back of a stuffed Manchurian tiger. Below him, on the floor of his tent, sat his astrologers and sorcerers, his bodyguards and the lesser Khans. All but one were Mongols. The one who wasn't, a young Moldavian prince wearing black and holding onto a curved dagger, was the traitor.

Batu looked over at Dimitri, curiosity in his narrow eyes.

"Untie him," he ordered.

Dimitri's ropes were cut.

"I admire your courage," Batu continued, and his words were quickly translated by one of the shamans. "I give you your life and your sword; go wherever you wish."

"Great Khan!" The traitor jumped to his feet. "This man is dangerous. Kill him!" There was hatred and fear in his large gray eyes. He pulled out his dagger; the ruby in his small golden crown shone brightly, like a drop of blood.

A huge Tartar bodyguard pushed him back to the floor.

"Dangerous?" Batu laughed. "No man is dangerous to the grandson of Temujin!" Now his attention focused on the Moldavian prince. "Except possibly you, my friend. But . . . you are not a man! Take the Russian out of my camp!" He screamed. "Let the feast begin.' "

Outside Batu's tent the Tartars, drenched in blood, were already building a pyramid of human skulls.

Dimitri crossed himself again and recited a short prayer. He looked at the sun, now even with the tops of the pines, listened to the birds, the soft murmur of the water. He felt satisfied, fulfilled. His task was finished; his manuscript was in safe hands. He was also sad. He knew that very soon he would no longer take his walks in the forest and play with his bear, or swim in the cold fresh water, or see the sun and the sky. He was in mortal danger and there was no escape. Here, in an uncharted forest, or anywhere else in the world, the dreaded Moldavian prince would find him. The time was growing near. He heard hoofbeats and whistles. He crossed himself once more. He thought of not returning, of fleeing deeper into the forest. It was no use. He picked up his basket, stood up, and walked slowly toward his cabin. Half a dozen Tartar archers stood in the clearing near the cabin. His bear lay groaning, mortally wounded by their arrows. Among the trees were other Tartars on horseback.

Dimitri walked past the archers into his cabin. He took his heavy double-edged Russian sword off the wall, the sword Batu Khan had let him keep. My dear friend, thought Dimitri, this is the last time I'll need you. He sprang outside with the agility of a much younger man and cut the Tartar nearest to him almost in half.

The other archers did not shoot. Instead, two horsemen, screaming wildly, raced out of the trees, coming toward him with a net. This was their mistake. Dimitri jumped in front of one of the horses; the horse reared up; the Tartar fell down, dropping his net. As he hit the ground, Dimitri chopped off his head. Four more horsemen appeared with ropes and nets, and after a furious struggle, they managed to disarm and subdue him.

"Greetings, Prince." He heard a voice behind him. He turned quickly and saw, smiling underneath a crown, the face he had not been able to erase from his mind for these many years.

Quietly, the Moldavian prince rode toward Dimitri. He looked exactly as he had in Batu's tent: the same hatred in his gray eyes, the same tear-shaped ruby in his crown.

Dimitri cursed and spat in his direction.

The nobleman looked amused. "A man of God? Shame on you, Dimitri." Then his face changed—his mouth twisted open, his words were like the hissing of a snake. "Hear me, monk, one of us has already been killed because of your writings. More are in danger . . . you and Setozar . . ." He fell silent, his hand on his dagger. That same dagger.

"Tell me who has your manuscript. Who has the last page?"

How in God's holy name did he know? Dimitri was astounded.

The nobleman's eyes were burrowing deep into his mind; it

seemed flames appeared in them. Dimitri felt weak, almost help-less.

"Go to hell, where you came from! I will tell you nothing."

"Oh, yes you will," the nobleman softly corrected him. "And you yourself will beg me to listen. And you will renounce your God and your homeland a thousand times before this night is over. Tell me now and I'll simply kill you. I only want what is rightfully mine, the last page." It was now getting dark in the forest and the Tartars were nervous. The wolves howled in the distance. The nobleman waited.

Just then, Dimitri's bear, still growling in a pool of blood, gathered its last bit of strength, crossed the clearing with two swift strides, and threw itself at the nobleman and his horse, knocking both of them to the ground. In the ensuing confusion, the Tartars left Dimitri unguarded for a second or two, long enough for him to bend down, pick up his sword, and plunge it deep into his own left side.

Later that night, a silver fox, another friend, came over and sniffed Dimitri's body and howled sadly at the full moon.

The Moskva River murmurs softly through the dark forests, as it did centuries before the coming of man and as it will centuries after man is no more.

Several hundred miles away, near the great city of Novgorod, Father Gleb was reciting his prayers in a village inn before going to sleep. He said a special prayer for his brother, Dimitri, whose manuscript he carried so carefully. From Novgorod, Father Gleb planned to travel south across foreign lands toward the foothills of the Carpathian Mountains, to a small monastery in Moldavia, to deliver the manuscript. Father Gleb was puzzled about the burden he was to carry on his journey—a handwritten history, or letopis, which narrated some of the tragic events of the previous half-century. The last page had been left blank for some reason. Gleb finished his prayers, climbed into the sleeping alcove above the wide Russian stove, covered himself with sheepskins, and closed his eyes.

Tired as he was, he couldn't sleep. The night was disturbingly bright, the horses were restless, and the dogs were barking. He decided to read the letopis again. Perhaps there was something in it that he had missed.

Not wishing to disturb anyone, he read it by the light of the moon. Now the words and the meaning were quite different. He felt that his very soul was being strangled. He wanted to throw the dreaded manuscript away, to burn it in the stove. But he had given his word and had to keep it. His hands trembling, he assembled the thick yellow pages, put them carefully inside a black leather pouch, tied it, and hid it in a secret pocket of his coarse cassock.